DECEIVED

DECEIVED

A KELLY PRUETT MYSTERY

MARY KELIIKOA

CAMEL
PRESS

KENMORE, WA

CAMEL
PRESS

A Camel Press book published by Epicenter Press

Epicenter Press
6524 NE 181st St.
Suite 2
Kenmore, WA 98028

For more information go to:
www.Camelpress.com
www.Coffeetownpress.com
www.Epicenterpress.com

Author's website: www.marykeliikoa.com

Design by Rudy Ramos

Deceived
2022 © Mary Keliikoa

ISBN: 9781603818650 (trade paper)
ISBN: 9781684920105 (ebook)

Printed in the United States of America

For Robb, Always

Acknowledgments

Thank you to my editor, Jennifer McCord, for working with me on the plot and prose to make Kelly and her clan shine. To Kate Pickford whose input and keen observations on this novel were monumental. To my critique partners Dianne Freeman, Jaime Lynn Hendricks, and Cynthia Goyette whose insights and recommendations push me to dig deeper. To my beta readers Jessica Jett, Bonnie Matheny, and Karenza Corder, who make me feel like a rock star. To Detective James Lawrence (retired) and current Clark County Sheriff Deputy, who is always ready with the answers I need to make my stories believable. If I've missed the mark on the procedural side, that's all on me for not asking the right questions.

To you my readers. Thank you for buying, reviewing, and sharing my novels, and for reaching out to tell me how much you relate to Kelly. Your emails and the recognition this series has received has been humbling. You drive me to work even harder to get my stories right. I hope you enjoy— this one is for you.

And last, but by no means least, to my husband, Robb, who makes every day an adventure. Having his support and continuous positive outlook helps me move through this world and this publishing journey grounded and excited for the future. This road would not be nearly as fun if I didn't have him to share it with. Forever my heart, Mr. K. Aloha nui loa.

CHAPTER 1

Life turns on a dime. My dad, Roger, had said that more than a few times. My life had done enough of that to cause whiplash over the past two years. The first turn happened when I divorced my childhood sweetheart and moved in with my dad. The next was when I lost my dad to a stroke and inherited my childhood home off Belmont in Portland, Oregon and his detective agency R&K Investigations. K is for Kelly Pruett—me.

The other turns were solving my last two cases—or "near-death experiences," as my ex-mother-in-law Arlene liked to remind me—and I felt like a legit private investigator. While no significant investigations had come my way in a while, process-serving, skip-traces, and following the cheating ex had picked up. I had a bit tucked away to cover me for the unforeseen, and I made enough to pay the bills and keep me, Mitz and our basset hound, Floyd, in peanut butter, pancakes, and kibble.

After years of yearning for my father's approval—doing everything in my power to have him acknowledge that I was capable in the detecting department—I was finally "one of the boys." If only he were around to see it.

Don't get me wrong, I was Mitz's mom, and Kyle's girlfriend—and my own best advocate—but PI work is often considered "guys work." So, to get a call from Bernie Sokol about "a delicate matter which requires a pro" was validating—although not a complete surprise.

Bernie's firm had been a longtime client of R&K Investigations. My dad had been called to Bernie's home many times over the years to handle cases for him, but most of the work I did came from his assistant in the form of serving documents. This call had come direct from Bernie to me, and that said he had more than process serving on his mind. Now I was

1

cruising through his well-to-do neighborhood, with its McMansions, heated pools and security systems, after dropping Mitz off at school.

Raindrops laced with snow dripped from the gray January sky, and my droopy-eyed and musky smelling friend, Floyd, lay curled in a ball on the passenger seat. I came upon Bernie Sokol's S emblazoned wrought iron gate fast and skidded into the driveway, hoping the four million cameras hadn't caught my less-than-graceful arrival. I hadn't mastered my new-to-me Ford Focus, purchased after my Triumph Spitfire had an ending that rivaled an installment of *Fast & Furious*. Easing up the circular drive, I parked under the wide columned portico. A valet dashing out to greet me wouldn't have felt out of place.

It was a good thing I'd dressed for the occasion, opting for black pants and a white blouse instead of my usual grey Nike warmup jacket and blue jeans. I was the CEO of my own agency now—time to act like it. I ran a hand over Floyd's bony head and down one of his long ears, ignoring the butterflies taking flight in my stomach.

"Back in a jiff," I said.

More than a decade younger than my thirty-two years, a girl dressed in grey sweats answered the door. She had light freckles across her upturned nose and had a baby boy in blue-footed PJs perched on her hip. He pulled on the long blonde braid she'd thrown over her shoulder.

"Mrs. Sokol?" I asked. I'd never known much about Bernie's family life other than what his assistant, Carla, had shared. Word was he'd traded in his first wife, Katherine, who had forty years of marriage on the clock.

The girl rolled her eyes so hard they almost disappeared into their sockets. "Yeah, no. I'm Morgan." She tilted her head and yelled. "Mom." She turned back to me. "She prefers Candy Appleton, by the way."

My face flushed at the misstep, even as I wondered if the child on Morgan's hip was her son or her half-brother. I was afraid to ask. The kid coughed, sounding croupy. Morgan rocked him and kissed him, patting his back. "Bad cold," she said.

The real Mrs. Sokol, or Ms. Appleton as I'd been informed, jogged out from a back room of the house dressed in hot pink stretch pants, pink sparkle sports bra, and black heels. She'd pulled her red hair into a messy bun that sat on top of her head like a giant tarantula. Large hoop earrings hung from her ears.

Her bracelets jingled with each step, and her five-carat ring shot shimmers of rainbow colors around the foyer. "Morgan, don't be rude. Let the lady in," she directed.

Morgan huffed and stepped aside so I could enter the marble foyer that divided two living spaces. To my right, low slung couches, and sleek, modern lines; to the left, French provincial, matching the furniture I'd seen at Baumgartner & Sokol's offices—a house divided, not just by age, but by taste—or lack thereof. I checked myself. She was Bernie's wife, and I'd done enough sneaking around in bushes and peering through windows to be aware that wives often knew what was happening in their husband's lives long before they hired me. I couldn't alienate her.

Ms. Appleton smiled with her blinding white teeth. "You making a delivery?"

"No, ma'am. I have an appointment with Mr. Sokol."

"Oh, God, don't call me ma'am. I'm only forty-nine."

"And a young forty-nine at that. Right, grandma?" Morgan bounced the baby on her hip.

Candy smiled, but her jaw flinched. "Honey, show the lady up to your dad's office."

"Dad?" Morgan said.

"The man pays for your education. Show a little gratitude. It's the least you could do."

Morgan met my eye, her mouth held in a tight curve. "Follow me."

I wasn't the only one with the occasionally strained family relations—except I didn't have to live with my ex, Jeff, or his mother, Arlene, who happened to be my neighbor. But Bernie's new wife was an interesting choice, and given the amount of jewelry and *education* he sprung for, I wondered if Candy was in it for more than love.

We climbed the grand staircase, red oriental carpet running up the middle cushioning our footsteps, while I made scrunchy faces at the little guy on Morgan's hip. He mimicked them back at me.

"Your son's a cutie. What's his name?" I said.

"Thomas, but we call him bubbles because he likes it when I blow bubbles into my soda with a straw. Don't we, bubbles?" She rubbed her nose on his and the kid burbled right back at his mom, pulling her braid harder.

I missed those years when they were focused so tightly on every action; a sound could get a giggle. My mom had a thing she did with spoons and a piece of aluminum foil that used to crack me up when I was a toddler—that's what my dad had told me—but I couldn't think about that. I was here on a matter of business, not a walk down memory lane.

Three mountains worth of staircase later, we reached Mr. Sokol's office.

Morgan pushed open his door. "Some chick's here to see you." She didn't wait for his response and took off down the hall. Cool, I was a *chick*.

Mr. Sokol leaned back, an old-school phone in one hand and a cigar in the other. He set the receiver down and peered over his wired spectacles. He rounded the desk wearing a burgundy warmup suit with a white stripe down the legs. His salt and pepper hair had a precision cut. Except for dark circles shadowing his eyes and a slump to his shoulders, he hadn't changed much since the last time I'd seen him, which was at my dad's funeral.

"Ms. Pruett, my apologies for not greeting you at the door." He nodded at his phone. "Trying to settle a case ahead of trial."

I extended my hand. "No worries, and it's Kelly."

He had a firm grip that was friendly and not overly familiar. They say a lot can be told about a person by their handshake, and they're not wrong. Bernie was clearly in charge of his world.

He motioned me to sit and returned to his chair behind the desk. He spent a few seconds puffing on his cigar, sizing me up and assessing whether I could handle the job.

I shifted in my chair. "What can I do for you, Mr. Sokol?"

"It's Bernie." He balanced his cigar on the edge of the ashtray. His elbows rested on the arms of his chair, and he drew up his fingertips, forming a steeple close to his mouth. "I could always rely on your father. He was thorough and got the job done every time. Hell of an investigator. But he's not here and I need your help at the women's homeless shelter, Loving Grace."

Bernie told me about founding Loving Grace and how it had been inspired by the drug-related death of his sister—Grace. I'd learned as much when prepping for the meeting. But it was good to hear him tell the story as I knew how grief could shape a person from my own experience of losing both parents. It also might help me understand why he called me. Even decades after his sister's death, the tears came readily and he had to stop to compose himself. I'd be in the same emotional state if I allowed myself to talk about my parents, which I didn't. "I'm sorry for the loss of your sister."

"Appreciate that." He pulled himself together so he could continue. "But she's not why you're here. My granddaughter Amber has been missing for the last five days…." He took off his glasses and pressed the heels of his hands against his eyes. "Drugs…"

Surrounded by wealth and splendor, with a snazzy new wife downstairs, the man was still grieving. He continued, "I can't lose another…"

"What do the Portland police…?" I began.

Bernie let out a wry laugh before I could finish the sentence. "Amber Moore's just another homeless drug addict as far as they're concerned. The police asked a few questions, wrote down what I told them, but she's 18. Let me translate that for you: they don't have the time or the inclination. They filed the report. Case closed."

The news reported almost daily that drugs and addiction were an epic problem in Portland, but my newly promoted Portland Police Detective boyfriend, Kyle Jaeger, might be able to provide more information on that report.

I was about to share that fact, but Bernie shook himself, seeming to come back to the moment. "That's why I called you."

"You'd like me to find her?" I said.

He waved me off, wrangling his emotions into a tiny box. "No. It's more delicate than that. Amber was only twelve when her mother left. I did my best, but a girl needs a mother."

That fact hit home since I'd lost mine when I was young. I kept my face straight and looked at him as he continued with his story.

"As a teen, Amber fell in with the wrong crowd and the downward spiral began. By the time she was fifteen, she'd dropped out and was dodging my calls and shooting up in alleyways and abandoned buildings. The best I could hope for, I thought, was that she had a safe place to retreat to when things got too rough. She had a permanent bed reserved for her at Loving Grace." He stubbed his cigar out without taking another puff.

There was something in that gesture. I leaned in, trying to home in on what he wasn't saying. "She'd even gotten some assistance at the pain and rehab center across the street. She didn't know I knew, but I kept an eye out. About six weeks ago, I saw she'd checked herself into rehab for a spell." He shook his head. "I actually slept a few nights after that. Not worrying. Do you have any idea what that's like to worry all the time?"

"I have a nine-year-old daughter," I said.

"Then you do."

One hundred percent. Mitz had been born deaf, a result of Waardenburg syndrome. We had our own special language, even though we weren't always together because Jeff lived closest to her school. During the week, it made the most sense she was with him. But when I wasn't working, all I wanted to do was be with her. I couldn't imagine a life without her in it.

"Well, my grandbaby made it through rehab and found herself a little job as a filing clerk. Not fancy, but honest work. I couldn't remember the last time she'd had a job. I didn't get in touch. She's like a cat. She needed to come to me." His eyes filled again. "Then, out of the blue, she did. Two weeks ago, she called to say she was clean and had sworn off drugs and was learning some new skills—pulling her life together. She sounded good and I believed her." He frowned. "It was short lived."

First his sister, and now this…it didn't sound good.

"Her last calls to me say she's in trouble. It's not the same old same old. This is something new." He reached into his top drawer and pulled out a handheld recorder and pressed play.

"Papa. I'm close. They're definitely dealing. Now I have to work out who all's involved. Don't come down here. Don't come looking for me." There was a crinkling sound in the background like she had crunched a candy wrapper in her hand and thrown it in the trash. "You stand out, Papa. And, anyway, they prepare when you do a visit. Hide things. Go underground. You need to let me ride this one out. I'm so close. Promise me you won't come or send the police? I'll have the evidence soon. I love you, Papa. Thank you for being on my side. Now let me do this for you." There was a hitch in her voice, like she was swallowing or holding back tears. "I'm almost there. I just have to make sure they don't find me."

He stopped the recorder, flipped it open, reached into his desk and found a second cassette. *Old school.*

I waited, hands folded in my lap, brain working overtime and forming several questions. Why weren't the police interested in a drug bust if Amber was right and drugs were being sold at Loving Grace? Why hadn't Bernie gone down there himself? I'd be dragging Mitz out whether she liked it or not. What was Amber trying to tell him about the shelter? What was she trying to do that put her in danger? Had he played this cassette when he called the police?

"This one came in at midnight the last time I heard from her." He clicked play again. Amber's voice was a whisper. "They're onto me, Papa. They know. Gotta go." That was the end of the message. She'd hung up without saying that she loved him or what she'd found or anything that could remotely be construed as a lead.

Bernie came around his desk and propped himself up beside me. "Whatever Amber found at Loving Grace, I believe it was so damning that she's gone into hiding."

I didn't want to state the obvious, but if there was a drug ring as Amber suggested, I had no choice. "Are you sure she's alive?"

"Yes. And I intend to keep her that way, which is why you can't go looking for her," he said. "She's scared. She's in danger. People are watching her."

Those facts were something for the police, surely: drugs, threats, missing girl.

"I went after Grace and look how that ended."

His sister had OD'd. I had a horrible feeling I was about to learn more about how and why.

"She'd spiraled out of control." He squeezed his eyes shut, tight. "We got her into rehab. Best place. Top-notch. Doctors available round the clock. Therapy. The works." He stared at me without seeing me; the hole in his heart showed through his eyes. "Once released, she worked for me in the law offices. She kept her head above water. Even started dating." He rubbed his face like there was something that wouldn't come off. "I didn't see it coming."

"I'm sorry." The statistics on recidivism weren't encouraging. People relapsed. There was a particular danger for people who'd gotten clean but remained close to their old friends. They had to get out of the old circles of influence if they were going to make a clean break. Many didn't.

"She called me."

I nodded, not sure which *she* we were talking about.

"Grace said she was sorry. A hundred times. That she didn't mean it. That she would try again." He stared at the curtains, the carpet; anywhere but me. "I told her how disappointed I was. How she'd let me down. How she was weak and…"

Ouch. On the one hand, I got it. Grace had gotten clean only to fall right off the wagon. If she overdosed after *that* conversation, I could see why he was reluctant to let me go after his granddaughter.

"I can't mess up again, you understand? I only want you to find out if things are a foul at Loving Grace. If people are dealing drugs inside my shelter, then you tell me exactly who they are." Bernie returned to his side of the desk and plopped down, helping himself to another cigar. "When they're gone, Amber will see that she's safe." He lopped off the top of his Cuban. "You see where I'm coming from?"

Despite his logic, it came down to: don't find Amber because of mistakes he'd made in the past. I did see, but I didn't agree that sending me in on a fact-finding mission would be enough.

"You look like him, you know," Bernie said.

"Sorry?"

"Your dad."

"I do have his eyes." Although mine weren't as wise as my Welshman father, I had my mother's round chin, her smile, and long wavy hair.

"Not just that. He looked at me the same way when I asked him to do something he wasn't sold on. But I listen to my gut and I'm usually right. Wish he was here to confirm that for you."

I wished that too and hoped that didn't show on my face. "I'm glad my dad trusted you and you him."

"That's what it's all about," he said. "Trust."

"I hope you'll learn to trust me in the same way, Bernie."

He held my gaze for far too long. "Me too."

If I hadn't been one hundred percent committed before that look, it sealed the deal. I wouldn't let this man down. He'd seen enough disappointment. I'd find the people who were dealing drugs. Once he cleaned house, I'd convince him to hire me to find his granddaughter.

We talked a few more minutes about the details of my going in, about my fee, and I agreed to stay in touch with him via phone. He also provided me a picture of Amber with her short brown hair and wide innocent eyes. It was taken when her mother was alive. "It was the last time she was truly happy," he said as he escorted me to the door.

Now I just had to find a way into Loving Grace and come up with a plan to begin my investigation.

CHAPTER 2

Being called to help Bernie was a big deal, and a lot was riding on it. Not only my future ability to get work from his firm, but a young girl was out there, clearly scared from the messages she left her grandfather, and in hiding. I couldn't mess it up, which meant educating myself on what I'd be walking into beforehand.

My interactions with drug dealers had been limited to buying a joint from the high school pothead, Tyler, with my now-ex-hubby, Jeff, at prom. Tyler was a pleasant sort, which ensured he had a steady stream of customers. But high school potheads had nothing on the hard-core drug dealers of the real world.

I needed someone who had that kind of experience, and I knew where to start.

Finding a dog park for Floyd to stretch his legs, I let him romp the fenced acre with a whippet dressed in a yellow rain slicker while I retrieved my phone. I found my favorites and clicked on *Hot Stuff*. Kyle had changed his name in my contacts late one night when we were messing around on the couch. It wasn't what I would have called him, but it was too funny and so opposite of anything I would ever call him, that I didn't change it.

Several years ago, we'd met at the courthouse when my dad had sent me down to check on some warrants on a missing person. I'd run into Kyle, literally, on the stairs, sending his coffee skyward before it drenched him. Over a million apologies and another steaming mug, we'd become friends—or more like friendly acquaintances as I'd continued to see him around the courthouse.

It wasn't until a few years later after he helped me on my first murder investigation that the occasional coffees turned into an ongoing relationship that had become important to me.

He answered on the third ring. "What's up?" he said, his voice hushed.

"You busy?"

"Just finished a meeting about my next rotation." As a new detective, Kyle rotated through the different departments, teamed with a coach in three-month stints. The "up" team, as they were named, was always on call. Sometimes those calls didn't amount to anything. Other times they kept Kyle out of touch with me for a couple of days. The last quarter rotation had been robbery and assault. This quarter he'd been assigned to homicide.

"Who's your lead?"

"Detective Enloe. And he doesn't like me on the phone too long."

"This shouldn't take but a minute."

"Shoot."

I quickly broke down my conversation with Bernie and that he'd asked me to go undercover to find out about the drugs. I informed him of my plan to dress like a homeless woman who needed a place to stay. I briefly mentioned Amber, but since she wasn't my actual directive yet, I kept the conversation tight.

"Undercover is one way to ferret out a drug ring," he said. "You up for it?"

"I am," I said, as Floyd had lost interest in the whippet and turned his nose to a mound of dirt—probably a mole. He burrowed his whole body into the mound before I could blink. I didn't want to think about what he'd smell like when I got him back into the car.

"You don't sound confident."

"No, I am. Or I will be after this conversation. I'll be starting tonight." I told him the particulars. One thing I'd learned in my last two cases was the importance of someone aware of my planned location and when I'd be there. That was even more necessary when that someone was a cop I was dating. "But I need your expertise on what to look for because honestly, rooting out drugs is a first for me."

"Good to know."

I laughed. "Seriously. Are there any blatant signs to watch for? Should I inspect everyone's eyes to see if they're dilated? Listen for slurred speech? What?"

"If you're looking for users, then yeah. If you're trying to catch a dealer, they're likely to be a bit more discreet and not use up their inventory when they could be making a profit. What kind of drugs are we talking about?"

"Not sure." Although Bernie alluded to heroin, he hadn't been specific. I didn't want to get focused on only one kind.

He paused, probably thinking. "Then look for baggies and packets that are handed off to a dealer or user. That's the most common way for delivery." Muffled voices came from his end, and he'd put his hand over the phone. "Enloe wants to roll, but be careful. Check in later?"

"You know it." I clicked END as Floyd dove in again to that mound of dirt. "Floyd, stop rolling, will you?"

* * *

The city bus stopped a quarter mile from the Loving Grace Women's Shelter. I stepped from the relative warmth of the bus into Portland's trademark drizzle. I made a mini tent out of the free real estate paper I'd found on my seat to shield myself from the rain, which involved raising my arm. I'd done my best to try and look like a homeless woman. I'd forgone the deodorant, so the moisture brought out my rankness. The newspaper disintegrated, drooping over my ponytail, making me look disheveled, broken, and on the skids.

There were cracked cement walkways on the street in front of the women's shelter. The single-story building had a non-descript vibe, and its dull amber lights barely lit the few barren trees that surrounded it. The shelter, along with a four-story building across the street that could be the pain and rehab center Bernie had mentioned, anchored a mixed residential and old commercial section of the city.

Women of all ages hovered under the eaves of the shelter, their cigarettes illuminated like fireflies in the dusky light. I didn't scan their faces as I walked through their wall of smoke with my old high school backpack slung over my shoulder. All eyes were on me, though—new girl in town curiosity maybe, or my drenched rat fashion statement.

A fifty-something woman met me just inside the propped open door. Dressed in black polyester pants a few shades darker than her skin tone and a long, striped sweater, she gave me a warm smile. "I'm Nettie. Welcome to Loving Grace. Are you on the list, honey?"

"Yes. Kelly Robertson," I said, using the name of my daughter's favorite teacher. Only Kyle and Bernie knew my identity while undercover, and Nettie didn't request ID to prove otherwise.

Nettie ran her finger down the paper. "Any drugs or paraphernalia on you?"

I shook my head.

"Weapons?"

"No." The can of pepper spray in my pack wasn't going anywhere, for Nettie or anyone else.

"Sign next to your name," Nettie said.

That was it? I half expected a pat-down. Without that, women could sneak anything inside these walls. I'd have to be careful as I assembled the information on how this place operated. It wasn't only rumor and speculation that Loving Grace was a place to score. Kyle told me it was a known fact; and it couldn't have been easier to infiltrate.

"Are you high now, or have you done drugs today?" She inspected my face. Okay. That was better.

A standard question, but with my focus on finding a drug dealer inside these walls, I scanned her face back. "No, on both counts." Coffee and peanut butter didn't count.

Her eyes narrowed. I'm sure she had heard that from everyone and believed no one. Her sudden smile revealed crooked teeth. "Come in, then."

She led me into the building and pointed to the back corner. "Toiletry kits are available and showers are open for the next few hours. I suggest you use them."

There'd be no need. I wouldn't be stripping down.

She continued, "The doors are locked at ten. House rules state no in, no out after. Got it?"

I nodded as she talked and took the opportunity to check the basic surroundings of scuffed floorboards, vinyl wainscotting that reached waist-high, all topped off with the unmistakable smell of bleach.

"Laundry's available, but you need to be here much earlier if you plan to get in line for that. Questions?" she asked.

"Not so far," I said.

We stopped at the edge of the dining room where a buffet ran parallel to the long rows of tables crowded with women of various ages, no children.

Some of the women were unkempt, others well-groomed. Some stared blankly into space and others had their heads down. They were putting the food into their mouths at a rapid pace. Many carried on full conversations with themselves and a few to each other. Some were thinner than others which told me that a place that offered a hot meal would be a magnet to many homeless women.

Kyle had prepared me for some of what I'd seen. What he hadn't prepared me for was how many women were here, and I couldn't wrap my head around how that was possible. One could be down on their luck, and things could go wrong with no family or friends. Women could also be a victim of domestic abuse and even be abandoned by a spouse; but how could this many women have nowhere else to turn?

I had to stay focused and do what I came here to do: assess the situation and discover who the low-life drug-dealers were and then inform the man who'd hired me.

I turned back to Nettie with a nervous smile. "Are all of these women regulars?"

"A few, but beds aren't promised. We're not a residential, stay all day facility. If you're on a list, that helps, but you must check in on time, and if you're late, there are no guarantees. We open at four in the afternoon. If you want a bed, come earlier rather than later."

I nodded, looking again on the dining room. Where did I even begin to get answers?

"We're serving dinner." Nettie placed her hand on my shoulder. "Get something to eat. You'll feel better. I can see you're fairly new to the streets."

My dirty clothes hadn't made me look any less like a newbie. "That obvious?"

"The deer in the headlights look wears off after a while. It becomes more internalized and hardens you. You, however, have that shock in your eyes. You're wondering how you got here. But there's no use crying over spilled milk, as they say. You're here. Warm and dry. Make the best of it. Now go, get some food, and find yourself anywhere you'd like to sit. You'll be fine here."

Except people weren't always *fine* here.

Someone in here knew something about Amber, but Bernie's orders had been quite clear: this was a fact-finding mission, no heroics, no going it alone. I was not to do anything that might spook Amber (and/or the people who'd scared her into hiding). If I did my job, Bernie might trust me with more investigative work.

All I had to do now was blend in and find someone who would talk to me. There's one in every group, and they're never that hard to find—at least not in the world when standard operating rules applied and where safety nets were in place. Perhaps it was different once you fell through the cracks; only one way to find out.

I shrugged the pack off my back and looped the strap over one shoulder. A stack of gray trays piled high started the buffet line. Despite having eaten a few hours ago, nerves had my stomach growling. What I wouldn't give for a spoon of peanut butter.

Tray in hand, I fell in line behind a tall brunette. Her polyester pants hung off her waist and her shoes, which could have fit Big Bird, were held together by duct tape. She smelled sour. She looked sixty but could be forty. It was hard to tell. Sadness, addiction, weather, and mental illness had to take its toll out on the streets. I looked thirty-two. If I had to spend time out here, my looks would change fast. This lady's tired eyes had none of that deer in the headlights look.

Dinner was beef stew, with chunks of potatoes, celery, and carrots. It smelled delicious. A hawkish woman with glasses dropped a roll onto my tray and grunted, indicating that I keep it moving. There was a holdup around the dessert, which was a choice of orange or green Jell-O. A dollop of Cool Whip was its only redeeming feature.

The line started to move again. I balanced the tray with one hand, grabbed the marshmallow-filled orange version, and was clearing the line when an elbow slammed against my shoulders. As I turned, a hand slapped up under my tray, sending the stew flying into the air and then raining down on my shirt.

So much for blending in.

CHAPTER 3

A woman, the size of an NFL linebacker, crowded into my face. "What the hell you looking at, Bambi?"

I'd been perceived as weak in my last case, and almost burned to a crisp because of it. That wouldn't happen this time. I straightened to my full five foot seven inches and glared. "Excuse you." I yanked a napkin from the table and removed a carrot chunk from my shirt. "Why'd you hit me?"

The woman's pale blue eyes narrowed below the swirl of gray curls poking out from under her stocking cap. "Did no such thing." She stepped on my foot, shifting her full weight onto my big toe, and then moved back.

She acted like she could squash me like a bug, but I was no lightweight and could handle myself. The extra pounds I'd gained when I was pregnant with Mitz hadn't gone anywhere. Kyle had insisted on a self-defense course due to my work, however, this was not the place to show how I could defend myself.

Making a scene and getting tossed out on my first night wasn't part of the plan so I suppressed the urge to shove the linebacker chick back ten steps and out of my space. No staff member had come to my aid. Either they hadn't seen what happened, or they ignored scuffles among the population. *Noted.*

I forced a smile. "Then sorry my back hit your arm and your hand hit my tray."

"Hmph. You got a lot of attitude, girlie. That ain't going to serve you around here." She straightened her oversized flannel shirt. "Haven't seen you around on the streets. Where'd you come from?"

Process-serving for my dad had taught me some coping skills—one of them being to play innocent when dealing with difficult people.

"I was fortunate to get on the list. I've heard this is the place to be for a hot meal and a safe place to sleep. That's all. Not looking for trouble." I smiled, the very picture of a meek and mild newbie. I even lowered my eyes for a couple of beats so she'd think she was top dog.

She looked me up and down like she had the same bullshit meter that I was employing. Hers was blatant; mine was subterranean. She must be a regular here, or if not here, on the streets. She also might have information to share or be the muscle for a drug dealer. My last year of investigating had taught me that human nature was complex and fickle. People were often not what they seemed. A big old teddy bear might reside underneath that flannel and in need of a hug—not that I'd give her one.

She hissed at me. *Disgust? Resignation?* I couldn't tell, but it was delivered with a tiny spray of saliva. Her breath was surprisingly minty fresh, but it took everything I had to resist the urge to wipe my face.

In contrast, a wave of foul odor drifted over my shoulder. The woman in front of me in line with the big shoes now stood inches from my neck. "LuAnn, leave her alone. You're always getting up in other people's business. Why is that?"

LuAnn went to the top of my mental list of potential suspects.

"Just asking her a question." LuAnn was confident, cocky, not a shadow of shame or defensiveness in her tone.

"Yeah, you're full of it. No one gets in here without permission. You don't need to be giving her the third degree."

LuAnn shrugged like she didn't care but stepped out of line and strode back to a table where her tray of food waited.

"She the welcoming committee?" I asked my new ally as I grabbed another tray and a fresh bowl of stew.

The woman walked away without responding—maybe not an ally after all. What was the pecking order in this place? She might be a rung above LuAnn making her, what? I had no idea on how to read the women or how they ranked in relation to one another. It wasn't like when I investigated at an office and could see the Louis Vuitton bag next to the Goodwill pleather special. If I intended to find out who ran things in Loving Grace, I'd better learn how to decode who was who.

"Thanks for that." I followed the tall woman. I had to start somewhere.

"She was testing you."

LuAnn's challenge had felt like a test. Uncertain of whether I'd passed or failed, she was at least leaving me alone for a minute.

My new friend took a seat away from the others. I set my tray down across from hers. "You mind?"

She dug into her stew, head down. It seemed to be an unspoken rule that you didn't make small talk while eating because they were hungry. I had to remember their daily life was very different than mine.

LuAnn sat three tables away, her forearms resting on the top as she focused on her plate. She'd left an entire tray of food to come over and bother me. People knew not to mess with her stuff. That could have been the message she intended for me. My right shoulder throbbed from her shove.

I took a bite of potato. "I appreciated your help back there."

The woman didn't raise her eyes to look at me.

Good thing I didn't give up easily. "I'm Kelly."

"Judy," she muttered.

"Nice to meet you." I nibbled on the soft roll. "How you'd end up here?"

"Lucky, I guess."

I moved a beef chunk around in the bowl with my spoon like my sweet daughter, Mitz, when she didn't want to eat something. "If it weren't for bad luck, I'd have no luck at all..."

That got a slight smile out of Judy before she focused on her food again.

"You stay here often?" I asked and then cringed. If she didn't already suspect I was a plant and a spy, she'd work it out soon unless I got my act together. "I mean, it's better than living under the bridge, right?"

She didn't respond at first, then glanced around her. "Eat," she said under her breath. Her hands were red and weathered. She had spent too much time in the cold without gloves.

I took a few more bites. "What's the story with LuAnn? She test everyone who comes through the door?"

Judy's hand clenched around her spoon as she finished off her stew. "Don't ask so many questions. They frown on that."

"Who does? Who's 'they?'"

She looked around the room in reply.

I'd take that as everybody. *Everybody* frowned on asking questions. *Interesting*.

Judy had moved onto her Jell-O—the green variation. It looked... green. She finished it off in three spoonful's, took a final drink from her milk carton, and jumped up out of her chair. She dumped her tray's contents in the trash and without another glance my way headed to the back corner of the building—the shower area.

My acting skills might not be Oscar-worthy, but asking more about LuAnn's harassment or saying I was glad to have found Loving Grace should have been harmless icebreakers. Did this place inspire fear in the women who came here?

I'd thought this gig would be a straight up-and-down find out about this place and report back to Bernie: no bullets, no burning buildings, nothing to make the people who cared about me throw their arms up about my work.

But my assignment wasn't shaping up to be as simple as Bernie had said it would be. Bernie lived on an estate with spacious grounds and a cook and a cleaner, and a new wife. He had even less understanding of a woman's homeless shelter than I did.

Out of the corner of my eye, I saw LuAnn palm a folded piece of paper and stuff it in her top pocket. She could have been wiping some of the delicious stew from her shirt, but my conversation with Kyle had paid off, as I knew what to watch for. The chase, as my father used to say, was on.

CHAPTER 4

I finished my dinner alone, put my tray in the designated place, and wandered through the shelter. On the other side of the sprawling building was the laundry service. Two sets of machines bounced and gurgled with activity, and clothes teetered in piles next to them. At the left back corner of the complex were the dormitories.

I wasn't looking forward to sleeping in a room of strangers—or a night without Floyd and his floppy ears and stinky breath and ability to take up half the bed, even though he was a short-legged hound dog. After cleaning him up from the dog park, I'd taken him to Arlene's for the night. She insisted on it these days when he wasn't with me, and Floyd loved it. He might miss me, but not as much as I missed him.

The shower stalls were around the corner from the laundry, as Nettie had pointed out earlier, but I skirted those, careful not to be seen. I didn't want Judy to accuse me of following her. A row of offices were located by another set of bathrooms. I tried a couple of the office door handles. *Locked.* The admins having done their duty had gone home to their lives. If I didn't manage to get Judy, LuAnn, or anyone else talking, I might need to engage in a bit of lock picking and file cabinet rummaging.

I strolled back through the main dining room and ended up in the TV room. About a dozen women occupied the area. One woman, over in the corner chair, was reading a well-thumbed paperback. Her formal posture, black-rimmed glasses, and coifed hair had me thinking of a librarian. Several middle-aged women were watching a CSI episode from the plaid-printed sofa. A couple of tables, stacked with tattered boxes of *Clue* and *Sorry!* and *Risk*, were shoved against the walls.

A puzzle had been started but abandoned half-way through. Another woman with tangled long hair, the grey outnumbering the black, talked to the spider in the web about two feet above her head.

Where were these women's families? Their children? Was there truly no place else for any of them to go? The woman talking to the spider needed help—kindness. I was no doctor, but she likely had a mental health condition that medication might at least help with.

My attention came to rest on the youngest girl in the room. If anyone could know about Amber, maybe she would. Curled in a chair, feet tucked and hair hanging over her face, she wrote furiously in a floral-covered journal. My nine-year-old daughter, Mitz, had similar strawberry-blond hair but with the addition of soft curls. Seeing that young girl had me longing for the weekend when it would be my time with Mitz again.

Was anyone missing this girl? The spider whisperer in the corner was sad enough, but a teenager? How had she ended up here? Who was at home right now, worried sick about her? She looked far too young to be out on the streets—and alone.

She looked my way but quickly lowered her gaze to her journal.

I headed to the puzzle table next to her. "This looks interesting," I said, inspecting the one-inch pieces covering the flat surface. The box pictured a rustic red barn and a churning water wheel. "Do you mind if I hang with you?" I had to connect with someone who'd trust me enough to break the silence. She might be a good bet since she didn't seem as hardened as the older women.

"Suit yourself."

I rescued a folding chair from behind the door, hunkered down at the table, and began putting it together. "I'm Kelly Robertson."

"Robyn....Baker." She continued to write.

The pause made me think full introductions were not the norm; I filed that away for the next time. "Nice to meet you."

"Haven't been on the streets long, have you?" Her attention had shifted to my hands.

I pulled them back. They didn't look like the other women's hands in the shelter who, like Judy's, were calloused, chapped, or stained. It was clear my choice of clothes or backpack had little to do with my ability to blend in. "Not long, no. You?"

"Few months."

A newbie herself. "What brought you out here?"

"The atmosphere," she waved her hand at the room.

I chuckled. That sense of humor would hopefully go a long way in protecting Robyn on the streets. "Right, who wouldn't want to spend time here?" That got a smile. "I meant, what brought you *here*?"

"What brought you?" She went back to her journal.

"Asshole ex took all my money and kicked me out. I lived out of my car for a week in Seattle, but the rain drove me crazy. So, I came south and then heard about this place."

"No family to bum off of?" she asked.

I arranged the puzzle pieces, pushing the blue ones to the upper corner and the red ones to the left. "No. I lost my mom when I was young—my dad more recently." My chin trembled, which I hadn't expected.

She looked me over and worked her jaw. "I lost my mom, too."

"I'm sorry. It's hard," I said. "How did she die?"

"Cancer."

"Rough."

"You're telling me. I still have my dad if you can call him that. He's pretty much a drunk when he's home and grounds me to keep me away from my girlfriend. That's why I left."

Teenage angst aside, a few months was a long time to punish people for not approving their love interest. "You left with her?"

She nodded.

Yet Robyn was in a shelter, and I hadn't spotted another young woman her age. "Things didn't work out?"

Tears rimmed the bottom of her eyes. "Thought they were. We were staying in a church parking lot until she took off weeks ago with some slut."

I arranged more puzzle pieces around, unsettled that this young girl was out here on her own. "How old are you?"

"Twenty-one."

I side-eyed her.

"I have the ID to prove it."

"So did I at your age."

"Fine. Seventeen, but I'll deny it if you rat me out." She shot a look at the door.

She was too young to be on these streets, too young to be on her own. "I wouldn't. But can't you go home? Your dad must be panicked and has reported you as a runaway, right?" Every maternal instinct in me revved up, desperate to protect her.

She rolled her eyes. "Yeah, right. Dad's a long-haul trucker and never there anyway. When he is, like I said, he's drunk and screaming or punching something. Me included."

My dad had been many things, unfaithful, gruff, hyper-focused, overly-protective, but I'd never wanted to run from him. Not everyone had that choice. "I'm sorry."

"Is what it is." She acted like it was no big deal. The fact she wouldn't meet my eyes said it was.

"No other family you could stay with?"

"All Bible-thumpers. I'm a sinner, don't you know?"

"No, you're not."

"Whatever."

"How about a school counselor? Maybe they could help you get into a place where you could keep up your education." The need to fix this was overwhelming. It wasn't my job nor the reason I'd come to Loving Grace, but every cell in my body was in Momma Bear mode and I couldn't turn it off.

She sniffed and shook it off. "If it was that easy, I would've done it by now."

Message received. I was trying to repair things I knew nothing about and it was time for me to hang back. She was the only person willing to chat so far. Maybe she could provide me with some insight into how this place really worked.

I pushed some more pieces around the table as we talked for another half hour. I mostly listened. People need to be heard, especially those who've been kicked to the curb by the precise people who were supposed to love and protect them, no matter what. Unconditional love was part of the parental code. So what if she wanted to date girls? Big deal. I wanted to put her under my wing and take her home. She wasn't Mitz. But without guidance, without a mother figure…

While I didn't know Robyn Baker, I wanted to make sure she'd be okay. "What are you writing about?"

"Right now, I'm just making notes. But I plan to write a novel someday about my adventures." Her face and mood lightened at the idea.

"I love to read…"

Her face flushed. "I don't let anyone touch this. Ever."

I'd hit a nerve. I smiled. "I get it. I'm like that too about certain things. When your book comes out, I'll buy it."

She tilted her head back and had a quick comeback. "Yeah, with what money?"

"Oh, this is just temporary," I said. "I expect to be back on my feet real soon." I pretended to inspect the puzzle while thinking of her notes, which could mean she'd been observing. Like she had noticed my hands when I thought she was immersed in her journal. "You come across any colorful characters to write about?"

She wrinkled her nose. "Only a few dozen."

"I bet. Ran into one myself tonight. Or she ran into me."

She snickered. "LuAnn?"

"Yeah. Is she always that pleasant?"

"She's nice. She's learned how to play the system. If you're going to survive on the streets, you've got to know the system," she said.

"What system?" I tried to keep my voice light.

Robyn doodled in the margin of her journal. Eyes and flowers as far as I could tell. "Bully the bullies and keep the authorities sweet."

"Is that what you do?" My heart was in my throat. It sounded like a terrible way to live.

Robyn looked up at me and flashed a smile. "I'm young enough that I don't count."

What did that mean—that she wasn't seen, wasn't bullied, that she didn't have to suck up to people if she wanted them to treat her well? What?

"They all want to be the mother they never were," she added.

I hoped that statement wasn't aimed at me, but it told me a lot about what she had seen and experienced.

"They think they can make up for their screw-ups by being nice to me. It won't last long, but as long as I remind them of their daughter, someone will have my back."

"Are there many other young women in the shelter system you've come across?" I asked. This could be an opportunity to find out more about Amber and Loving Grace.

"Not many." Robyn had drawn an eye as big as a page, giving it lashes so long they would have knocked you out in the real world.

"I heard about a girl who was here just last week. About your age. Did you meet her?"

"Which one? They come and go."

I frowned at the idea of that. "Amber something. Not sure."

"Yeah, no idea." But the way she held her body a little straighter, her mouth tighter, her pen harder as she swiped another lash on that big eye, I wasn't convinced.

"Might have gotten into drugs, or so I heard," I continued.

Her gaze slid back to her journal. She took long strokes with her pencil, shutting down as Judy had. "I'm not into all that. What's your interest anyway?"

I stumbled for a second. I'd pushed too hard again. "Just want to make sure this is a safe place, is all." It was time to move the conversation to another topic. "Anyone I should be careful of—besides LuAnn? I don't want to get myself into trouble. I'm sure you've figured this out, but the streets are scary enough. Drugs. Rape. It doesn't feel like it's ever safe anywhere."

She didn't respond.

I was crashing at the first hurdle. "How about on the streets? Any advice on places to stay away from?" Bernie thought Amber's drugs had come from the shelter, but maybe the drug dealer hung outside at the curb—or in the park down the street.

The backlit shape of a woman filled the entrance to the recreation room. "Lights out in ten," Nettie said.

I picked up a piece of sky, found where it belonged, and locked it into place with a snap. "Nettie seems nice enough."

Robyn grimaced. "They all do." There was that word *they* again—the one in Amber's voicemail message. And in Judy's—*they* who didn't like questions. "Until—"

"Hey, girlies." LuAnn shadowed the entry right after Nettie disappeared. "She said lights out in ten. That means move it." LuAnn stared at the two of us.

The other women in the room hustled out. I smiled, looking for that nice side LuAnn supposedly possessed. "Just wanted to finish this last part."

LuAnn *Hmphed* and disappeared.

"Until what?" I said, sure Robyn had been about to tell me something important.

She stood, tucking her journal under her coat. "Nothing. Just keep your head down and do as they tell you when you're inside these walls and you won't end up like...."

"Who?" I said. "The girl who disappeared?"

"Just don't *need* anything." She gathered her stuff and raced out of the room.

Between *don't ask questions* from Judy and *keep your head down* and *don't need anything* from Robyn, something was going on around here. I jumped out of my chair with the plan to find a bed close to Robyn and learn more about this place. I had made some progress but not enough.

CHAPTER 5

The sleeping quarters had cots lined up five across and twelve deep. With an army-green wool blanket rolled at the foot of each bed and a pillow, it reminded me of a military barracks. The thick clear plastic covers revealed a thin, striped mattress that barely kept the coiled springs at bay. It was going to be a crunchy-crinkly, backbreaking night. Then again, I had no intention of sleeping. My mandate was to observe, track, and report back to Bernie ASAP. I'd had a half-sighting of LuAnn *maybe* accepting drugs, but I'd need more proof of what was happening here regarding drugs being dealt and by whom.

Robyn had already secured a cot near the front and against the wall. She glanced my way a couple of times, giving me a small smile. For all her tough bravado, a trait I also took some pride in, she looked scared. However, my intention to bunk down close to her so we could talk was a no go. Other women who'd thought farther ahead about their sleeping arrangements were in the beds surrounding her. My choice was the middle or the end.

LuAnn came from behind and hit my shoulder with hers, forcing me to take a step to avoid falling. She pointed. "Back there."

If LuAnn was the resident dealer, perhaps even the person who'd sold drugs to Amber, you'd think she'd be friendlier to a potential client. But if she didn't have that in her, I'd pick-up the slack. "Didn't mean for us to get started on the wrong foot."

"Hmph," she said, her trademark sound. Useful insofar as it didn't give anything away.

"Seems like you know your way around here pretty well. I could benefit from that."

She saw right through my attempt at flattery, tsked, and pointed to the back of the room. "Lights out in two."

At my bed, I dropped my backpack just below my pillow with the intention of wrapping myself around it to keep it secure. Homesick already, I grabbed my phone out of my pack, turned it on and tossed the thin wool blanket over my hands while I texted Mitz. After my last case, we made it a point to say goodnight to each other every night. Assignment or not, I wasn't about to let that slide.

If I were at home, I'd be signing with her over video chat, but I looked rough and didn't want to scare her. Texting would have to do. I made it quick. A bright light under a cover would draw the wrong kind of attention. The less information people knew about me and what I owned, the safer I'd be.

Good night and sweet dreams xoxoxoxo. I wrote.

Face time? Mitz replied within seconds.

Working my love. Tomorrow?

Unhappy face followed by one of those sideways teary ones. Laughing? Emojis stumped me sometimes. Then: *JK. Love you.*

JK. That one I saw a lot. Just kidding. *Love you too silly girl. xxxxxxx*

Next, I texted Kyle that all was well and I was safe. Hopefully, I'd have info to share with him tomorrow. I hadn't seen blatant signs of drugs, but the night was young, and a lot happens under cover of darkness.

Kyle responded, *sounds good.* I shot back a heart and got one in return.

Switching my phone to silent, I tucked it into my pack. I lay on my stomach and scanned the room, taking shallow breaths. The combination of street filth and body odor was overwhelming. The stew that had landed on me earlier acted like cheap perfume wafting up my nose. I pulled off my long-sleeved shirt and laid it at the foot of my bed, hoping the wool blanket wouldn't irritate my skin.

Robyn had turned to her side, her bag filling the space between her and the concrete wall, her journal open as she scanned the room and jotted down more words.

If Robyn was half as observant as I thought, her journal could be a gold mine of clues. She'd blanched when I mentioned Amber by name. And the timing lined up: Robyn had been here for about a month, she'd said, and Amber had last called her Papa five days ago. They definitely overlapped at Loving Grace. While there were women of all ages, teenagers were not the norm here. Amber would have stood out every bit as much as Robyn did.

LuAnn had settled in and looked comfy on a double cot pushed against the farthest wall. What was her role in this place—a dealer—a go-between the dealer and the homeless women? Where did Nettie fit? No one stepped in when LuAnn roughed me up and threw her weight around the way she did. Was that at Nettie's direction?

The other women in the room messed with their bags and crawled under their covers. LuAnn got up and stepped out of the room. I took that as an invitation to get a few more minutes with Robyn. My feet hit the floor at the same time the lights dimmed and a loud "Shhhh" came from LuAnn's corner. She had only stepped out to turn off the overhead fluorescent lights, which held a light glow on their way to blackout, enough for me to watch Robyn lower her head on the pillow and close her eyes. I'd try in the morning.

I nestled down under the covers and stared at the ceiling. The clink of dishes rattling and water running came from the kitchen. The night crew was cleaning up. A cup of coffee sounded good and would help me stay awake and keep tabs on possible nighttime sales. But LuAnn was reading via penlight under her covers. No way I'd get past her.

Within minutes, snores filled the room. I snuggled closer to my backpack and forced my eyes to stay open and to stay alert, but I could imagine Kyle curling his body to mine. His breath in the back of my hair. His spicy cologne tingling my nose.

I shook myself awake a couple of times but despite my best efforts, I succumbed to sleep because the next thing I knew, my eyes flew open and the lights above were humming. A woman with long, grey-black hair hovered two inches from my face. My heart jolted. I tried to scoot away but only backed up against the pillow. "What the…"

"Barb. Wake up. We got to get out of here," the woman whispered.

Barb? That was my mom's name. If it hadn't been for the fluorescent lights and the woman being close enough for me to smell the urine coming off her, I'd have sworn I was trapped in a nightmare. They came with alarming regularity. There was the one about the night my mother died, then the one where my dad collapsed in his office and I couldn't resuscitate him. Less frequent, but no less alarming, were the episodes where I'd been shot—or burned alive. Worst of all, when I was about to die in my dreams, it only confirmed my greatest fear: I was a terrible mother, leaving Mitz behind.

This was no nightmare.

My eyes focused on the woman who was nose-to-nose with me.

My heart pounded harder. It was the same woman who'd been talking to the spider last night in the TV room. "Hey there, I'm Kelly."

The woman pulled herself upright and tilted her head. "Don't mess around, Barb. They're going to find out. We need to go." I rolled off the cot and stood, her intensity and utter conviction that there was a problem, and the fact she was about the age my mom would be if she were alive, rattling me. Unstable or not, she believed she and Barb needed to escape. "Go where?"

"Away."

"Why? What's happened?"

"They know," she hissed.

It was eerily like what Amber had said to Bernie on the answering machine. "Know what?"

The woman shook her head.

I reached my hand out to touch her forearm, but she jerked it back like I'd burned her. "It's okay. I'm Kelly. What's your name?"

"We don't have time for this, Barb. What's wrong with you?"

Mental illness was complex, and I didn't have the expertise to handle this situation—except through compassion. "You're confused. I'm sorry, I'm not who you think I am."

Her eyes bore into me. She reached out a rough hand and touched my face, my hair.

"For God sakes, Ruth Comfrey, leave the girl alone." A woman's voice came from behind me.

Ruth jumped back, her eyes wide in fear. "Sorry, ma'am."

"Now get moving," the voice said.

I turned, expecting LuAnn, but Nettie stood with her arm at her side, a long knife clutched in her hand. Kathy Bates' menacing look in *Misery* flashed through my mind, which led to the memory of my last case and sent a shiver through me.

"Breakfast in five," Nettie announced and turned her back, slipping out the door.

Ruth hurried to her cot, repeating, "I want Barb. I need to see Barb. I like Barb," her voice getting quieter and quieter until she was back to mumbling to herself like she had been last night.

My heart slowed to a regular beat as the other women rolled out of their beds, roused by Ruth's confusion and Nettie's announcement. LuAnn's cot was empty, her bedding already rolled and set on top of the pillow. Robyn's cot lay empty too, her blanket piled in the middle. Her bag was gone. An early riser. She must be getting ready for the day. If I intended to finish the conversation that LuAnn had interrupted last night, I'd better do the same.

Slipping back into my smelly shirt, I grabbed my bag and headed to the facilities, my face, arms, and neck itching. I scratched them through my long sleeves. Robyn wasn't in the stalls or the showers. With my backpack hanging off my shoulder, I made my way to the TV room. I paused outside the door and rolled up a sleeve to find little red bites. "Damn it." *Bedbugs.* They must be in the blanket.

A morning show blasted from the caged TV hanging from the ceiling. A few women sipped their coffee and listened to a very stylish morning star tell them about the latest in-home décor or gourmet pasta or something else utterly divorced from their present lives. The corner chair where Robyn had been last night was empty.

Over by the front doors, Nettie was getting into it with a young woman I hadn't seen last night. She raised her voice, but Nettie seemed to be holding her ground.

Was I about to see what I'd come here for in the first place?

Whatever the topic, the way the younger woman's body leaned toward Nettie—her bulky down jacket open, her hands tucked into the pockets of her size too-small jeans, along with Nettie's rigid stance—indicated the conversation was not pleasant. Taking a step closer, I noted the girl's red hair, shaved on one side and long on the other. A track of gold and diamond studs lined her exposed ear.

The women trailed behind me from the dorm room to the cafeteria, ignoring what was happening up front. I kept one eye on Nettie, the other on the food line where a volunteer spooned scrambled eggs onto the breakfast plates. Judy appeared from the back of the facility and joined the line. There was no sign of Robyn or LuAnn.

Nettie's voice rose a notch. "She's not here."

"Where is she then?" the tall girl asked.

"How would I know?"

"Well, someone must. I got a text from her after midnight saying it was urgent I meet her at Farragut Park. She never showed."

Who was "she?" Could this girl be looking for Amber? Farragut Park wasn't far from the shelter.

"She checked into the shelter and was here when the lights went out at ten. We have a rule of no in, no out, but we don't cage people like animals. If she left, that's on her."

Okay, so not Amber.

"You're telling me no one heard her leave or saw her go? What kind of shelter are you?"

I moved closer to hear the answer.

Nettie didn't notice me and the tall girl didn't glance my direction. "Like I said, we don't police the front door. It's locked from the outside for their protection, but if they want to leave, I can't stop them."

The young woman slammed her hand against the table. All eyes shot up at her, then darted away. "Something happened. She hasn't taken my calls for over a month and, suddenly, I get a panicked text which means she was in trouble. Get it? So what kind of trouble was she in? What went down here?"

She had to be referring to Robyn. She was the "girlfriend who'd run off with a slut" who Robyn had mentioned last night. Nothing from my discussion with Robyn suggested she'd be calling her ex any time soon. What had changed during the previous eight hours?

Nettie shook her head and glanced at her watch. "Nothing 'went down' as far as I've been told. I left at eleven to go home and was back here at five. I can check with Gordon, the night manager, but he didn't report any problems either."

Nettie kept her tone soft and even, but her body language suggested she didn't like the questions. I hadn't seen a man since I'd arrived, but Bernie had mentioned a Gordon when he briefed me on who I would meet and need to investigate. Amber had left the premises after dark. Why had Robyn bolted? What happened at night that had driven them both out?

The tall girl stood straight. "Where's this Gordon? Let me see him."

"He's not here. Give me your number, and I'll have him call you when he arrives."

"Sure you will." Her tone dripped sarcasm. "Tell me when he'll be here and I'll come back."

"No idea. Take your chances, leave your number or don't. That's up to you."

Women were wandering about the shelter and the place buzzed with activity. Nettie was busy, but her attitude was on the defense. She appeared strangely unconcerned about a young missing girl—or maybe it had happened too many times.

The young woman grabbed a piece of paper off a nearby table and scribbled down her info. "Call me if you see her. If I don't hear from her soon, you'll be answering to the police," she said and stormed out.

All I saw as she left was another homeless girl not much older than Robyn on the streets. While I knew nothing about Robyn or her ex's relationship, after spending time with Robyn, I leaned toward a theory that the two of them were confused and miserable at being grownups.

Who didn't have problems navigating those early years? I had trouble wrangling my feelings into order at my age, how much harder was it for them, and add dealing with their sexual orientation and their families' reaction.

Whatever they had going on, Robyn calling her ex-girlfriend meant something had changed. I had to talk to the girlfriend. Before I could get more than a few steps, sweet, muddled, Ruth came into view again. "Barb?"

I side-stepped her and made it out the door just as a brown, early eighties Datsun hatchback accelerated away, leaving a trail of thick black exhaust in its wake. I ran to the curb expecting to get a license plate at least, but the cloud of smoke made that impossible.

I trudged back inside, annoyed at myself. Robyn was the closest I'd come to making a connection and now she was gone. I'd have to start over again. Worse, if she'd disappeared in the night like Amber, I was looking at a pattern. Either way, I didn't have enough information to take to Bernie or to convince him to let me launch phase two of my investigation: tracking down these missing girls.

Nettie had stepped behind the oatmeal pot like nothing had happened. She pinned the paper the young woman had given her to a small corkboard behind her. I fell into line and made my way to her.

As I waited, a tall, dark-haired man appeared next to the cooks. His ample stomach hung over his jeans, and he wore a black Izod T-shirt. I put him at forty. He was attractive in your best friend's nerdy dad kind of way. He directed some of the staff to put things in the refrigerator while he tasted the eggs and motioned for another to start the dishes. He appeared in charge to me. If that was Gordon, Nettie must have known he was here when that young girl asked about him. Why had Nettie lied about it?

"Morning," I said when I reached Nettie. "Is he the chef?" I nodded to the kitchen.

"That there's Gordon. He cooks, among other things. Your sleep was good, I trust?"

"Yes, thank you. I appreciated the place to rest my head."

Gordon placed a hand on one of the women's shoulders and pointed at a stack of plates in the background. His hand lingered before his fingers brushed down her arm. She appeared to bristle before walking over to the dishes. I was on high alert. This was a women's shelter and a place of refuge. If he was hassling women, then that was another problem for the shelter.

Gordon turned his attention to the produce delivery guy that had arrived. Good looking in a commercial model kind of way, the man flashed his smile at one of the cooks and reduced her to a giggling schoolgirl. It became clear how vulnerable these women were, and how easy it would be to sway them to break the law. They had nothing and nowhere to go, desperate for money. It made sense they'd be open to running what appeared to be errands of a packet of whatever LuAnn had palmed at dinner to someone.

The vendor stopped Gordon and whispered something in his ear. They turned away from me but I watched the delivery man hand off a small packet to Gordon. Gordon promptly slid that packet into his front pocket. It was the same move that LuAnn made last evening.

There it was—another possible exchange of drugs. It could be that they came in with the produce and went out via Gordon. That was something to inform Bernie and Kyle about.

"Remember we close after breakfast and reopen at four," Nettie said, getting ready to scoop a serving of gruel in my bowl.

I waved her off, deciding to eat later and save the food for the other women, but I couldn't leave quite yet. I'd witnessed a potential drug buy in broad daylight. I had to stick around a while longer. If I could chat with Gordon, perhaps I could learn if he saw Robyn leave the shelter.

I smiled at Nettie. "Thanks for the reminder." A coffee pot was next to Nettie. I filled a cup.

The men turned back around; the produce guy was laughing.

"Hey, I overheard that woman asking about Robyn. I haven't seen her this morning either," I said to Nettie.

Nettie stirred the oatmeal with some vigor. "Hard to keep track of them all. Like I told her, she'd probably already left. Some like to get a head start on their day."

"Before breakfast?" I asked, when what I wanted to say: before seven when the doors were supposedly locked? If she'd gotten outside and couldn't get back in, why had no one noticed? Was that it? Gordon would have been around all night—he should have.

"Can't speak to what people are thinking."

Whatever the reason for Robyn's departure, Nettie either hadn't been clued in or didn't intend to discuss it with me. "Very true." I focused on the paper Robyn's ex had left with her number on the board behind Nettie. *Trinity* was written there in bold block letters along with a phone number that I repeated in my head until I had it down.

"Let's keep the line moving," Nettie ordered.

I finished my coffee alone. Judy wouldn't make eye contact. She'd wedged herself in the center of a table full of women making it impossible for me to approach her privately. I dove into my backpack, fished out my toiletry kit, and headed to the bathrooms.

The office doors, which had been secured last night, were open. One looked to be a supply closet. Another might have been a secretary's office or maybe Nettie's. The last one was unoccupied, and a tweed jacket hung over the chair—a man's office, then—Gordon's?

It had to be. My eyes scanned his desk, and I froze. Just to the left of his keyboard was Robyn's flowery journal.

CHAPTER 6

Robyn had clung to her journal and wouldn't let me touch it when I'd asked. No one touched it "ever," were her exact words, which meant she wouldn't have left it behind voluntarily. With how attached she'd been to her journal, the idea of her forgetting it didn't make sense either—nor did the possibility of it dropping out of her bag without her noticing—unless something caused her to run—or someone.

The fact it was on Gordon's desk might be a stroke of luck for me since I had wanted to read its contents, but that didn't answer why Gordon had it or when he'd come into possession. If Robyn's notes inside implicated him and he had time to read it….

Robyn had called her ex-girlfriend and then not shown up to meet her.

Amber had called her Papa and disappeared.

Loving Grace looked a lot more sinister this morning than it did when I first walked in the door.

I picked up the journal and slid it inside my backpack. Robyn and Amber both running out in the middle of the night could be a coincidence. I had no clue. Until I knew more, Robyn's journal would stay in safekeeping with me.

When I returned to the common area, the wall clock read seven and the doors had opened. Not only did the homeless women fill the place, but suddenly there were more employees, vendors, and volunteers.

The PI in me was itching to stay and find out what was going on here, but Bernie only wanted info on who was dealing and nothing more. This was a private matter between him and his employees. He'd drive out the bad guys and hope Amber emerged from hiding afterwards—not my choice if it were me.

Gordon had joined Nettie at the front door. "Have a blessed day," he said. His eyes were warm, but they lingered. Maybe I could get him talking. Even one more snippet of information might help Bernie. Tired and dirty, he might peg me wanting to score drugs. That could work. I smiled as I passed him. He reached out and placed his hand on my shoulder, leaving it there a couple of beats too long.

"Maybe we can talk?" That sounded more like a pickup line than how I imagined you scored drugs.

Gordon smiled. "Be back here when the doors reopen, and we can certainly find time for that."

"Now?" I let a little desperation creep into my voice.

Nettie shot him a look. I had no idea what it meant.

"I'm afraid we have a busy day ahead of us," he said. "Find me this evening. We can chat then."

Not wanting to push too hard, I nodded and walked away, keeping my eyes on him.

He cleared his throat and turned his attention to the other women behind me, continuing to recite the exact words as one by one, the women of Loving Grace filed out of the double doors and onto the streets.

Our interaction had been brief, but he employed his lingering hand routine on the shoulders of a couple more women, although a few stepped out of line and avoided talking with either Gordon or Nettie. If his touchy-feely approach was his usual MO, I didn't blame them.

I was glad to be outside and on the sidewalk—especially glad for the fresh air. The women dispersed around me.

A movement in a top window of the four-story building across the street caught my attention. Was it someone in a white coat? I cupped my hands over my eyes for a better view. It was only a white shade, half drawn. That had to be the rehab center, "Saving Grace." The irony didn't escape me. Bernie should have sent me in there instead of the shelter. However, it would be harder to fake being a junkie.

Sending me to the shelter had been the right choice, and I had enough to report. There were now potentially two women who disappeared in the middle of the night at the shelter. There was also a hint of fear if one asked too many questions about the place. Bernie couldn't sit back and wait for his grandbaby to come to him. Once I confirmed for him that his gut instinct was right—it appeared drugs were being delivered and passed on to employees at Loving Grace—he'd agree.

That was unless he wasn't telling me something—there always was information left out in cases that involved family. But I was determined to provide him with a report that would make him listen and see sense. Those girls were out there on their own and predators like Gordon and the good-looking smiley produce guy were picking them off one by one.

I couldn't get home fast enough to clean up, burn my clothes, call Kyle and bring Bernie up to date.

Before I even took a step, someone slammed into me from behind, and my shoulder lurched toward my chin. My hackles raised, certain LuAnn had made a reappearance. But it was Judy, passing me in a hurry. If she'd wanted my attention for a chat, she didn't show it. She took long strides down the street, her bag flung over her shoulder.

She'd made it clear she wasn't interested in answering my questions last night. Away from the shelter, she could feel differently. I jogged after her, but she darted across the street and ducked into the passenger side of a gray work van before I could catch up. It took off the moment her door slammed shut and the dark plastic covering the license plate made it unreadable from my distance.

As I turned back to the shelter, Ruth emerged from the building. She hadn't bothered me at breakfast and I didn't want to give her another chance.

Tri-Met's Route 7 pulled to the curb, and the hydraulic door swooshed open. I hopped on and made my way to the back of the bus. As I did, a white van pulled up in front of the rehab center. At least a dozen people got off and headed toward the front door. Homelessness and rehab never end.

I took a seat and dropped my bag next to me, my thoughts on Loving Grace and the vulnerable position the women were in there. I had a place to fall back to when I hit a rough patch. My dad had left me his house when he died. My ex-mother-in-law could be difficult, but her living next door blessed me with a live-in babysitter for Mitz and a dog sitter for Floyd. I could say no to being a drug mule because I had choices.

If drug dealing was occurring in the shelter, as it appeared to be, Robyn's journal might hold some more clues. I dug into my bag and retrieved the journal, uncomfortable with the thought of looking through her private thoughts and breaching her trust.

She was out there on her own. I turned my attention to outside the bus window, aware this young woman had struck a chord. Was Portland drearier, danker? Was the world less rosy now that I'd spent a single night with a million bloodsuckers and a handful of broken women?

The truth, the world wasn't always kind to people who'd fallen on hard times. Robyn was in trouble, and I cared what happened to her...to all of them. I had no choice. I flipped open the first page.

Her handwriting was a blocky print, no cursive like I'd been taught, but the i's had hearts and the borders were decorated with cute, wide-eyed animals, swirling flourishes and dainty flowers. Her heart might have been broken and she might be on the run from her dad, but she hadn't given up hope of a better tomorrow.

Trinity says we're going to have a house one day.

There were pages and pages of "Trinity says" entries indicating Robyn had been head-over-heels in love with the young woman...and they were making plans.

Trinity says we can have a dog.

Trinity says we're going to be rich and famous, sell our story to the highest bidder.

Trinity says...

The Trinity says entries trailed off, but what little she'd said looked promising. I skipped ahead. There was a poem about bedbugs. A stream-of-consciousness piece about chilly cheese dogs. There was a rant about the cost of clean clothes and how demoralizing it was to be dirty all the time. A ton of doodles had wide eyes with big lashes, cars, people, and insects.

I'd be writing rants about laundry if I had to live like this for long. Bernie had more than just human trash to take out.

Robyn had been adamant that no one see her diary, but the contents didn't appear to incriminate anyone that I could tell on my first reading, apart from herself. If she was right about her family rejecting her because of who she loved, then all the *Trinity Says* entries would have been a problem. Was there something else in the journal that I'd missed? I didn't think so at this point. After gaining more information, I'd reread it.

I tucked the journal back in my bag and watched the neighborhoods switch from dingy to respectable in just a few avenues and I dismounted a couple of stops before my street. It wasn't that I cared what the neighbors said. It was Arlene, my ex-husband's mother, who was the issue.

Arlene's house was next door to mine, and a staircase joined our two properties. It got the most use when Mitz was over at one of our places or if Arlene was watching Floyd, or when she wanted to bring me a hanging basket. It used to be she liked to meddle. That had been on the decrease since she'd started dating Detective Kuni, with whom I'd worked in my last case.

But for all the flaws we bumped against in each other, Arlene adored Mitz, and she was partial to Floyd, which meant we'd made an unspoken pact that mostly involved me not telling her what I was doing when it came to my investigative work. That meant she couldn't see me like this.

I was all set to sneak into my place and get cleaned up when I spotted an unfamiliar sedan backed into Arlene's driveway. The trunk was wide-open; a stack of boxes and a large blue suitcase were sitting outside it. Detective Kuni couldn't have already decided to move in. Man, I was pathetic if Arlene was ahead of me in the relationship department, not that she and I competed, but Kyle and I weren't even close to cohabitating. A toothbrush in a cup and a dedicated underwear drawer weren't what you'd call compelling evidence that we'd entered that next stage of our relationship.

Floyd appeared at the top of the stairs and flew down them, launching himself at my legs, slobbering kisses all the while. He didn't care that I smelled like a hobo. In fact, he was thrilled. I, on the other hand, was not as chipper. Why was Arlene leaving the front door open like that? I thought to remind her about Floyd's hound dog traits that could get him into trouble quickly.

But my clothes. My hair. The stench. Talking to Arlene would have to wait.

"Come on, boy," I said. I turned toward my house but was stopped dead by the laughter. That wasn't Arlene. But it couldn't be who I thought it was.

My face wrinkled in confusion as I turned around. "Hannah?"

"Sis." She trotted down the stairs and hugged me. It was her turn to wrinkle her nose. "Nice look you've got happening. How've you been?"

I pulled myself away. Last I'd heard, she was in the Seattle area. "Fine, but is that your car in the driveway?"

"Yup. I'm baaacck," Hannah sing-songed.

What did it mean she was back—for how long, why here? All questions I wanted to ask but where to begin? "Where have you been for the last year?" I said instead, unsure how I felt about seeing her. She reminded me of some of my father's past choices that I'd tried to forget.

"You know me, I'm always around."

The last time I'd spent any significant time with her was after my first case that involved her other half-sister. That's how Arlene had met her as well. They'd hit it off at my dinner table. None of that explained why she was at Arlene's with a suitcase and boxes.

While we were chatting, Arlene had arrived at the top of the stairs and had been listening to our conversation. She gave me the once over—a couple of times. I braced myself for a commentary on my clothes, but she said, "Hannah is moving in for a while, dear."

My jaw must have fallen open, as I couldn't get any words out.

"Don't look so thunderstruck," Arlene said. "It's only for a short time."

"Yeah, big sis. Arly here offered her basement for a few weeks until I can get my feet on the ground." Hannah climbed the stairs to stand next to Arlene.

"Arly?"

Arlene laughed. "That's her term of endearment for me."

"Endearment?" I wasn't handling this well or able to stop my mouth from parroting these outrageous words.

Floyd darted back up the stairs to Hannah and sat at her feet. Even he liked Hannah?

"It's only for a month," Arlene said.

"Are your parents okay?" I stared at Hannah for an answer.

She bent down to ruffle Floyd's ears. He was almost smiling. "They're good. They're remodeling and I got my job back at Casa Diablo. Sometimes it's just easier to have space, you get that I'm sure?"

I did, and I was relieved her mom, Georgine and Chester were okay. She was my half-sister because of a situation with my dad and Hannah's mother. Her mother was fortunate that her husband, Chester, had accepted Hannah as his own because my dad, her real dad, not so much. Clearly, I struggled with it, too.

"Arlene, can we talk?" I met her gaze with one of my own.

"No worries," Hannah chimed in. "I'll get my stuff into the house and get settled."

Arlene nodded and when Hannah was back at her car, came down the stairs to me. "Change for you is hard, I realize this, but please be kind to her. She is my guest."

"Your guest?"

"Yes. She called me a few days ago. She was coming into town and needed a place to land. I don't mind. It gets lonely here. You rarely come by to stay and visit, and Jeff and Mitz aren't here nearly enough. Not all of us believe we have to go it alone. Some of us like company. Even seek it out."

"But Hannah?" I was guilty as charged as far as visiting. I didn't come by "just to visit" or "say hi" nearly as often as I probably should. I wasn't the hanging-out sort. I liked to be doing and Arlene understood—I thought;

I'd vastly improved on going it alone. My bringing Kyle into the loop on my current investigation had been a huge leap forward in that regard.

Arlene chuckled. "She's your sister."

"Half," I answered. "And where's Detective Kuni? Aren't you two hitting it off? I thought it was him moving in when I saw Hannah's car."

Arlene blushed. "We're doing fine, thank you. But let me ask you, where's Kyle right now?"

"He's working. He gets a lot of overtime since being promoted to detective." I knew where she was going with this.

"Precisely. David has a similar job, only he's over thirty miles away. He can't just stop by for a booty call."

"Booty call?"

She waved me away. "That's what Hannah calls them."

This was more information than I wanted to hear. The fact Hannah knew details about Arlene's love life with Detective Kuni, and I didn't, was almost more than I could take.

"Want to tell me about your latest case?" Arlene pointed at my hobo ensemble.

"Maybe later."

"Suit yourself."

She headed back toward her house. I waited and then followed as far as the garage where Hannah was removing more boxes from the trunk of her car.

"I understand why Arlene invited you, but she's been family to me for far longer than you and I won't let anyone take advantage of her." I never thought those words would come out of my mouth, but there they were.

"Wouldn't think of it, sis," she said. "I'm here for you, too."

"Hmm," was all I said. I'd heard that a time or two from various people in my life, which usually meant they weren't.

Hannah's behavior during my first case involving her family led me to believe she had flaky qualities. Whether that remained the case was to be determined. I found myself being protective of Arlene. She might want company, but I wouldn't let anyone use her—even my half-sister.

I had to admit—I was frustrated at Arlene for letting Hannah so close, maybe even more at the ease in which they interacted with each other, at Floyd for liking Hannah—although he'd returned to my side as I trotted down the stairs. But I had my work and that was enough to keep me busy for a while.

I had to fumigate myself, and then I had a job to do—calls to make—and most importantly, missing girls to think about.

CHAPTER 7

I stripped at the bottom of the stairs, emptied my backpack, and shoved it and my clothes into the dryer. A google search said I didn't need to burn everything to get rid of bedbugs. Thirty minutes on high heat would do it. To be on the safe side, I set it for sixty.

I raced for the shower with Floyd on my heels and stepped into the steaming spray. Whoever invented hot, running water should win every science award. I poured a handful of oatmeal-based soap into my palm and slathered it on my arms and legs, soothing the bites immediately. Almost half an hour later, grateful and humbled, amazed how something so simple could make me feel that good, I dressed and called Bernie and gave him my report.

As soon as he heard that Gordon was the possible dealer and possibly harassed some women, he wanted to get off the line and go down there to hand out pink-slips.

I reminded him what Amber had said, that they would "clean up" all evidence of wrongdoing if he showed his face.

"Not your concern," he barked. "You did what I asked you to do…"

I cut him off. "It's not enough for a conviction. All I saw was…"

"You're not listening," he shouted. "I don't need a conviction. I need them out of there."

There had to be something more he wasn't telling me. He'd offered me a case that didn't add up, and now it was only getting weirder. "Bernie," I said in the voice I use when I need Floyd to stop what he's doing immediately for his own good. Bernie shut up for a second. "What's going on? What are you not telling me?"

The other end of the line was silent. I worried that he'd cut me off, but the seconds were ticking away, which meant the call was live.

"Is it money you want?" he said.

Wow. I hadn't expected that answer. "No, I'd like you to let me continue to find out what is going on at Loving Grace though."

"I'll pay you to stay away."

Right. He *was* holding something back. "Bernie." This time I used my gentlest, most convincing tone. There were bad men out there—as in evil men—and vulnerable women who didn't know how to take care of themselves. "I was only there one night. I saw a couple of low-level deals. But there is more; the vibe is off. They're not talking, except to say to be careful of *them,* but no one would tell me what that meant. They're shifty, restless, scared, and there's bullying that goes on in there. The doors aren't secure. A boatload of vendors have access to the place. Gordon is only the tip of the iceberg."

I had an ace up my sleeve—the thing that would tip him into hiring me to find his granddaughter. "And another young woman, in addition to Amber, has possibly gone missing."

The line went dead. I stared at the phone, incredulous.

That wasn't at all how it was supposed to go.

I stomped around my bedroom, unable to get the adrenaline out of my system. Floyd liked this new game and trotted after me, headbutting my ankles every third step. "What are we going to do, bud? Are we going to let him make the same mistake again?"

My boy looked up at me, head cocked to one side. I found it best to put my thorniest problems to Floyd. Dogs always had the right answers. No matter how far out one went, they followed. The world should be all dogs, except Mitz and me...and Kyle. He was shaping up to be *the one.*

"You think so? You think I should do a little digging?" I said to him.

Floyd panted, all love and floppy ears and slobber.

"You're right. We should. Good idea." I scrubbed his head and gave his ears a scratch. He flopped to the floor, ready for a follow-up belly rub, but I was already scrolling through my contacts.

I shot off a text to Kyle, aka Hot Stuff.

Know you're working, but real quick. Any women, homeless or otherwise, reported missing in the parks or vicinity last night?

Maybe Robyn's girlfriend had gone to the police by now.

Maybe arrested? I added just in case.

I expected a phone call with that question. Instead, a few minutes later I got: *Nothing reported.*

My thumb hovered over the keypad. He was busy, but I was antsy and irritated and in need of someone with a solid head on their shoulders. Since we'd already consulted about the assignment, he was the perfect person to talk this through with me.

Any chance you could come by? Missing you. Could do with some face-to-face time.

He'd say no. It was the beginning of his day. I stared at my phone for a full thirty seconds, my stomach in knots, before his sweet reply popped up.

*On my way. Wild horses…*plus a music emoji.

While our relationship had become more official in the past few months, slowly, it was nice to know that nothing could keep him away. That cheered me considerably, enough to make a few more calls to the local hospitals and cover my bases. I made my final notes on the case and dried my hair.

The smell of marinara, cheese, and garlic wafted from my kitchen by the time I'd finished. It was an odd combination for the morning but left no doubt who was at the stove. I grabbed my robe and raced downstairs. My mouth watered as I walked into the kitchen, and not only because *Hot Stuff* had a pan of sauce bubbling on the top burner. His muscular legs stretched the fabric of his black shorts, and a WSU T-shirt stopped me in my tracks.

"Hey, sunshine," he said. "You rang?"

"Are you trying to win my heart with food?"

He frowned. "Thought I already had that in the bag."

"Oh yeah." I smiled and touched his face, the heat of the skillet radiating between us. "I'm so happy you're here. I've had quite the last twelve or so hours. I thought you were on duty?"

"I'm getting a reprieve because we handled a case last night," he said. "And before you ask, I'm figuring you didn't eat great last night. That's why dinner for breakfast, so food first."

How'd I get so lucky? "Actually, I need your brain first."

He lowered the spaghetti into the boiling water. "Of course you do. All the women want me for my brain."

I laughed. He'd come over as soon as I called, and here he was, easy and laughing and putting the world to rights. I sat at the kitchen table, Floyd on my feet, and waited for my meal.

"Well?" He shot a look over his shoulder. "How are you going to handle my grey matter this time?"

"It's about that case we spoke about yesterday."

"Right, missing granddaughter and possible drugs." He tasted the sauce, nodding for me to go on.

"Exactly. I gave you the rundown, but not all of the particulars, which is that she also has or had a habit."

"We're not talking about origami, I take it?"

"I wish. Probably heroin."

"Okay. And you've determined that she's a runaway at this point?"

I shook my head. If I intended to work out what Bernie was hiding from me, my detective boyfriend had to be cranking on all cylinders, which meant I had to retell him everything from the beginning. I relayed the tale, leaving out no details and ending with my theory. "Bottom line. There might be hard drugs, and missing girls, and the two things must be somehow related. But I have no hard evidence yet."

Kyle shrugged. "Maybe they are and maybe they aren't. We don't have enough info either way."

"What about Bernie hanging up on me—after telling me to back off? What's your take on that? It doesn't pass the smell test."

The bowl in front of me sure did—a steaming pile of yum with grated parm coming down on the sauce like snow in the Rockies.

"He's a rich man." Kyle took a seat across from me. He grated slightly less cheese on top of his marinara, but not by much. The only difference between us when it came to cheesy deliciousness was that he had more self-control when it came to his diet. "He's used to getting his way."

"But it's his *granddaughter*. Why would he keep me from finding her?" I slurped up a fork full of noodles.

"He's a criminal lawyer, right?"

I nodded.

"Then he's going to brush elbows with criminals. This is a fact."

"Yes, but family…"

"Wait…" He put his fork down. "I'm not done. Let's say he knew about the drug dealing out of Loving Grace. Did he turn a blind eye? Did he get a cut? Was he in on the action?"

I shook my head this time with some vigor, but he didn't let me get a word in.

"Let's say he either pretends it isn't happening or is making a profit for years." He held up his hand. "Just for the sake of argument. I get that you don't believe it's possible, but let me paint you a picture. He's fine with drugs going in and out of Loving Grace until it hits his family. Then there are repercussions. There are consequences. He hears that his granddaughter—you said her name was Amber?—Amber is looking into his shady business dealings."

"It's not like that," I said. "Bernie's sister OD'd. He'd never be involved. But that's not the point. It's like he's scared."

Kyle raised his eyebrows. "You make my point for me. He's scared of being implicated."

"I get what you're saying, but again, not like that. He believes Amber's in danger and that if he goes crashing in there, she'll be…" What did Bernie believe? He'd said he was overcome with guilt and didn't want to make the same mistake he'd made with Grace. That didn't rule out the scenario Kyle had painted.

He waited, the smile around his eyes just a little annoying. He sensed I was coming around to his way of looking at the chess pieces currently in play.

"Okay. Let's say, for the sake of argument, he's got pressure from someone else, with the emphasis on him. They don't know about me," I said.

Kyle dug back into his spaghetti. "True. That is to your advantage."

My turn to smile. "And based on that, what's to stop me from trying to find the girls?"

He looked at me again, his smile askew. "Nothing, except they're homeless and missing. It's an impossible combination."

I wouldn't accept that. "Perhaps on my own, which is why I need your help." Look at me go. I had not only consulted and kept Kyle in the loop, but I was asking for more of his help. "Is it possible for me to file an official missing person's report for Robyn so that we can all be searching?"

He sighed and reached for my hand.

Oh-oh. "You're about to go even more devil's advocate on me, aren't you?"

"Isn't that why you like my grey matter?"

"I suppose it is."

"But this time, it's something else. You're a bulldog, something I find very attractive about you, by the way, but I'm debating whether to give you this piece of information."

I pulled my hand out from under his. "What?"

"I dug into your request after we hung up. The department got a report from Trinity Abrams earlier today about her missing girlfriend."

It had to be the same Trinity that had driven off in that smoking Datsun. "She came by the shelter first thing. Good. I'm glad she filed."

"It is good, although it's too early to do anything about it and like I said, the homeless are consistently in survival mode or taking off because something scared them. We don't assign a lot of resources to a case like this because there's no point. The homeless are transient by nature and skilled at disappearing. Many don't want to be found."

"I'm not convinced this is one of those situations. Another favor, please?"

"I'll do my best to help, but it depends." He'd gotten very serious, very fast.

I bumped him with my knee. "C'mon. It's easy. I'm only asking that you check on whether any weird things have happened with other girls at Loving Grace. Like other missing person reports in the past few months that show their last known place was the shelter."

"For what purpose?"

"Maybe nothing. But I want to make sure there isn't some unseen pattern that not even Bernie is aware of."

"The only issue is it sounds like he doesn't want you on the case."

I took a bite. I'd thought some about that. "Remember during my investigation in May when I found out my dad had taken it upon himself to help find a missing child?"

He nodded.

"Some cases aren't about the money. Some you undertake because it's the right thing to do."

He reached for the cheese and the grater. "I'll give you that. But if you think she or any street person is going to dish about the latest problem they encounter in a shelter, you're wrong. They've decided their voices don't ring as loud as others. They're used to being dismissed. Which is why I hesitated to mention it."

"I hear you. But I have to do this. So you'll look? See if other girls have gone missing?"

He took another bite of food. "On one condition."

I wasn't a fan of conditions. "Okay…"

"I'm not going to tell you what to do. I have my opinions, but you're a pro, and I trust your judgment." I could have kissed him right then. "But be very careful. If you're right and girls are disappearing because of some drug deal gone bad, you don't want to be sitting in the middle of that."

I reached for the parmesan. My snow-topped mountain wasn't snow-covered anymore. "I promise."

Kyle's phone rang. He put his finger up for me to wait, scooted back from the table and disappeared into the living room. I took the dishes to the sink and rinsed them. While he was on the phone, I ran upstairs and changed into some well-worn jeans and a pair of shoes that had some thin tread. I shoved a thin blanket into my backpack, so I didn't have to use the shelter's bedding.

Kyle's footsteps on the stairway stopped short of the doorway where he leaned, his arms crossed over his chest while I stood there in my jeans and bra.

I wiggled my eyebrows at him.

"I wish. That was Enloe. We got another case." He strode in and wrapped his arms around me, his warmth and skin against me.

I could have melted into him. "So much for a break. One of these days, we'll get to sleep together again."

He nuzzled his face into my hair. "Tomorrow night if one of us isn't out sleuthing?"

"Sounds like a date." I laughed.

"In the meantime, play it smart and keep me posted."

"That I will do," I said as Floyd and I watched him disappear.

I'd thought many times over the past year that my dad would have liked Kyle. Since my last case, we'd come to an understanding where he recognized the pitfalls of my job but supported me anyway like I did his. I'd never had that from anyone—not my dad who'd protected me or Jeff who'd judged me. Kyle's support gave me confidence.

Back downstairs, I grabbed my phone. We were ready for action, but a solid lead to chase in finding these girls would be nice. Bernie didn't want me looking for Amber directly. Until I understood why, I'd honor that part, but Robyn had given the impression that she knew Bernie's granddaughter. Finding Robyn might accomplish both. I punched in Trinity's number from memory.

Hey, Trinity. My name's Kelly. We haven't met, but I know Robyn. I backspaced over that last part. I didn't "know" Robyn, I talked to her for a little while. *I met Robyn at Loving Grace. I want to help you find her.* I waited, rolling one of Floyd's toys with my foot. *No response*—it was time to bait the hook. *I have Robyn's journal. I think she must have dropped it. I know she'll want it back.* I hit send.

CHAPTER 8

Loving Grace wouldn't open its doors for several more hours, and I had nothing to go on until I talked to Trinity and got some ideas of where Robyn could be. If the stars were aligned and he got a break, Kyle would call me with stats about missing girls.

In the meantime, it was Tuesday, an official workday. I had to make a living and that included two documents that needed serving. After settling Floyd in my car, we tracked down the two respondents. It took me all morning and three stops at the Mini Mart for fresh coffee. They were uneventful.

The harasser in the first case looked at me and said, "This is just an example of fake news. Always somebody making something up."

I ignored his reference with, "You've been served."

The default document was an easy hand-off to a forty-something trying to re-write his parenting plan. He deserved what was coming. Nothing was worse than someone who skips out on their kid.

I checked the time. Mitz was in class, but she carried her phone. I texted her a couple of hearts and flowers. I had Robyn's journal on the brain, it seemed.

It was three-thirty when I pulled in front of my office located in the northeast part of town, where if Portland were anatomically correct, would be considered the armpit. Speaker-busting rap blared from cars bouncing down the street at any given time of day, and its where I had my own group of homeless people using my doorframe as a urinal periodically. Despite that, I'd always loved this run-down brick building with its green-striped awnings.

I hadn't been here much after my first case, but I'd been making my way back to my home away from home slowly. I'd worked with my dad in this building. It had history, and the good memories outweighed the bad. I'd begun to learn my trade under this roof.

Now, I was on the precipice of being what my dad would have called "The Real Deal," and I was proud of that fact. I wouldn't let something like a client's trepidation get in the way of me solving a case, which meant finding these girls. My dad would never have given up on a just cause and this qualified as one. A missing motherless girl had been his Achilles heel and, apparently, mine.

With Floyd at my side, I unlocked the building, and pushed open the door, shifting the pile of envelopes and postcards that had formed in front of the mail slot. I carried the stack into the office, dropping it onto my dad's worn and weathered desk.

I sorted through the junk, retrieved the checks, and powered up my computer to complete a couple of Affidavits of Service.

As I waited for them to print, I leaned back in the chair and ran my finger in the ruts of my father's desk. We'd shared this very spot, and he hadn't lived to see the investigator I had started to become—or at least what I thought I'd become. Whether I'd believed being called to Bernie's house had meant something, the answer to my statement about my father lingered in my mind.

"Hope you'll learn to trust me in the same way," I'd said to Bernie.

"Me too," he'd responded.

But he didn't trust me. I'd become so involved and driven to prove myself with this case that I'd ignored that Bernie didn't want me on it. Did he suspect I was nowhere near as good as my dad? I'd believed that about myself more than once over these past two years. It's not that Bernie didn't want his granddaughter found. He simply didn't think I could do it.

Grabbing the affidavits from the printer, I shoved them in my bag. Locking up, Floyd and I climbed back into my car.

I had thought at the very least, by working in his office, I had a chance of finding out that I might be as good as he'd been someday. Others would see that too, but it became clear that having this office made little difference in how I was perceived. Something to think about.

I flipped open my glove compartment and grabbed some peanut butter crackers I'd picked up from the store, breaking off a square for Floyd. Nothing replaced my love of peanut butter straight from the jar, but sometimes this was easier.

My phone buzzed with a text: Carla, Bernie's assistant. My heart jumped, a tiny sliver of hope that it was a summons from Bernie, but it wasn't. Carla had papers that needed serving. Could I come and pick them up today?

On my way, I wrote. With any luck, Bernie would be in the office and I could have another go at convincing him to bring me into the loop officially.

Baumgartner & Sokol was located in another questionable part of the city, Northwest Third and Davis in Old China Town. Despite its grittiness, I loved this part of the city with its old-world charm, Asian fusion restaurants, and red lanterns hung high above. The Shanghai Tunnels ran under this area and connected to the newer business district. Certain parts of the tunnels were off-limits, but other sections offered tours. When Mitz got a bit older, we'd be on one of those tours. My girl loved adventure, and it would be a fun experience to do together.

After securing Floyd in the car, I walked the distance, aware that being showered and wearing clean clothes made a difference to my attitude. At least the women I'd spent the night with didn't have rain to contend with today. I was hopeful that Robyn was somewhere safe and dry too, and that when I found her she'd lead me to Amber.

The two-person law office was on the first floor of a two-story brick building. They owned the entire building, but legal files were required to be kept for a long while and, apparently, bankers' boxes of years' old cases consumed the upstairs. The reception desk chair was empty, but men filled the glass conference room behind it. One of them was Tony Baumgartner, the other named partner of the firm, but no Bernie. The others were all business in their suits, including a balding man with his yellow bowtie who had lawyer written all over him. Their taut faces and creased foreheads said they were discussing a serious subject. None looked my way when I passed the conference room.

Bernie was behind his desk and on the phone when I poked my head inside his office. He held up his hand, indicating he'd be a few minutes. At least he hadn't glared at me. I took that as a positive sign.

I went looking for Carla, who I found punching keys on her computer. Client files stacked two feet high teetered next to her. Another larger pile sat on the credenza behind her and were interspersed with photos of Carla and her friends and family standing in front of a black limo. The feathered hats and bright colors said "wedding" rather than "funeral."

"Ms. Kelly." She glanced up and waved me in with one of her floral tattooed arms. Today's hair color was deep auburn cut sharply at her jaw and she wore a billowy top…very boho chic.

In my father's day, she wouldn't have been able to land a law office job. Those days were over. Now it was all about what you could do, not what you looked like—viva progress.

"You know where to find those docs," she said.

"Perfect." The document filer was attached to the wall above a couple of *Donation* boxes half-full of clothes and shoes. They'd been there for years and I'd never asked why—obviously for the shelter. I grabbed the papers, an Injunction for Harassment, not one of my favorites since the defendant to be served had boundary issues. The second was a hearing subpoena in a domestic relations case. I slid them into my shoulder bag before dropping into the chair directly across from her.

"Mind if I hang here until Bernie frees up?" I asked.

She smiled and gave me a thumbs up. We weren't buddies. We'd never hung out or gone for a drink, but we had a great working relationship. I didn't want to press. She was Bernie's assistant after all, and this was her livelihood, but if she knew anything about Amber, it would be helpful. I didn't have to broach the topic. She did it for me.

"You're investigating drugs in the shelter?" Carla asked.

I nodded, glad she knew that much. "I spent the night."

"Oh, that must have been interesting."

"And irritating." I pulled up my sleeve to show the red bumps on my arm.

"Are those…" One side of her lip curled.

"Yep." Seeing them made me want to scratch and take another shower. "I get everyone here is busy practicing law, but come on."

She shuddered. "It used to be better when Bernie and Tony were more involved. They haven't run their charities for at least fifteen years, though. They leave the day-to-day operations to the people down there." She shook her head. "Not my place to say whether that's a good thing or not…" She leaned over the table and whispered. "But between you and me and the wall, it's not great. You need to stay alert. Keep your eye on people. If they don't think you're watching, they get up to all kinds of shenanigans."

"You were here? Back then?"

"Sure. I've worked for the guys since before they founded the charities. I met Bernie's sister, Grace, a couple of times."

"Bernie said he gave her a job. I had no idea you knew her." It made sense, though. Carla would have been in her late twenties then and I couldn't remember a time when she wasn't with the firm. "Did you work with the shelter and the pain and rehab center, too?"

She shuffled a file off her desk and dropped it into a drawer. "Here and there. Bernie's ex-wife, Katherine, has always been the accountant." She opened her eyes as wide as she could. Good for her, letting me in on the dirt. She didn't have to. Her loyalty was to Bernie, not me.

"It must have been a nightmare when Bernie and Katherine got divorced," I said.

"Tell me about it." She tapped at her keyboard. "Some people shouldn't work together. Relationships have a way of souring over time when you do. You have to know who you're getting into bed with." She gave a cheeky smile. "Whether it's bed-bed or business-bed."

"Some people do okay." I wanted to keep her talking. Anything she could tell me about Bernie's life could be useful. "My mom used to do some light bookkeeping for my dad and they seemed to get along fine, until she…" I couldn't say the last part.

"I know." Her face flushed and she appeared flustered. People get weird when you mention the dead. Uncertain of what to say, they don't say anything. She grabbed back the file from the drawer and then gained her composure.

"You knew my mom?"

"We met."

"When?"

She flipped the file open and fingered through the pages, looking for something. "I think she did the books for the charity, Loving Grace."

"My mom?"

She nodded, distracted. "She worked under Katherine a year or so before her accident. Sweet lady."

Ruth, from the shelter, thinking I was my mother, had rattled me. Now to learn that my mother had once worked with the shelter was shocking. She'd paid the detective agency's bills, but the fact it had morphed into more than that was news to me. A surge of grief gripped my chest. I'd been so careful to guard my heart against the pain of her death that I hadn't paid enough attention to her life. I clamped it down, afraid the pain would sear straight through me if I let it out.

I cleared my throat of the frog that had moved in. "All these years, you've never mentioned knowing my mom."

Her face remained red, embarrassed. "I assumed you knew, I'm sorry. That's how your dad came to work for Bernie in the first place. Bernie was looking for an investigator on a case and Barb mentioned that her husband was a PI."

I was always a step behind knowing my family's history. But a question came to mind. Ruth had been so convinced I was Barb. Had she been homeless all those years ago when my mom was around? "Did my mom ever work in the shelter with the homeless women directly?"

Carla frowned. "The offices are separate and always have been. I don't imagine she did."

Ruth clearly had mental issues; that didn't mean she hadn't encountered my mother at some point. My mother could have shown her some kindness and she'd recalled it when she saw me. Mom had always been a gentle soul... I glanced at my watch again. "I should get moving and see Bernie."

"I'll have a couple of subpoenas for you later too. Big trial next week. Genuine bad guys. Portland's answer to the mafia. Guns and bribery and payoffs to people in high places. Fun stuff." She rolled her eyes. She'd seen it all. Even the thought of going up against armed thugs didn't faze her. When I grew up, I wanted to be like Carla. Minus the tattoos, but only because I didn't like pain, not because I didn't think they looked cool on her.

"I'll check back on Friday, then." I got up. "Hope the guys realize how incredible you are and treat you accordingly."

"Oh, they do. I make sure of that." She chuckled before crossing behind me and closing her office door. "But real quick, and this didn't come from me, okay?"

I was on the edge of my seat emotionally but kept my arms relaxed, and my back slightly slumped. "My lips are sealed."

"If you really want to get to the bottom of all this, talk to Katherine Sokol."

"Bernie's ex?" What did she have to do with anything?

Carla nodded. "I can't say more, but if you want information on where Amber is..." She paused. "Or could be... Talk to Katherine." She opened her door and returned to her desk.

That's it? Wasn't she going to say more?

Carla glanced at her phone. "He's off now." She held her finger to her lips. "Not a word, you hear? I won't lose my job over this."

Stunned and confused, I left Carla and made my way down the corridor past a few unused offices, another small conference room, and back through reception.

Bernie waved me in when I appeared in his doorway. He'd replaced the warmup suit he'd worn in our first meeting with black slacks, a white button-down and a red tie.

"What can I do for you, Mizz Pruett?" Bernie asked, colder than an iceberg in the dead of winter.

Where to begin? How about *what the hell is going on here?* "You have a bedbug problem." I rotated my arms for him to see.

His jaw tensed. "I'll make sure that's taken care of right away."

At least he was talking to me. I hadn't been summarily dismissed. "I'm sure the women will appreciate it. Although it brings up the question what your house manager and director have been doing down there."

"Yes it does."

"One thing was clear," I continued, "a lot of people are in and out of that place, despite the locked door policy between 10 and 7, and no one seems to pay much attention. Case in point, and as I mentioned before, I met a girl last night who said her name was Robyn Baker. She disappeared before breakfast and left her journal, yet no one seems to have noticed. I want to go back there, Bernie. I want to find her and Amber."

My request hung between us as a loud rap came on Bernie's door and Tony Baumgartner strode in without waiting for Bernie to answer. He was a decade younger than Bernie and looked slick in his charcoal pants and pink Oxford minus a tie. He'd always been polite and professional towards me, but everything about him said power, money, and no-nonsense.

"Got a minute?" he directed his question to Bernie and nodded at me.

The tension between them filled the room making me shift.

"Please excuse me." Bernie followed his partner out.

While I waited, I looked around and scanned his desk. Case files, and an opened envelope with what looked like statements from a bank and an unopened one from Multnomah Circuit Court records caught my eye just before Bernie marched back into the room, his face bright red and perspiration forming on his forehead. I hadn't heard any yelling, but Bernie's blood pressure had skyrocketed from what I assumed was his exchange with Tony.

"You'll have to excuse me. I have another matter to attend to."

"I need answers, Bernie. This doesn't add up. My father would have asked you the same questions. Put bluntly, what are you hiding and why? What don't you want me to know?"

Before he could reply, his wife, Candy Appleton, burst in. She whisked by, leaving a trail of perfume in her wake. I sneezed.

"Bernie Boop," she said, ignoring me.

He leaned away from her. "Please Candy, I'm busy." He swept his arm across his desk and ended his gesture toward me.

"Oh." She turned my direction. "You're the girl that was at the house yesterday."

I stood. "Nice to see you again."

She flashed a fake smile before returning her focus to Bernie. I might need to start calling her crabby Appleton. "Hon, me and Morgan are off to the beach for a few nights." She presented her cheek for him to kiss.

He obliged but was distracted and took to shuffling the files on his desk.

I cleared my throat, resigned to the fact I wouldn't get anywhere with Bernie at this point—which was fine. I knew my next step. "I'll be leaving now, Mr. Sokol." He didn't answer as I showed myself out.

Morgan was in the waiting area, her baby fast asleep in the carrier she had set on the chair next to her. "They having a kiss fest in there?" she said, grimacing.

I shrugged, and she rolled her eyes at me. She didn't think much of Bernie and her mom together. But that wasn't the question on my mind. I was headed for a meeting with Katherine Sokol just as soon as I could land an appointment.

CHAPTER 9

Once outside the law offices, I checked my phone: nothing from Kyle, nothing from Trinity, a couple of ::heart eyes:: from Mitz in response to my earlier message. My heart smiled, and the rest of me with it. She was the best of me, and I could hardly wait to see her on Friday. Perhaps I could finagle a visit sooner—like, now? Parking Floyd with someone I trusted before I dove into round two of my investigation would be better for him anyway. With or without Bernie's directive, I intended to do that.

I didn't like asking my ex, Jeff for favors, but he wouldn't begrudge me one night of dog sitting. Also, if Floyd stayed with Mitz at Jeff's place, it would save me from having to face Arlene and Hannah, whose sudden living arrangement had me off balance, with the bonus of seeing my girl.

I did a quick search for Katherine Sokol and found her info unlisted but readily available to those who know where to look. I dialed and waited as a machine picked up and a computerized voice directed me to, "Leave a message after the tone."

"Ms.," I began uncertain what to call Bernie's ex-wife. "Katherine. My name's Kelly Pruett. You might have met my father when he worked for your husband. I mean, Bernie." I trailed off. *Damn.* She probably didn't want to be reminded of Bernie. "Anyway. I'm looking for your granddaughter, Amber, and hoping you could answer a few questions." I left my number and hung up. Not my finest moment, but we were talking about her flesh and blood. She'd return the call.

I'd made it back to my car when my phone buzzed. *Hot Stuff.*

"You've found something?"

"Nice to hear your voice, too," Kyle said. It was light, but it was a tap on the nose. He knew me better than that. I wasn't using him. Girls were missing and the clock was ticking. I waited for him to talk.

"A girl was found in Farragut Park over a week ago. An autopsy was conducted and the toxicology reports came back as overdose."

"Autopsy?" My heart thumped in my throat. "Not Amber?"

"Not Amber. Maria Castro."

A small relief that it wasn't either of my girls, but not what you'd call good news. "Was Maria homeless?"

"Unfortunately. One of the patrolmen who works with the community down there recognized her. She'd been seen more often up on Filmore, but more recently down on Lombard."

Lombard was close to Loving Grace. It was starting to look like Amber had been telling the truth—she'd been onto something. "Was it heroin?" That would explain the packets I'd seen at the shelter.

"Fentanyl. There were no witnesses. A jogger and his dog found her. She'd been dead for a few hours according to post."

"I'm not as familiar with fentanyl. Is it for pain?"

"Pain management, yes, but recreational use has been on the rise over the last few years. It takes less to get high and cheaper to manufacture. It's often used to lace other drugs —heroin, cocaine." I could sense him tapping his toe on the other end of the phone, and I knew what was coming before it arrived. "These are hard drugs, Kelly."

"I understand that."

"And while you didn't buy my theory about Bernie being caught up with the wrong crowd, this adds credence to my hypothesis. I said I support you as a PI and your decision to work this case, and I do. And I will. But…"

"I don't intend to wrangle directly with a drug dealer. That I can promise. But the girls…"

He sighed. "No one ever intends for bad things to happen, yet they do."

"You've known about this need to succeed trait in me from the get-go, Hot Stuff," I said, playfully.

"How did I manage to fall in love with a danger seeker? I'm going to need anti-acids at this rate."

Woah, danger seeker—is that what he thought I was? "Well, I could say the same since being a cop is no less dangerous."

"Touché."

"But I hear you. I also worry about you too, so I'll check in with you regularly. Deal?"

I could see him rubbing his gorgeous forehead. "I appreciate that," he said.

We were in a new place with each other on this. That part of me that had always loved independence, had committed to compromise and on some levels accountability to him. The protective cop in him was committed to honoring my profession. But he'd said danger seeker. I had never thought of myself like that. Danger found me. It's not like I asked it to.

Regardless of how it came down the pike, at this moment, with a dead homeless girl in the park, especially one who'd spent time at Loving Grace; and with Amber's phone call to her Papa; and Robyn's call to her girlfriend, Trinity, followed by both of their disappearances, I had a case and it added up to Amber and Robyn could be in trouble. That had to be my priority.

"Love you," he said.

"Me too," I said before clicking off.

Floyd was staring at me, waiting.

"Nothing's changed. Onward we go. Let's go see Mitz."

At the sound of her name, his tail thumped against the door. I was only eleven miles from my old house, the one where Jeff and my sweet Mitz lived, as well as Linda and her little one.

Floyd could stay there overnight while I spent another night at the shelter and I'd come by first thing in the morning to pick him up. Even if I wasn't keen on seeing my former friend, it made sense.

I texted Jeff. *You home?*

On my way, why?

Need a favor. Can you watch Floyd?

Sure. Mitz will love it.

Well, that was easy.

Thanks. Be there in fifteen. I tossed the phone near my gear shift and drove.

Twenty-five minutes later due to heavy traffic, I pulled in front of the light gray craftsman I used to call home. Jeff and I had bought it a couple of years into our marriage, and it's where we'd lived for eight years before our divorce.

I'd fallen in love with the rock veneer, tapered columns set on bluestone bases, and eaves lined with clear cedar. At the time, it felt like the perfect place to create a marriage and bring up a child. I'd picked all the paint colors inside, and the furniture. Jeff and I had set the tile in the guest bathroom over a pizza and a six-pack of beer. Mitz's baby room had been painted, complete with a mural of daisies, and decorated by me. If only all of life could be lived inside four protective walls.

The truth was I had never fit in with the luxury car-driving neighbors and their white-collar career paths. I hadn't really found my place in this world. The only solid part of me was being a mother to a fabulous daughter—a daughter who gave me purpose when nothing else made sense. The fact that she would be home by now was the reward for coming here—and knowing Floyd would be with someone who loved him as much as I did.

However, Jeff's Subaru Outback was not in the driveway. Instead, a minivan took up one side indicating that Linda was in residence. The only time we'd spoken since her arrival back into town was last May when her suggestion had helped me unravel my case. That hadn't fixed the fact she'd slept with Jeff, and now had his child.

Then they'd moved in together, a recent development I hadn't seen coming or adjusted to. The tightness in my gut at the prospect of seeing her again, despite the reward of Mitz, had me rethinking my strategy.

Enough so that I had my hand on the gearshift to put the car into drive and take my chances with traffic and Hannah, when my red-haired, freckle-faced reward came running up the sidewalk towards me. *Too late now.*

I shot off a quick text to Jeff of *thought you'd be here…?* and got out.

Mitz barreled at me, dropping her pack at my feet. "Mama, you're here," she signed, wrapping both arms around me in a hug that I returned, laying my head on top of hers and following it up with a kiss.

When she unglued herself I signed, "Just for a second. I was in the neighborhood and wanted to say hi. But…" I began to tell her I wouldn't be able to stay long when the front door swung open.

"Hey Kel," Linda said, with her towhead son perched on her bony hip. I had yet to meet him. He had Linda's eyes and Jeff's nose. Wearing an OshKosh jumper, he was cute, as two-year-olds often are. His hands were tangled around Linda's waist-length flowing hair. "Jeff said Floyd is spending the night?"

Mitz read lips well enough to get excited. "Floyd is staying?" she signed.

Might as well go with it at this point. "Yeah, Ladybug," I signed, walking to the other side of the car and letting Floyd stretch his long body out. He proceeded to hit the wet grass and roll, rubbing his back into the ground, while I grabbed a baggy of kibble I used for treats from the glove compartment. "Just for the night while Mom works." Floyd stood, shook off a spray that landed on me, and his wiggle took up double time when he homed in on Mitz.

Arms up and palms facing her cheeks, she shook them in a wave motion. The sign for *yay*, along with the smile consuming her face left me no options.

The three of us walked to the front door, but all the way I cursed my decision to come here.

At the porch, Linda smiled. "It's good to see you and glad we could help. It's important for us to work as a family."

My stomach about lurched into my throat. She'd been living with Jeff for just over a month. Now we were family? "Yeah, thank you. I appreciate it."

"Mommy Linda loves dogs," Mitz signed. "She and I will take really good care of Floyd. Mommy Linda, can we make dog biscuits for him?"

"Of course." Linda reached out a free hand and rubbed it over Mitz's hair, sending a ripple through my muscles. I wanted my daughter to be in the care of someone who loved her. But why Linda…Mommy Linda of all people. Where was Jeff?

"Thank you." I forced a smile and signed to Mitz. "I know you'll take great care of him, sweetness. That's why he's here."

"Is it?" Linda said. "Or is it because of your conversation with Jeff?"

What conversation with Jeff? That didn't sound good. I just shrugged, not wanting to look stupid or get into anything in front of Mitz. "Just dropping Floyd off. No hidden agenda."

"Well, I'll make sure Mitz sends you postcards from Disneyland."

The blood rushed into my face. We hadn't talked about Disneyland. Vacations were supposed to be mutually agreed upon.

"Ladybug," I signed, "please take Floyd and give him a potty break in the back, okay?" I handed Mitz the bag of kibble. It would be enough for a couple of feedings. Floyd's food and my peanut butter were items we never left home without. Then I gave Mitz a hug that lasted too long as she squirmed out.

Mitz nodded and waved at Floyd to follow her.

I was past being hurt by Linda's betrayal of our friendship, but she was being high-handed, and that never set well with me.

After Mitz had disappeared into the house, I said, "Jeff hasn't spoken to me about any trip, and I don't appreciate him setting us up like this because clearly you think he did. But if he wants to discuss it, have him give me a call."

"Fine, but did he mention—"

"I'll swing by tomorrow morning for Floyd," I said, cutting her off. "Thanks again."

I marched to the car as the front door slammed. Behind the wheel, I texted Jeff. *Thanks for the lack of communication.*

He didn't respond.

Today was not a good day to talk to men, perhaps. I was running at a fifty percent success rate. Bernie was being paranoid. And now Jeff was cooking up some trip that he should have cleared with me before talking to Mitz. At least Floyd and Kyle were solid, but probably a good thing I was spending the night at a women's shelter.

Traffic hadn't eased and it took me longer than usual to get to Loving Grace. I parked a few blocks away. Backpack on my shoulder, I hustled across the city streets and arrived at the shelter five minutes after six. I pushed open the double doors. Nettie stood with her back to the entry and near a long, empty table speaking with a group of kitchen staff. She bristled when she saw me and strode over. "It's after six."

"Right, I'm sorry. I'd hoped to be back earlier."

"Doesn't matter. Your bed's taken."

"I don't take up much space. I could sleep on the couch in the TV room?"

"Not how it works. I warned you this morning. Try tomorrow. If you're late again, it'll be the same thing."

"I understand." I didn't, but I wasn't going to argue and get permanently banned. "But can I use your bathroom? I'm dying." It wasn't a lie. All that coffee earlier in the day was pressing down hard on my bladder. If I could get past her, I could do a run through the premises to see if Robyn had come back.

Nettie set her hands on her hips. "Make it fast."

I hurried back to the far part of the building, my backpack bouncing against my shoulders. Before I made it to the bathroom, I did a quick look through the sleeping room, empty, and once Nettie disappeared into the kitchen, tracked back to check the TV room. There were no signs of Robyn, LuAnn or even Judy anywhere. Ruth, the woman who'd come nose to nose with me this morning was back in her corner, staring at something high on the wall.

Nettie came out of the kitchen. I waited until she disappeared down the corridor and then headed to the laundry area. The machines shook with action, but the room was empty; next, the shower area. A few women were cleaning up, but no Robyn. Worry set into my shoulders again.

I was shuffling towards the admin offices when a man's muffled voice came from that direction. I ran back to the bathroom entry that hid me from the hallway, my heart pounding. I'd stepped out of sight just as a door clicked open and the man's voice became clearer.

"Thanks for coming by," Gordon said, in a hushed but intimate tone.

Bernie hadn't fired Gordon? *WTH.* Kyle was right. Bernie was implicated, but in *what?*

I squeezed against the doorframe, peeking down the hall. Gordon ran his hand down the arm of a woman a few years older than me. Her brown hair framed her flushed face. Her eyes were teary as he slipped something into her hand and she slid it into her front pocket.

"This didn't come from me, got it? Nettie finds them and you're on your own."

"Yes, sir."

"And don't use them all at one time. Make it last."

My stomach tightened at the way he touched her. I wanted to run down the hall and body slam him away, to see for myself the drugs he was doling out. My head said stay put. I forced myself not to move or say anything—or worse.

Gordon was dealing to the young women. Had he given the girl from the park, Maria Castro, the drugs that ultimately killer her?

The woman left, her footsteps echoing down the corridor, but I didn't hear Gordon's office door close. I waited in the doorway.

Gordon's footsteps moved towards the bathroom area. This was not cool, buddy— ladies only.

"You still here?" Nettie said, her voice up an octave.

"No, ma'am," I said, jogging past her all the way to the double doors and out.

There was no reason to stay. I'd seen enough—heard enough. Gordon's warning, "Don't use it all at one time" clearly had to do with the drugs. Maybe he'd grown a conscience and didn't want to see her OD like Maria.

I texted Bernie on my ride home.

Confirmed. 100% this time. Gordon is the drug dealer. Do something about it or I will.

CHAPTER 10

I slept fitfully even though I was in my own bed. Giant bugs chased me all over downtown Portland, waving their mandibles and telling me I was a fool and a loser and I'd never measure up.

I woke, tangled in my sheets and immediately checked my phone.

I'd sent a goodnight text to Mitz, and a *home safe and sound* to Kyle, but no one had called—or texted. I was dead in the water. I couldn't wait for a lead; I had to go out there and shake the trees myself.

Problem was, the homeless aren't in the phone book, listed or unlisted. I had to figure out where they went during the day. I'd been far too passive. I'd let Bernie direct my steps instead of taking charge of the investigation from the start. That had to change.

I plodded downstairs in time to hear a knock at the front door.

It was kind of early for a Wednesday morning, but I answered and found Jeff on the step, Floyd on the end of a leash.

"Morning," he said.

I took Floyd from him as I ran my hand through my wild hair and stood there in my sweats. Despite being annoyed with his lack of communication, his girlfriend, and his vacation plans, he had done me a favor. "Morning. Thanks for taking care of my boy. I would've been happy to come get him, but I appreciate your bringing him home." I started to close the door.

"Can we talk?"

I was appreciative, but that didn't make me any more in the mood to chat. But I couldn't complain about him not talking to me about things like vacation plans and then blow him off. "For a few minutes." I didn't invite him in. I did have a case to keep moving on.

"I'm sorry Linda blind-sided you. I should have told you. I didn't…"

"Yeah, talking about going to California is something you and I should be discussing, not her."

"Right. You good with it though?"

"Not a hundred percent. No."

"Well, it was her idea and we're just talking about it at this point."

He and I never even had a vacation to chat about. Early on we didn't have money, later it was time. Maybe the fact he was having these conversations in his new relationship was a good thing. "Yeah, I get it. Disneyland would be fun for sure, but it's a lot of money." The Mommy Linda angle would bug me for a while. She would get to experience that first with my daughter, and admittedly, that was the hardest part for me to get over.

"Did she say anything else?"

"That seemed to be enough, but I did cut her off…. Why, is there more?"

"We're talking about a full-on remodel of the house."

"Huh, seems soon," I said, not sure what to make of that. Did it matter that everything I'd chosen for the house would be removed—and changed by another woman? I couldn't get a read on myself. Maybe I didn't want to. "Anything else?"

"And I'm hoping I can bring Mitz by Saturday. We're having dinner with Linda's parents Friday night and—"

"She wants them to meet Mitz." A part of me knew that would be coming at some point.

He nodded. "If you don't mind. I realize it's your night."

"No worries," I said, although it was more information for me to process. Linda's parents were great people. I couldn't hold her choices against them since Linda and Jeff were a couple now. "Okay, how about now? Are we good?"

He seemed to want to say more, but he only nodded.

I glanced at my watch. "It's okay Jeff. Navigating all this new stuff with new people in our lives might take some work, but we'll figure it out. I promise."

I closed the door and followed Floyd who strolled into the kitchen. Floyd plonked himself down beside his bowl. Mitz would have made sure he had breakfast, but if Floyd could work it for more food he would. I poured him some kibble, filled his water bowl and grabbed a jar of peanut butter from the cupboard.

With that sticky goodness on board and Jeff forgiven, I felt better and the way became clear of who to ask for guidance.

Jessica Webster and I had been friends since high school. She'd gone into social work right after college and we were overdue for a lunch date. She was always good at staying in touch—leaving messages on my phone about going out for drinks—and I was terrible at returning calls, a fact she never held against me. I texted her and invited her to join me for coffee at one of our favorite locations—a place where Floyd would be welcome, too. If nothing else, Jessica might be able to give me a different perspective on where I could start looking for Robyn and Amber. She had to be up on where the homeless hotspots were in the city.

I waited for her response, but not for long. She sent back an enthusiastic *YESSSS!!*

Within the hour, Floyd and I walked through the front of Java Hound, a fully stocked pet supply store with a coffee shop in the back. His tail and nose went into overdrive. Whenever Mitz and I wandered Twenty-Third Street during the summer, we brought Floyd with us. My boy had a steel trap for a memory and never forgot a scent. He dragged me past the toys and dry food aisle to the bucket of beef tendons across the store.

With a treat purchased from the clerk to keep him busy, we made our way to the back corner of the store near the cat section where the smart shop owner had built a coffee bar. *Have a Cup and Feed your Pup* was scrawled on the chalkboard above the register. It sounded like a good plan to me.

While I scanned the menu, Jessica rushed in wearing blue slacks and a chunky white sweater. Her short legs taking long strides always reminded me of a corgi wanting to get somewhere fast, but not having the wherewithal to get there.

"Girl." Jessica swooped in for a hug. I barely got my arms around her before she squatted next to Floyd. "Hey boy, you taking care of your mama here?"

He flopped over in response. She ran her hands over his belly and gave him a good scritch. Her fingernails were gnawed to the quick. She'd chewed them ever since third grade. My coping strategy was peanut butter by the spoonful, hers was chewing her nails. We all do what we must to stay afloat.

"It's been too long," I said. "You look great."

Jessica stood, letting out a weary sigh. "It has. Truth is I'm exhausted and I feel it. You buying?"

I smiled. "Of course. I appreciate your running out to meet me on such short notice."

"Then I'll take a double caramel latte. And no problem. I was planning to visit a few of my clients later today. Your timing worked out perfectly."

Jessica found our corner table with Floyd, and I joined her a few minutes later with her frothy caramel coffee and my triple shot mocha.

Floyd took up with his chewy tendon at my feet and Jessica and I took a moment to enjoy our drinks and some chit-chat. She'd been at my dad's funeral, but I hadn't seen her since. I also hadn't kept her apprised of my work, which included my gunshot wound from my first murder investigation, or my near-barbecue experience in my missing person's case last May. Some things were better not rehashed.

"How's life treating you?" I asked.

"Crazy. I'm working with elderly shut-ins now." At this news, my heart sank a bit. I tried not to let my disappointment show, as Jessica went on. "I make sure they have the services they need in their homes. Partnering them with other agencies to get their medications on track, their checkups in. It has me running everywhere, but helping an older person with their quality of life is rewarding. Especially because my personal life is non-existent these days. No time. When I do have time, I sleep."

"Tell me about it. Sleep is a premium product these days." I sipped my coffee. "You always had a big heart."

"Thank you for saying so. It gets me into trouble." She tapped her sternum. "Feeling all the feels, as the young people say."

"Is that why you're no longer working with the homeless?"

"Exactly. It got to be too much. You'd help one woman and she'd be replaced by two more. In the end you're exhausted. Too many times my heart was broken." Her eyes had that weary sadness one gets when they lift the carpet and see the underbelly of the world. Serving subpoenas and restraining orders had put me in touch with enough bad guys to know how overwhelming it could get if you did it for any length of time.

Jessica bounced right back. "Talking about hearts. You seeing anyone?"

I blushed. "Kyle. He's incredible, smart, a new detective."

She smiled. "Do tell. Is he more supportive than Jeff, I hope?"

"He is." I found myself smiling. "But..." I rubbed my face.

She laughed. "I can tell by the way you're itching your cheek there's something else."

No one had told me that I had a tell, but that was one drawback with having life-long friends: they knew and noticed stuff no one else did. Did Kyle know this about me, like I'd noticed his eye twitching when he was holding back? I put my hands in my lap. "It's complicated."

"Especially when you're a bulldog, like your dad."

My tenacious ways had been evident since I was a kid, I guess. Maybe what Kyle had said was true. "Jess, am I a danger seeker too like my dad?" I wanted her take because I didn't see it that way at all.

"Well, you never had a problem jumping from the highest branch on a tree if that's what you mean, but seeking danger out?" She scoffed. "Jeff said that, right?"

"No, that wouldn't be a shock. It was Kyle."

"Oh." She looked at her coffee, as if it held the answers. "Remember that girl in school. The one that stuttered?"

"Beth. Of course I do."

"And do you remember that group of horrible boys that teased her every time she went to home room?"

"Scum," I said.

"Yup. What I remember most about that is you walking Beth to her class every day, just to catch them in the act so you could put a stop to it. Which you did by the way."

"Hmmm…Yeah, leave it to me to take on the biggest bully in the class." Kyle *was* right.

"Yeah, he was bigger, meaner, but to me, you didn't seek that out for the sake of a fight. You had courage. You've always known what was right, and nothing stopped you from making sure Beth felt safe. I call it having a pair that most people will never have."

My cheeks warmed. Yeah. I did have those. "Thanks Jessica." I cleared my throat. "Anyway. I didn't drag you down here for all that, but I am hoping you can help me."

She took a drink. "Wondered when you'd get to it. You know I will if I can."

"My client asked me to go undercover in his homeless shelter after his granddaughter went missing."

"Oh." Her face crumpled. She knew the stats. It wasn't good.

I told her about Maria Castro, the dead girl Kyle had mentioned, about the fentanyl and heroin, about Robyn missing. "Bernie's granddaughter, Amber, has been MIA for going on a week now and no one's heard from Robyn for nearly two days. I'm concerned there's a pattern. I was hoping you could give me some advice on how to track these girls down."

"Have you checked the registry?"

"For Loving Grace?"

"Loving Grace is part of the homeless network registry. It's statewide. Once a person gets in the system, they can be tracked if they move around.

There are, of course, private shelters not a part of that system, but the ones that are often won't allow anyone in that's not on the registry. Perhaps your client can help you with that search."

I'd been under the impression when Bernie put me on a list it was only for his shelter. "Yeah, that's not likely to happen. Do you have access so we can check if Robyn or Amber have gone somewhere else?"

Jessica leaned back in her chair. "I don't personally, and there are strict rules about doing things like that. As in people could lose their jobs." She stared at her cup again. She lowered her voice. "Although I do have a friend working with the homeless who I might be able to convince to bend the rules a tiny bit and search. Maybe even flag her if she does show up."

"I get it's a big ask."

"At the end of the day, we just want to help these people. I'll see what I can do, but no promises on that end. At the very least though, I can ask around and find out if those names sound familiar. Everyone talks. Perhaps a social worker has heard something, because if either of them are in a private facility…."

"Right, they wouldn't show up. Who would private include?"

"Those run by charitable groups like churches. Granges. There's an assortment really."

"Takes a village, right? I'm starting to see how prevalent homelessness is…"

"And getting worse." She shook her head. "What are their stories?"

"Robyn left her dad's house with her girlfriend. Abuse and alcoholism, and an inability to accept Robyn's sexuality, seemed to be the issues there. Her mother died a few years ago. She's been lost, but then she gets out here, and the girlfriend takes off with someone else." Even though Trinity had been looking for her girlfriend, which suggested she cared, I went with Robyn's perspective.

Jessica frowned. "Such a common story. Kids think that getting away on their own is the answer. Unless they're prepared for it, financially, emotionally, they're often left to fend for themselves out here on the street."

"Amber's mom died, too." I turned my head for a second. Motherless daughters going off the rails. There was my pattern, right there. "She turned to drugs. She'd been through rehab a couple of times. She told her grandfather she was close to finding who was dealing drugs at the shelter, then she went underground." Or, she was made to disappear. That part was undetermined.

"I bet the fact they both lost their moms is ringing all kinds of bells with you."

Jessica had been at my mother's funeral, too. I cleared my throat. "It's not that." It was, but I didn't want to discuss it.

She scoffed again. "C'mon. You act tough, but I'm trained to see down a couple of layers and girl, you're a hot mess."

I drank my coffee and grimaced. "I think I do okay."

"You do." She reached out her hand and patted mine. "But if you ever need to talk about your mom, since you never have, I'm here."

"I couldn't. Dad…"

"Just don't let it blind you, alright?"

I wasn't sure where that came from and that damn frog had crept back into my throat. It was time to steer this conversation away from me. "Really, my concern is that Robyn left in the middle of the night. Bernie's granddaughter did the same thing and both called for help. In fact, can you check on Maria Castro? Kyle gave me the rundown on what happened to her, but I'd like her story beforehand. Who was she? Why she was on the street? Was she an addict?"

Jessica took a long drink and set her cup down. "I can try. But on the other, let's face it, drugs are everywhere and the homeless are transient and disappear all the time without a trace. Can't tell you how many people I tried and failed to find during my time. Sometimes it's as simple as they caught the next bus out of town. You could check with the hospitals to make sure she hasn't been treated there. And check with the police to see if she'd been arrested."

"All checked and double checked."

"Good. There's also roaming shower services and the tent cities. Some choose not to stay in the shelter for various reasons. Someone's bothering them. Or the fact that it's four walls. The long-timers get so used to the street they can't bear the confines of being inside or the rules."

"But it's only been a couple of months for Robyn." I went on to tell her about the journal that she wouldn't let me touch and that Trinity had shown up at the shelter concerned.

"Leaving the journal is strange. The homeless cling to their possessions. I had one woman who nearly committed suicide when the police left her red boots behind to put her in jail for the night. Her grandmother, the only woman she felt ever loved her, had given them to her. Then they were gone. I hit garage sales on the weekend trying to find something comparable. I came close and hoped the gesture would show that someone else cared."

Jessica only confirmed my fear that Robyn leaving her journal behind was too alarming to ignore. I took another sip, thinking. "So many places. Where do I start? I need to get this search off the ground."

"If it were me, I'd begin at *Shower to the People*. They're a good outfit and they see a lot of people from various shelters."

"Got it. That's what I'll do." I finished my coffee. "By the way, when you were working with the homeless, did you ever hear anything good or bad about Loving Grace?"

"Not specifically, but they all have their issues. Low wages, high turnover. Compassion fatigue and burnout. Same deal with the rehab centers. You've seen there's one across the street, right?"

"Saving Grace, yes."

"Talk about heartbreak. They're detox only, not sure why they even have 'pain management' as part of their description because that's not anything I've heard they addressed. Anyway, I placed a couple of short-term clients there in my day, but they're not great for long term since they don't have steps."

"What do you mean steps?"

"Many centers have housing or treatment programs that participants can step down into after initial treatment. But Saving Grace puts them back out on their own. As a social worker, that usually means our clients will go back into treatment again and again. It was a huge factor in why I left and took this elder care job. Even though my clients will die, it feels more hopeful. What time they have, they put to good use. I can make a difference. I stopped feeling that with my homeless clients. They churn through the system, trying to find a way to a better place, but without steps it's all a game of human ping-pong."

"Sounds like putting a Band-Aid on a gaping wound."

She wiped some foam off her top lip and offered it to Floyd. "There are good intentions, generally, but the police barely manage it. And of course, there's abuse and those who take advantage of the vulnerable." Jessica's eyes were pained.

I bent down to Floyd, who was working on the last of his chew. Homelessness was an epidemic. It was disheartening to think even the people on the front lines weren't optimistic.

My thoughts returned to the woman Jessica shopped for. "Did it help getting the red boots for that girl?"

"She's the only one I gave my number to when I left. She's graduating an online course next month to be a nurse's aide." She smiled. "She's an exception to the rule. If that girl Amber was a drug addict and has relapsed, its possible she's dead. Or she may resurface out of state after being arrested. The people on drugs rarely make it through without a few interactions with the law. Regardless, you can't beat yourself up for their choices. Sometimes out on the streets, an addict can be too trusting and it gets them into trouble. I always told my clients to beware of people who pretend they want to help you unless you truly know who they are."

I'd heard variations of that a lot since taking on this case. I was beginning to think it was a mantra. Be wary of everyone and everything. I didn't want to think about Amber being dead. Bernie didn't believe that or he wouldn't have sent me into the shelter in the first place.

When we got up to leave, Jessica pulled me in for a hug. "Remember. When you're ready to talk about your mom, I'm here for you."

I loved her to pieces but I couldn't get out of there fast enough. She was right, I was searching for these girls because of my mother, but despite her thoughts about me having courage, I was too chicken to admit that out loud.

CHAPTER 11

I launched google on my phone and searched for *Shower to the People*. They had a simple website listing where they'd be and on which days, which made my job easier.

Floyd and I drove straight over to Big Lots and pulled into a space near the back and about fifty yards from my target. A line of men and women snaked out and around the mobile truck. Some pushed grocery carts full of their possessions. Others had everything they owned strapped onto their backs. They all were in need of soap and water.

A woman about my age stood to the side of the three entry doors with a notepad. She was bundled in a long jacket and matching stocking cap and gloves. The passenger side of her truck was open, and a thermos and a half-filled cup of coffee sat on the seat…a girl after my own heart.

I left Floyd in the car and approached with my hand out. "Are you Leslie?"

She didn't look up. "Sure am. You'll need to get in line, but I'll get you on the list. What's your name?"

"Actually, I'm here to ask a few questions about your services."

She lifted her eyes and tucked the pad under her left arm. She smiled. "I love to talk about what we offer. What would you like to know?"

I had the distinct feeling that the occasional news reporter had stopped in to do articles. Bringing services out to the homeless, rather than making them hunt and peck their way through the city for assistance was a cool concept. I was curious myself. "How did you get started?"

Her smile widened. "It began as my senior class project and a way to give back to the community. Homeless people and their plight, along with society's blind eye towards them, has always rubbed me wrong. My dad worked in the RV industry for years and he had this old box truck out on our property for nearly as long. When I approached him about making it useful, he was excited to help."

"That's great." I turned away from her and gazed at the long line. "You serve a lot of people."

"I do. I could do more, but local businesses have a thing about the homeless being too close to their front doors and scaring patrons away. I only come to the business district a few days a week. Mostly I stick to church parking lots. But it's a community problem and we all need to figure out how to make it better."

I was getting somewhere. Finally. I'd plugged into a crucial part of the homeless network. "Are you familiar with most of the people that spend time around here?"

"Not all for sure. I have my regulars, but new people show every time. Or they come a couple of times, and I never see them again."

I nodded and pulled out one of my cards. "I should probably tell you who I am," I said, handing it to her. "I'm looking for a Robyn Baker, a young girl I befriended at Loving Grace a few nights ago. She's gone missing. Before that, an Amber Moore. Maria Castro before that."

"You're a private investigator?"

"Yes." I waited as Leslie stared at my card. Maybe she'd never met a female PI before?

When she finally looked up she had tears in her eyes. "The first girl you mentioned, doesn't sound familiar, but Maria was a regular for a long time. I was sorry to hear about her death." She took a deep, shuddering breath. "Amber used to come here, too, but I haven't seen her lately. I hope nothing's happened to her." Her hand rested on her chest.

What were the chances she knew two of my girls? "When did you last see Amber?"

"Oh..." She handed a miniature toiletry kit to a woman to my left. "At least a week ago? I'm not sure."

"Did she seem agitated? Concerned? Did she have anything on her mind?"

"I'm sorry, I don't have time to pay attention. Like when you came up, I wasn't even looking at you. It's enough to keep everything functioning on the truck. The water. The soap system. Making sure people aren't shooting up inside or deciding to stay there all day. I try to engage with them when I can, but that's not often."

"I hear ya. But anything you noticed could help."

"I wish I could tell you something, but nothing struck me as out of the norm. She often had that glassy-eyed look in that 'I've been using' kind of way." A loud noise came up from the truck, and a vibration shook the body. "Damn it," she said. "I need to go. They're using up the water today fast."

Dang. Amber had told her Papa that she was clean and I'd been operating on that fact. Was she?

I followed Leslie behind the truck. "Any idea where Amber might go? Favorite hang outs?"

She laughed. "I don't know about favorites, but the long-timers rotate through the churches."

"Rotate?"

She grabbed a wrench and hit a couple of pipes. "Soup kitchens are on different days, see?"

I did see. How depressing, but it answered why Robyn and Trinity had ended up staying at a church. As for Amber, she was too young to be on a regular rotation through soup kitchens. She could have been in a mansion with a personal cook and someone to do her laundry. What had driven her away? Why would anyone choose this life?

Leslie had crawled under the van and was tooling with the waterworks.

"One last question," I shouted. Amber had been seen—alive. I had to establish if it was before or after her call to Bernie. "Can you at least tell me which day you might have seen her?"

"We were here, outside Big Lots. In fact, that is when I saw her. So, Friday."

I wanted to punch the sky with joy. Amber had been seen after that call. "Thank you," I yelled.

She didn't answer so I made my way back to my car where Floyd greeted me, tail wagging. I'd only been gone ten minutes, but he was as pleased to see me as if I'd been on a three-week vacation.

Once again, I launched google on my phone. What did we do when we didn't have the world at our fingertips? I searched for "churches plus food kitchen." The good news—places to look were limited. The bad news—they weren't all concentrated in one location.

After giving Floyd a break, we hit the list. The first three churches I checked had plenty of people camping out, but no Amber or Robyn or the Datsun I'd seen speeding away from the shelter. The sun had started its dip down over the skyline and the homeless began bedding down for the night. No one was in the mood to talk to me. Some were outright hostile.

The fourth lot overflowed with cars, and it took me half an hour to inspect the premises and determine that too was a bust.

I rubbed Floyd's ears. "One more, my good boy. Then we'll head home. I promise." He wasn't amused. Apart from potty breaks, he'd been in the car all day. It had been selfish of me to bring him. I'd suck it up and leave him with Arlene tomorrow. I drove to the church on Davis.

After winding through several haphazard rows of parked cars, I hit pay dirt as my dad would say, when I spotted a familiar Datsun parked in the rear of the lot. Another slow cruise by determined it was the rusty-colored B210 that had disappeared in a cloud of smoke with Trinity inside. A sunshade with a bumble bee design had been tossed into the front window blocking any interior view.

Parking across the street, I kissed a tired and hungry Floyd, put my pepper spray into my pocket and Robyn's journal into my jacket. The chill of the night had my windows building with condensation, and that was with my heat on full blast. As I stepped out of my car, a shiver skittered through me. I zipped my warmup jacket to under my chin. "Won't be long. Scouts honor."

I passed vehicles which were shut up for the night with sunshades, cardboard, or clothes draped over and inside their windows. I approached the Datsun with caution. Scaring people could get me shot and Trinity might not be alone. At least, I was pretty sure this was Trinity's car. She could have borrowed it to come to the shelter. But today had been breaking my way. Fingers crossed my luck would hold.

Using my phone for illumination, I kept it aimed half to the ground and half toward me so whoever was in the Datsun could see me approach. I tapped on the glass with my knuckle.

It took a minute, but the window lowered a crack. "What do you want?" A groggy voice floated out.

"I'm Kelly. If you're Trinity, we have a common friend, Robyn. You probably don't remember me, but I saw you at the shelter looking for her. I texted you a couple of times."

The window cranked down further. The young woman with the red hair and row of earrings in the curve of her ear, slouched in the seat, rubbing sleep out of her eyes. "I got your messages. You know where she is?"

She didn't offer an explanation as to why she'd ignored my texts. I assumed it was back to that trust thing they all struggled with. "No. But perhaps we can help each other."

She eyed me up and down, hesitant. Maybe she was deciding whether I was safe or wanted something else from her.

I'd come prepared that she might not lower her walls easily and pulled out Robyn's journal.

She pushed herself into an upright position. "You really have it."

"Found it yesterday morning. Something doesn't feel right that she'd leave it behind."

Trinity leaned over the passenger seat and unlocked the door. "Get in."

My turn to feel uncertain. However, Trinity had opened her window and invited me in and I wanted answers. I rounded the car and slid into the passenger seat.

The interior had zero warmth and my breath hung in the air before it dissipated. "Holy crap." A shiver rattled through me again. "How are you not freezing to death out here?"

She pulled a handwarmer from her pocket. "I have these in my shoes, and any other places I could manage. I also turn on the car for a few minutes every hour. Which is about now." She started the engine.

Sliding my hands under my butt for warmth, I shuffled my feet back and forth over a hole in the floorboard and waited for the car's heat to kick in. With the age of the vehicle, and its thin walls, not to mention the hole, the space would never get comfortable. "From what I overheard you say to Nettie at the shelter, Robyn contacted you."

She nodded.

"I take it you've checked every place she might have gone?"

"Yeah. Her dad's house, which was a long shot, but he wasn't there. A couple of our friends, in case she contacted them. She hasn't. I've also hung out at some of our usual spots. But nothing. I told the police, but they only took a report."

"Tell me about when you last spoke with her."

"It was around midnight when I got her text saying she was in trouble and needed to meet. She said she'd made a mistake…but she never showed. She didn't answer when I called. Now the calls go straight to voicemail, like her battery is dead."

"Which park were you supposed to meet at?"

"Farragut. It's the closest to the shelter."

That made sense though it made my blood run cold. That was the park where Maria had been found dead. "Any idea of the mistake Robyn referenced?"

Trinity shifted in her seat. "Hopefully leaving me in the first place."

"She left you?"

"Yeah." Her eyes narrowed. "Why? What'd she tell you?"

I didn't want to get into the middle but finding out what happened to them felt important to determining whether Robyn had only been playing a game with her ex. "That you took up with someone else and abandoned her."

Trinity flushed. "That's not what happened."

"Relationships can be complicated."

"Look, things haven't gone as well as we'd hoped out here. I was supposed to get a job waitressing, and it didn't pan out. We ran short on cash and ended up here at this church. We get fed on Wednesdays and Saturdays. It's relatively safe. I'm not complaining. Hell, it's cold, but I can survive that. They bring us blankets when the forecast calls for freezing temps."

Except it was freezing now and Trinity didn't have any extra blankets on her. What exactly constituted "freezing temps" I wondered as I put my hands on the vent to soak in some of the heat before it escaped out of the floor. "Did Robyn work?"

"No. But she wanted to and that's when the problems started."

"She tried to get a job?"

"Not exactly. There's a mobile shower truck that parks up the street a few days a week. We went there for showers. It's nice and private. They don't give us time limits. It feels safer than running into some highway rest stop or state park where anyone can come in on you."

I hadn't wanted to jump into the showers at Loving Grace for similar reasons. "I get it."

"So, I'm taking a shower, and when I come out, Robyn is going on and on about how she met someone who was talking up Loving Grace and how great it was. They promised they could get her a permanent bed and she could earn money. So, she wanted to go."

My ears perked up. Bernie had mentioned Amber getting a job. Was it the same deal? "How was she going to earn money there?"

"The chick didn't elaborate."

"Any guesses as to what the job might have been?"

She snorted. "Nothing good. They don't offer 'permanent beds' at Loving Grace. It didn't sit right with me. I told her that they were going to ask her to do some shady shit, but she went on and on about making money and us getting a place of our own and how even if it was shady, she could suck it up for a short time."

"It was another homeless person who talked about the shelter?"

She shrugged. "I figure. Robyn didn't say it was a social worker type and seems she would have. But I didn't see the lady who talked to her that day." She was hedging, not telling me something.

"If it was a woman, why not go too?" I asked.

"Because we had a good setup here. We'd found it in a legit way that didn't raise any red flags for me."

"Let me guess: be careful of people who act like they want to help you."

"You got it."

Both she and Robyn had the same sentiment.

"So, she went and you didn't?"

She nodded.

"And the two of you didn't talk? Didn't text? That seems like a bit of an overreaction." I regretted the words as soon as they were out of my mouth.

Trinity bristled. "Look, she saw me out with someone I'd met recently." She sniffed. "She's pretty ticked off even though she totally got it wrong. I wasn't hitting on them…just being friendly. She misconstrued the whole thing." She rubbed her hands together and turned back to me, deadly serious. "Her calling me at all means something has gone very wrong. I wish she'd listened to me in the first place. I'd tried to warn her about going there, but she wouldn't listen."

"The red flag you mentioned?"

"Yeah. There's some broad down on Burnside who's always mouthing off about the place. She's kinda sneaky and gets up in your face. Smells bad."

I almost smiled. Things were coming together. I had a piece of string which linked A to B. Maybe. "What did she look like?"

"Her shoes are held together with tape."

I had not seen that coming. "Judy?"

"No clue. I didn't go there, remember? I've just seen her around."

"You're sure. Not a big woman in a flannel shirt? Stocking cap with her hair sticking out?"

"No. That sounds like LuAnn. She's okay. Looks out for the younger women."

That didn't sound like the LuAnn I'd met.

"No, this woman has huge feet. You can't miss them. They're so big you notice them."

Okay. So, Judy was mouthing off on Burnside. "Tell me about these red flags of yours."

"The way Bigfoot told people to go there because she ran the place and she had the power to get you a bed if you didn't get on the list. You know, not everyone has a phone out here, or access. Or commonsense. But she tells people go there and she'll take care of you." She stopped rubbing her hands and slapped the steering wheel. "She must have been the woman Robyn met at the showers. Why didn't I work that out? I'm so stupid…"

"Is there anything else you can tell me about that woman?"

Trinity had her hands over her face, but she managed to let out a muffled, "No."

It didn't line up. If I had put money on anyone throwing their weight around it would have been LuAnn. She'd done it to me at the shelter, bullied new inmates, ran the lights at bedtime. But here was Trinity saying LuAnn was okay.

Which left me with Judy who, come to think of it, had pulled rank on LuAnn at dinner. Then she'd shut me out, avoided me, had run for the van when we got outside. Was she in control? Was she bringing in the drugs that Gordon dealt? Or was she just working with Gordon to bring in potential customers?

"I'll tell you this," Trinity broke into my thoughts. "That journal is everything to Robyn. Leaving it behind could have been an accident, but once she discovered it was gone, she'd be tearing the world apart to find it. She thought she left it once at a rest stop and she made me turn back and spend an hour searching. The fact that she's not looking for that journal right now, says only one thing to me."

"That she can't."

"Yeah." She swiped at her eyes, then held out one hand for the journal. "Can I have it?"

I didn't want to part with the journal. I hadn't been able to resist reading it and there was no way Trinity wouldn't study it from cover to cover. It would be best to keep the number of betrayals and intrusions to a minimum.

"I think it should stay with me for the moment. It might hold more clues of how to find her." I handed Trinity my business card, a twenty-dollar bill, and the three packages of peanut butter crackers I had in my purse. "If you hear from her before me, call and I'll get this journal back to her personally. If I find her first, I'll call you."

She scanned the card. "You're a PI?"

"Yeah."

"How'd you end up in a homeless shelter? You got no place to live?"

I could lie or be honest. I had a feeling, too many had done the first choice, and I wasn't anticipating going back in at this point anyway. "I was hired to find out if drugs were being dealt at the shelter. Did Robyn ever talk about drugs there?"

"No, but they're everywhere else, why not there?"

I'd had that same thought since my first meeting with Bernie. "True. But one of the women who passed through there was found dead in the park a while back."

"You talking about Maria?"

I straightened. "You knew her?"

"I'd met her at the shower truck a couple of times. She was sweet. A little flighty."

I wanted to hear everything Trinity could tell me about this dead girl. "Heard she'd OD'd," I said, doing everything I could to keep any judgment out of my tone.

"That's what they said." Her voice had an edge.

"You don't think so?"

"She was clean last time I talked to her. Seemed like she'd intended to stay that way too. I was surprised, that's all."

The fact that Maria had fallen out of sobriety, according to Trinity, made me think of Amber. "Ever run into an Amber Moore up at the shower truck? Or anywhere really…"

"A couple of times. She always seemed nice."

That wasn't much help, but the puzzle pieces were coming together, even if I wasn't liking the picture. Robyn had been clean. Of that I had no doubt. I'd seen a scared seventeen-year-old, not a drug addict. According to Trinity, Maria had been clean but died of an overdose. While I couldn't confirm her sobriety, according to her grandfather, Amber had been clean and disappeared. Who was pulling the strings and why did no one care?

If they'd been through rehab, there would be records of that at Saving Grace. That had to be my next port of call.

When I got back to my car Floyd told me off for a good two minutes, which I deserved. We drove home, ate dinner, said our goodnights to Mitz and Kyle, then snuggled on the couch—my brain churning with questions upon questions—until I fell asleep.

CHAPTER 12

My teeth were fuzzy and my hair was a crow's nest when I woke up, but my phone was buzzing and the number looked familiar. "Kelly Pruett." I sounded vaguely human and they couldn't see that I looked otherwise.

"Ms. Pruett. This is Katherine Sokol's assistant. I'm returning your call. She is available at ten today, if that's agreeable?"

That was less than an hour from now. I took down the address, raced upstairs, found my white shirt, black pants, and blazer, and brushed my teeth. I raced Floyd over to Arlene's place. With no idea how the day would unfold, I owed him that for being couped up yesterday.

"Don't have time to talk. If you don't mind?" I offered his leash and Arlene took it. If I could get out fast, I might not have to see Hannah.

"I don't mind at all. Right, Mr. Floppy Ears?" Arlene cooed at my boy.

I smiled, despite my rush. "He's had breakfast, but he never minds extra treats. I'll be back in a couple of hours, or so." I threw a *thank you* over my shoulder and ran down the steps to my car before she had time to reel me into a discussion about avoiding my sister.

Bernie's house had been impressive, sitting high above the city in the West Hills, but Katherine's had my jaw on the ground as I pulled past her open gate. The property perched above the Columbia River on the Washington side and the views were spectacular.

The red brick mini mansion with white trim and ivy winding up the sides could have been plucked off an English estate. Skeletal wisteria vines that would be graced with flowers come spring formed arches into the garden. A barely clad, concrete woman holding a vase spewed water upward and anchored the circular drive. I parked and made my way up the boxwood-lined pathway to the entry.

I had no idea why Carla had told me to talk to Katherine and little clue how to shape the interview, but with a vulnerable, missing granddaughter there was no question: she'd want to talk to me.

Everything about the place reeked of money so I was surprised when Katherine opened the door herself. In her mid-seventies, her coifed cinnamon-colored hair—the kind only achieved by regular salon visits—was swirled high on her head with a jeweled butterfly pick stuck into one side. The floral chiffon Mumu with butterfly arms, which she wore over a patterned long-sleeve shirt, gave her an ethereal look. Her flip-flops sparkled, a bold choice for the coolness of January. She wore a bit too much rouge. My grandmother had done something similar, using lipstick on her cheeks, rubbed in little circles and barely blended. It looked clownish if done in excess, and despite Katherine's elegance, her cheeks were too red.

"Yes?" she said when she answered and looked past me like she'd been expecting someone else.

"Ms. Sokol, my name is Kelly Pruett. Your assistant said I should be here at ten. I called about Amber. I was hoping you could shed some light on her disappearance." A small part of me also hoped the fact I resembled my mother might spark recognition.

Her eyes narrowed. "No. I can't. It was a waste of your time to make the drive."

Her greeting was a mile shy of polite. Had her assistant failed to give her details of my call? I had to hold back my disappointment. "If you don't mind, I'd like to be the judge of that. I'm a PI. My father and I have done work for the law firm for years and Bernie, I mean Mr. Sokol, hired me."

Her face was a blank. She didn't twitch a single muscle. "And? What does that have to do with me?"

This wasn't going well. "As I said, Mr. Sokol asked me to check things out at Loving Grace."

She lifted her chin and stretched her neck. "Because of Amber?"

"It stemmed from that, yes. He had concerns of drug dealing inside."

"The fool," she said, her jaw setting before she closed her eyes.

She'd been involved with the charity for decades. Maybe that's why it didn't come as a surprise to her that there were drugs flowing through the system. "Why do you say he was a fool?"

"Why? It's going to be a scam. Amber is a conniving little miss. She's playing him. Like they all do."

That was news and required more details, much more.

"She and her mother were both lost causes," Katherine continued. "Bernie never saw it that way, at least when it came to Amber. We'd both given up on her mother years ago, but Amber is no better. He just won't listen."

Katherine's attitude was harsh but bitter people often dish dirt—especially those who have long felt aggrieved. She might tell me things Bernie would never say out loud. "Would you mind if I came in for a few minutes? I mean, I did come all this way."

She stepped back from the door, again looking over my shoulder. "If you can make it quick."

"I can. I will."

She led the way to an expansive living room. It contained the same heavy, ornate furniture that appeared to be her trademark. It remained in Bernie's offices and half his home, signaling an ambivalent relationship with his ex-wife—or a man who couldn't be bothered to go furniture shopping. No, that wasn't right. Half of Bernie's house had been remodeled by the new Mrs. Sokol, who wasn't "Mrs. Sokol." Candy Appleton had kept her own name. There was something in this furniture business, but I had to focus on what was in front of me and come back to it later.

Katherine's pad had a distant view of the Portland International Airport. She had a wrap-around deck which afforded a view of the planes flying up the river toward their landing. Or at least it would, once it had been re-stained. There were ladders and cans and workman's tools just outside the floor-to-ceiling windows.

They sullied the view somewhat, but I was here on business. Besides, the water ran dark and murky this time of year. During the summer it would be filled with water skiers and sailboats. Today it matched the gloom in the sky and our conversation. Katherine—and her attitude towards her daughter and granddaughter had me on edge. I couldn't imagine not loving Mitz with every ounce of energy I possessed.

Katherine motioned me to the flowery sofa and I sat while she perched on the edge of the matching chair across from me. Her dress blended with the fabric.

"Amber's disappearance must be very distressing for all of you."

She waved me off. "You sound like him. Here are the facts. Amber's mother was a foster. We say she was our daughter because we legally adopted her at thirteen. Bernie's idea. Amber didn't have much of a chance coming from that bad seed."

"That's what you said. What kind of trouble was Amber's mother?"

Katherine let out a weary sigh. "She arrived broken and stayed that way. There was no fixing her. I told Bernard, 'You can't battle Mother Nature.' But he was convinced that 'Love will save the day.' The argument over nature versus nurture was a constant debate for us."

That was useful data and gave me an idea for a lead. "Did Amber stay in touch with her mom?"

"Never. Said she didn't care to, but she was as broken and feckless as her mother had been. She hoarded objects and stole jewelry. You couldn't leave your handbag downstairs at night or she'd wipe you out. Bernard refused to put his foot down." She rolled her eyes again. "He's an easy touch. No wonder he's been lumbered with that gold digger and her bitch-welp daughter. They'll bleed him dry, just like Amber."

This was like nothing else I'd heard; not from Bernie, not from Carla, or Trinity. I wouldn't have expected Trinity to have this kind of detail about Amber's home life, but she seemed to like the girl. If Amber had the reputation of a sneak and thief, that would have been a "known thing" on the street, surely?

How was it that Katherine's version of the past was so out of kilter with everyone else's? Was *this* what Carla wanted me to know? That Bernie wouldn't truly look into Loving Grace because *Amber* was behind the drugs? All kinds of alarm bells went off in my head. It fit. Bernie hadn't taken action because he loved his granddaughter. Shivers raged up and down my arms.

"Her mother died," Katherine said, snapping me back. "Despite Amber seemingly not to care about maintaining a relationship, the idea that her mother's death left no future option of that had her going completely wild. Kids." She grimaced. "Quite honestly, I stopped paying attention to what she was doing. Bernie obviously did not." She stared at me, hard. She was unmoved by her own story and genuinely didn't care that Amber was missing. "Is that all?"

I took in a deep breath, trying to absorb the information. "I'll only take one more moment of your time." I stared outside at the water again. "You really do have a beautiful view."

She crossed her ankles and let out a loud sigh. "It is a lovely place. I grew up here. It belonged to my family. It's a money pit, but what can you do? Some things are hard to give up." She closed her eyes and drifted away for a few seconds. When she opened them, the soft jowls of her face tightened and she glanced at her watch.

I was running out of time. "It's not only that Amber is missing. I'm concerned because another girl staying at the same shelter was found dead by overdose in the nearby park."

"I see."

I was taking a huge gamble, laying my theory out for her. "Is there any chance Amber could have been dealing?"

She flinched, the first sign that she might care about what had happened to her granddaughter. "Of course she is. It's exactly the kind of thing she'd do. Like I told you, she's bad to the bone. Don't believe a word Bernie says about her. The man has blinders on when it comes to hard luck cases." She brushed her hand over her perfect skirt. "He's told you about his sister?"

I nodded.

"That shaped him for life. He never got over it. When Grace died she eviscerated her brother. It wasn't his fault but he blamed himself and he's been trying to make up for it ever since." Her lip curled. I wondered if she realized how much she was showing me, but I wasn't about to stop her now that she was on a roll. "He couldn't bear the fact that I didn't need saving. It made him insane. He needs a project, you see. Something to 'fix.'" She made little air quotes around the word fix. "People think he traded me in for a younger wife." Her smile was every bit as grim as the picture she painted. "That wasn't it at all. He just found someone broken and needy and allowed her to dig her claws into his bleeding heart."

Katherine walked to the window to shift the blinds downward. The sun wasn't shining. Perhaps she needed something to do.

I didn't know what to make of her story. It was a tinderbox, primed and ready to go. I steered us to gentler waters. "I understand you worked with my mom."

She flinched a second time then switched gears, returning to her ice queen self. "I've worked with so many people, volunteers, assistants, social workers… who was she?"

"Barb Pruett. She helped you with bookkeeping at Loving Grace I believe?"

She shrugged. "I don't recall. Are you sure?"

"Well, no, not really." Carla could have been confused. Ruth might have been, too.

"I…oh, you know, she may have. My memory isn't what it used to be."

"We look somewhat similar. Although she would have been slightly older than I am now."

She looked at me with dead eyes. "I'm sorry. Does she remember me?"
My heart sunk a little further. "I lost her eighteen years ago in a car accident."

Her expression didn't change. Not even a flicker this time. "Sorry for your loss."

It hurt my heart that Katherine didn't remember my mother. But had I done any better by not letting myself think about her often? I cleared my throat but found nothing to say. There was lots to process—but where to start?

She looked at her watch again and stood, heading to the door.

I followed and stepped outside. "I appreciate your time and candor."

The door shut behind me with no response. She certainly had wanted me out of there.

I dropped into my driver's seat, grabbed my phone and found Trinity. *Hey, Trinity. Kelly here. Any news on your end?*

She texted me a crying-face emoji.

I'm working all the angles.

That got me a star.

Here's a weird one for you. Any word on the street that Amber was a thief? Was that how she survived? By boosting stuff?

The dots pulsed while she typed her reply. *Not all homeless people are criminals. Amber was a nice kid that I remember. She likely had some demons, but don't we all? Just because she was out here doesn't mean she was BAD. Check yourself, lady. Your privilege is showing.*

That wasn't what I meant, but it was hard to get tone right in a text message. *Yeah, I didn't think so.* I added a couple of care emojis. *I'll touch base later. Thanks, Trinity.* I waited, but according to Mitz you don't have to sign off when you're texting.

"Only OLD PEOPLE do that…," she would say. "and only OLD PEOPLE use punctuation" I would punctuate the hell out of all my messages to make her laugh. I pulled up her contact and sent her a flurry of messages, telling her how much I loved her and how she was my Ladybug and always would be.

luv u mom. auntie hannie and floyd came over for a visit today. it was koooool.

Even though I'd taken Floyd to Jeff's house, I had a difficult time reconciling that Hannah had taken my dog there and hung out with my daughter and her…, *Mommy Linda.*

It was too much to deal with on top of the case. I'd separate those threads out and deal with them one at a time. First, find the missing girls. Then, and only then, face the fact that I was having a raging attack of jealousy for no good reason. Hannah adoring Mitz was a good thing. And at some point I'd have to come to terms that Linda would be a part of my life again. Despite telling her during my last case that that day would never happen.

I'm glad you had FUN, Ladybug. We'll talk tonight as usual.

My gut was in knots and I was shot through with adrenaline. I pulled up Kyle's contact and sent him a heart.

Sorry I've been so tied up. You staying safe? he wrote.

I'm safe. I responded.

No news on your missing girls, I'm afraid. I'll keep digging.

I would be a damned fool to let this one get away. *Laters?*

You betcha. Love you. – Hot Stuff.

I had to say it back…no, I wanted to. Even though sometimes it scared the bejeezus out of me. *Love you, too.*

::wicked grin:: he wrote. *You're getting there.*

I tossed the phone onto the seat and started my car. I couldn't stay in Katherine's driveway any longer. That would be weird. As I pulled out, a sedan pulled in. I couldn't hang out to see who Katherine had been waiting for without looking even weirder. It was enough that I knew Katherine hated Amber and Amber's mother and thought Bernie's new wife was broken and needy *and* in it for the money.

I drove a couple of miles and found a Mini Mart parking lot, bought myself a cup of coffee, and ran through my options. I had this strange profile of Amber from Katherine and it didn't add up. Bernie hadn't canned Gordon, which perhaps meant he knew something concrete about how the drug operation operated. Why else would he keep the man on board? Was Gordon connected to Amber's disappearance? If I went back to the shelter, perhaps I could get Nettie, or one of the regulars, talking. They'd know if Amber was a thief or not.

Then I'd take a solid look at the pain and rehab center, Saving Grace. There was something itching at the back of my brain that said that place wasn't kosher. I had no leads on that specifically, but my dad had said more than once that gut instinct was often the most reliable of all leads to follow. I'd started to trust mine over the past couple of investigations.

However, I had a few hours to kill. I dug in my pack and fished out Robyn's journal. I had intended to circle back to it as I got further into this case. If she'd left a clue, I might recognize it easier than when I'd skimmed through it before.

She had a couple of novel ideas outlined just like she told me. Character sketches of bad guys, one clearly based on her father—a long-haul trucker with a bad temper. Her mother was depicted as an angel, which had my eyes watering and my chest tightening. Robyn was lost before she was lost.

She had poems of love gone bad, sketches of cars and street signs, a doodle of the American flag. Below it said *red, white and blue, let them do what they do.* Perhaps it was a cry for freedom. On the next page, a line that bothered me:

They take advantage of our souls.

When it stops, no one knows.

I traced the wide eyes and long lashes she drew. What was she trying to say with the eyes? I had no clue. And what I didn't find was any direct references to drugs, drug dealers, Gordon's creepy ways, or anything about LuAnn, Judy, or Amber for that matter.

My phone buzzed. It was Hannah, the last person I wanted to talk to—well, maybe not the last person. I could go without seeing Katherine ever again. What a cold fish.

Hannah buzzed me again. I hit REJECT.

She rang a third time, so I picked up. "What?"

"You need to get over here."

My gut squeezed. "Why? Did something happen to Arlene?" Images of my last case flooded my brain.

"No. It's Floyd. He's not in the backyard." She was breathless and panicking.

"What do you mean he's not in the backyard?"

"After we got back from visiting Mitz, Arlene left to run errands and Floyd wanted a potty break. I let him out."

"And?" My mind raced. If a gate had been left open, or if he found a hole in the fence, and a scent caught his nose at the same time, he'd be gone. Bassets were all nose. One whiff had their brains shut down to commonsense and hyper-focused on the prey. It could be miles, and many crossed streets, before Floyd even looked up. It was one of the reasons I didn't let him go outside unaccompanied. Ever.

"I can't find him. I've been looking since we got back."

I pulled into traffic, got honked at, and floored it all the way back to Belmont. Floyd was microchipped. But if Animal Control had him, they would have called by now, the same if he had been taken into a veterinarian clinic. I dodged in and out of traffic, upsetting a few people. But it was Floyd.

Hannah was pacing at the bottom of the steps in tears when I arrived. We didn't have time for handwringing or reprimands. We had to find my best buddy.

"He has a favorite spot. Let's go." Tucking my cell into my back pocket, I ran. Hannah trotted behind and we crossed the road in silence, heading to a creek that ran parallel to Belmont and only accessible down a side street. My heart pounded with each step. One time when I'd let Floyd "lead the way," we'd ended up at that creek. Between rats, frogs, fish, and occasional trash, it was a dog nose's delight.

"I really am sorry." Hannah tried to keep up.

I didn't break stride. "Why are you even here in the first place? What's your end game?" I raised my voice to a near shout.

She jogged alongside me with a shocked look on her face like I'd smacked her. "What do you mean? You've known me in one situation."

"Right. Guess that hasn't changed much since you're not staying with your parents. You drop out of sight for over a year. You don't make any contact with me, and then suddenly you're living next door."

"I kept in contact with Arlene."

"Did not."

"Did too." For a minute we sounded like real sisters.

We were both out of breath.

"Floyd!" I shouted. "Where are you, boy?" What would I do if I couldn't find him? Or if he'd been hit by a car? My stomach clenched. I wouldn't let myself go there.

Arlene had asked me about Hannah a few times. Had she been hearing from my half-sister and fishing to see if I had been in touch with her? She might have wanted to save my feelings if Hannah hadn't been talking to me. I'd been doing *only child* for so long, I had no idea how to have a sister in my life.

"There he is." She saw him before I did—belly deep into the creek and standing with his drooping, somber face and brown eyes staring at me. Stuck in the mud. Literally. His tail swayed as his eyes met mine. He let out a long bay.

My heart jumped and I sprinted his direction with Hannah on my heels. At the creek bed, I waded in mid-calf and sunk to my knees. No wonder he hadn't been able to move. From where I stood, I could reach his collar. I got one hand on that and the other under his front legs. I lifted, but his seventy pounds of chunk barely budged. Hannah was suddenly next to me and between the two of us, we yanked him out to the edge at the same time we went backwards into the sludge.

"Damn it," I spouted and Hannah laughed. I scowled as I wiped the mud from my hands onto my shirt. We were a disaster. Floyd unleashed a full body shake that sent another layer of wet mud all over us. If it were Mitz and me in this situation, we'd be hysterical with laughter. But between Hannah not watching Floyd, and the niggling guilt that I shouldn't be relying on other people to watch my dog, even when they wanted to, left me an arm's length passed annoyed.

We trudged back up from the creek in silence. At least my heartbeat wasn't pounding out of my chest this time. I'd found Floyd and he was fine. I had to hang on to that. He was safe.

When we reached the house, Hannah put her hand on my arm and gave me her own version of puppy dog eyes. "I am sorry."

"He's a hound dog and hounds are all about scent."

"I'll make it up to you. I'll give him a bath and take good care of him for the rest of the day."

I should be the one taking care of my own dog, but the truth was I had to go to the shelter and see what I could learn about Amber then scope out the rehab center. Floyd couldn't come with me in his present state, and Kyle was too busy with work to come over. Hannah was my only option.

"Thank you. Please use the colloidal oatmeal soap. That's good for his skin. He's going to be itchy." I turned to go and then turned back around. "Please don't lose him again. He's my best friend." No, he was family. Was Hannah going to be part of my family? Her DNA said so but I hadn't figured this relationship out. I swallowed the catch in my throat so she wouldn't see what almost losing him had done to me.

She called after me, but I took myself off for a hot shower. I had to get cleaned up before I went undercover and got dirty all over again.

CHAPTER 13

Stakeouts were only an occasional way of life for me when I process served for my dad and R&K Investigations. He never let me assist with anything that had any teeth. Like some of the men in my orbit, he'd tried to wrap me in cotton wool and keep me away from real life. Kyle had done that originally, but not now.

Of course, I wanted to play it safe, or at least smart—I had Mitz to think about—but I also had a career and an agency and deep in my gut I wanted to do something that mattered. This time around it meant finding these girls before something terrible happened to them. I'd learned a little something about what went on at Loving Grace and now I also had the rehab center in my sights.

Since no one was out front of the rehab center, I parked opposite the shelter and down a little ways and waited to see if I could snag someone from there for a word about Amber and her alleged *thieving little fingers*. Judy was deep in conversation with Nettie. LuAnn was her usual boisterous self, directing traffic and telling people what to do.

The only person not standing with the clump of women at the front door to Loving Grace was Ruth, and she turned her head and looked right at my car. I slid down in my seat. I didn't want to be mean because she was clearly fragile. If she lived in the past—and my mother was there with a kind word and a helping hand—all the better. But for my purposes, she was an "unreliable witness." Within a short time, Ruth wandered past Nettie, lost in her own world, and the doors closed and the outside lights went dark.

Strike one. In spite of watching fifty women stream into the shelter, I hadn't managed to corner and interrogate one.

My next at bat involved staking out Saving Grace. I swung the car around and parked by the dumpsters outside Saving Grace where I could watch without being seen. The rehab center's windows hung like black squares in the building's façade. Not a light was on in the whole place. Jessica didn't think highly of the operation inside, but her criticism centered on the type of treatment protocols they engaged in, rather than the place itself. If I understood her correctly, they were setting addicts up for failure by having a rotating door. There was no—what had she called it?—no "stepped" facility for them to go to once they'd detoxed.

Unsure what happened in a rehab center, I tapped "detox facility" plus "Portland" into my phone and was deluged with high-end, lodge-like images of pristine getaways where you could confront your demons, deal with your substance abuse, face your stress disorders, and overcome your opioid addiction. Whatever plagued you, there was a team of specialists who could help you "ditch dope and regain hope", for a pretty penny.

I stretched my neck, letting it click and pop. The girls—sorry, young women—who'd gone through those doors didn't have oodles of cash. They were poor. Technically, Amber wasn't cash-poor, but she might as well have been for all the support she got from Katherine. Her grandmother hated her and had since she'd come into their lives. There was no chance the ex-Mrs. Sokol was footing the get-well bill.

No lights came on inside Saving Grace. No people appeared at the windows. There was no foot traffic. If deals were happening, they were being done in the dark, away from the windows, or simply not at night. Although despite the limited activity, it could be too early to tell anything definitive. Stakeouts were often a whole lot of nothing, right up until they became a little bit of something.

I texted Mitz good night and then Kyle. I'd been wanting to catch up with him anyway. We were supposed to get together one of these nights, but I should have texted him sooner. *I have to take a rain check for tonight. You busy?*

I waited for a response. My phone rang within a second.

"Hey stranger. What are you doing?" he said. His voice was warm and friendly. "I was hoping to spend the evening with a beautiful woman."

"That was the plan, but…"

"Duty calls?" he said, his laugh light.

"I'm staking out the shelter."

"No worries. I'm busy too. Criminals never rest and Enloe likes to make sure I'm getting well trained."

"Tomorrow?" I said. "Mitz has a thing with Jeff and Linda's family. I won't get her until Saturday."

"Let's shoot for that."

I took a deep breath. "I meant what I said before."

He laughed.

"No, really, I did."

"I know. I just want to hear you say it again."

"I love you."

"Was that so hard?"

I wanted to tell him that he was a jerk, but truthfully it was getting easier every time and never failed to make me feel warm and fuzzy. But I wouldn't give him the satisfaction. I blew him a kiss instead.

"Damn right," he said and hung up.

I punched off my cell and glanced in my rearview mirror. A woman's silhouette crossed the street from Loving Grace and headed toward Saving Grace. Based on the oversized coat and stocking cap, it had to be LuAnn.

I checked my pocket for my pepper spray and shoved my purse with Robyn's journal under the seat. I zipped the spray, along with my phone and keys, into my warmup jacket. I eased out of my car and gently closed the door, giving it a lean with my hip until I heard it latch. Then I disappeared into the shadows.

LuAnn rang Saving Grace's doorbell, and shifted on her feet, waiting. A light came on, providing a clear view of the space through the wall of privacy glass, but not so private at night.

A man in a white doctor's coat approached LuAnn. It wasn't until the man unlocked the door, and the light above shone on him more fully, that I saw his bowtie. While I couldn't make out every feature, he resembled the man I'd seen in the conference room at Baumgartner & Sokol.

What was he doing greeting LuAnn? I'd thought the meeting up front had to do with criminal work for the firm. Maybe it had been a board meeting, or maybe something else. Either way, the man's coat looked doctorly. Could be that LuAnn was a patient. I'd figured her for the drug dealer at the very least, but was it possible she was checking in there for the night? What little I knew of her indicated she wouldn't want anyone knowing her business. She might want to be discreet if she was using the rehab's services; although how did that add up? Poor women didn't get to check in under cover of night to protect their privacy. I'd been looking at too many lodge-spa-rehab websites. LuAnn was here to conduct *business*.

I crossed the street, staying wide of the streetlights, and pressed myself up against the building.

LuAnn and Mr. Bow-Tie remained in the lobby. He handed her a thick envelope which she tucked into her flannel coat jacket. My brain immediately had the envelope filled with money; big notes, lots of cash—a payoff of some kind? Or was it payment for services rendered? Was she the mule? I had to keep watching—and breathe. I didn't have the data yet, only supposition.

An exchange went on between them for a few more minutes with her doing most of the talking. She stopped abruptly, throwing her head back, and his body stiffened. He leaned in, his face inches from LuAnn's. Whatever they were discussing had become heated.

LuAnn turned on her heels and slammed the exit bar with both hands—the interaction that transpired had left her beet red.

"That's enough," she snapped.

"You listen here," he said.

"You don't know what you're talking about."

Again went the back and forth for a few seconds with no clue what they were arguing about. Mr. Bow-Tie caught up to LuAnn and grabbed her by the arm. "Don't mess with me, or you'll end up like the rest of them."

My stomach tightened. LuAnn broke free and kept walking. I was torn. I wanted to get inside Saving Grace and see what they were up to. I also wanted to catch up with LuAnn. I couldn't run out into the street after her with him standing there, and I doubted he'd invite me in. I'd have to wait it out. He followed and snatched her by the arm again and lowered his voice. I couldn't make out what he was saying, although it sure sounded like LuAnn growled.

Suddenly, his hand flew off her arm like she was on fire. He spat at her feet before marching back into the rehab building. LuAnn glared at the door until it closed behind him. She stood in the middle of the road, shaking her arms, perhaps trying to dispel the adrenaline.

If she went to the shelter with an envelope full of money, it meant *what?* That she was the low-level gofer, that the money was for Gordon or the good-looking produce guy? Then again, if she went north towards Farragut Park it could mean she was going to score. *Which is it going to be LuAnn? Pusher or intermediary? Senior villain or sidekick? What are you?* She neither went west nor north. Instead, she headed my way.

With only seconds to avoid detection, I darted ahead before she turned the corner and stepped into the alley between two buildings. She had the envelope tucked in her jacket. Maybe it didn't have money at all. It could be full of drugs, packets of powdered stuff since it hadn't been bulky like I'd expect pills to be. She could be going to make a deal. If that were the case, she could lead me to the dealer above Gordon, because Gordon was dealing something.

I hugged the wall as she strode past me. She was moving fast and breathing hard, the mist floating in front of her face. Once she'd reached the corner and crossed the street, I came out of the alleyway and jaywalked from the midpoint and stayed close to the wall, rounding the corner. The dim street lamps had me tracking her at nearly two blocks ahead. I picked up my pace.

I'd closed the distance to a block when she froze. Her head whipped my way. I flattened myself into a doorway, slapping my hand over my mouth to stop my own trail of frosty breath from revealing my location. The whoosh of my heartbeat crashed in my ears. If she came back my way, I wouldn't be able to hear her over the racket. I watched for approaching shadows instead.

After a few seconds, I poked my head out to see LuAnn climbing a cement stoop. She pulled a key from her pocket and inserted it into the lock. As soon as the door slammed behind her, I trotted over to where she'd been.

She'd gone into an old house with a rickety door. A light flicked on in the upstairs right corner window. The window only had a pale, sheer curtain, which acted as a shadow screen. I stepped away from the door, with its small porch light, and blended into the sidewalk in case LuAnn looked out. But she didn't. LuAnn's silhouette took off her jacket and pulled off her stocking cap before massaging her head. She stretched, arms overhead. Her actions indicated comfort, familiarity, home.

If LuAnn had a home, why would she spend one minute inside a homeless shelter? Did she live with someone? Or was the house only available sometimes and not others?

There was only one way to find out.

As I made the decision to ask her in person, the light in the window clicked off. She might be going to bed. But if I waited to try to catch her again in the morning, I could lose my opportunity to talk with her altogether. I didn't intend to sleep on her doorstep and wait for her.

I bounded up the stairs and rang the bell. There weren't any noises on the other side of the door. I waited and rang again with no response... then one more time for good measure. A few minutes later, there was still no answer, I stepped back out onto the sidewalk. There was no movement from the upstairs window, no light, no shadows. This wasn't the best part of town. A vagrant ringing her doorbell in the middle of the night might be a common occurrence. Perhaps no one answered their doors after lights out around here? Only trouble rang the doorbell. Anyone sensible would have called her phone.

Then again, there was every chance she'd seen me coming and had decided to not give me the time of day. Or was there a back door? Was she even upstairs right now?

The houses had alleys between them. If there was a back exit, I should be able to get to it from there. To be safe, I took my pepper spray and phone out of my pocket. My left hand gripped the cannister. Trying not to focus on the thump of my heart, I started down the alley, fiddling with the flashlight feature on my phone. My footfalls were accentuated with the crunch of broken glass under my feet.

A crunch came out of sync from mine.

Fear blasted a shiver through me at the same moment a stream of mace caught me square in the face.

CHAPTER 14

My eyes slapped closed with excruciating pain. My skin burned like boiling water had been thrown on me. Blinded, my hands flew out in front of me to protect my face from another spray. My chest tightened; my mouth, nose and throat felt like I'd swallowed hot coals. I began to whip around, trying to track my attacker. But I hadn't even made a full rotation before I was slammed from the side, sending me crashing into a bay of garbage cans.

Lids popped and bags of garbage spilled out as my body hit them. My own pepper spray and phone flew out of my hands. Footfalls running away from me echoed in the alley.

My eyes were latched shut as I began to drool, my nose running and my ears tearing. I gasped for fresh air and all I got was a mouth full of chemicals.

I scrambled onto my hands and knees, listening for whether my attacker, who had to be LuAnn, was coming back. But I didn't hear anyone around.

I turned myself enough to drop onto my butt and picked off what had to be week old sludge, given the sour stench, from my jacket. Helpless—all I could do was wait out the effects. My defense class had prepped me for the reality of being incapacitated for a bit, and not to panic, something easier said than done.

What they hadn't prepared me for was the ten-out-of-ten pain raging around my face. Being tased was less agonizing, and that was no picnic. It took every ounce of my will not to scrub my eyes—and to not feel sorry for myself.

But feeling duped and annoyed that I'd been rushed was short lived. I could wallow or I could do something about it—or at least use this situation to my advantage.

I wasn't high, but I sure felt like hell. With what would soon become bloodshot eyes, combined with smelling like I'd landed in something gross, I was confident I looked rehab worthy.

When I felt able, I pushed myself up and found my phone which had landed right in front of me. What I couldn't find with my inability to see clearly, even with the flashlight feature, was my spray. I'd have to come back for it later. If a kid got to it, that would be bad and I couldn't risk that.

Once on my feet, I made my way across the street and back to Saving Grace. I rang the bell several times, until a woman's silhouette showed up in the entry.

She opened the door. "You look like you could use some detoxing, hon," she said.

I'd dispute that once upstairs. "Okay," I said, walking past her and following her into the elevator.

She held her breath as she punched a floor button.

I didn't blame her. My senses were starting to come back and with it the reality of how rank I smelled. I held my breath for a few seconds, before a cough rattled my chest.

The woman, a nurse I assumed at this point, led me into a room, and set me on a bed, where she left me. Through narrowed eyes, I could tell the room was small with no windows. Everything blurred beige and white like a hospital room, but without the electronics. A cloth chair sat in the corner next to a tall cabinet. And a sink. The minute she left, I headed there and rinsed my eyes out, the cold water taking some of the pain with it down the drain.

While better, it would be a while before I could see without it stinging. Instead of sitting back down, I poked my head out and looked around at what appeared to be a nurse's station and neighboring rooms. I expected to find a lot of activity, or the man in the bowtie who'd given that envelope to LuAnn. LuAnn who had attacked me. But I didn't see anyone meandering about.

Where was everyone? I was about to investigate further when a woman in her mid-sixties, based on her gray shoulder-length hair, saw me.

"Get back into your room, please." Her faced wrinkled with annoyance. She was dressed in blue scrubs and her name tag read *Nancy K.* Her voice indicated she was the same woman who'd met me downstairs and put me in this room, but I could see her more clearly now.

"Yes, ma'am. But there's been a misunderstanding." I slunk back into the room with her on my heels and hopped onto the bed.

"That's what you all say. What did you use? Did you shoot heroin? Or was it Fentanyl? You look like you used that. Your eyes… or did you snort coke or something else?"

"Shooting fentanyl?"

"That's it?"

"No, I mean people do that?"

"Oh yes. From the patch. You people do all sorts of things. I can always run a test to find out…"

"No, no, no. I'm good. Someone sprayed me with mace and I was confused. That's all." I slid off the bed, but felt dizzy.

"Uh-huh."

"No seriously, I'm not an addict. In fact, my name is Kelly Pruett. I'm a PI."

A young blonde girl appeared in the doorway, a clipboard in her hand. She frowned.

Addicts must have given similar stories in the past for me to get that condescending response and weird looks. But I had no desire to argue. "I just needed a place to pull myself together. I appreciate your bringing me up, but I'll call for someone to get me now."

"We can't let you go anywhere. You can use the phone for patients in the recreation room as soon as we fill out the paperwork and get you settled."

Not what I had in mind. "I won't be settling anywhere. Like I said, I'm a private investigator, on a case." I reached for my phone in my pocket.

She straightened, her face stoic. "What kind of case?"

I was sitting in the rehab center where Amber had been at one time. Perhaps Maria. Telling them Robyn was missing might not get me anywhere. The others could. "I'm looking into the disappearance of Amber Moore and the death of Maria Castro. Names sound familiar?" I watched for signs of recognition.

Her eyes flashed before she became stony-faced again. "Never."

Her expression and words didn't match. "You sure? Both were supposedly clean and sober. Did they come here for help with that?"

She cleared her throat. "Even if they had, HIPAA would bar me from discussing it with you."

That sounded like an admission. "Right." I stared at her hoping for more, but nothing came. "My boyfriend is a police detective. I'll be calling him now."

"We don't want any trouble, but it's not our usual protocol to let you out at your own discretion once you've come in."

That didn't jibe with what Jessica had told me about them detoxing and letting people go. And I wasn't even detoxing. "Is this a prison?"

"No. We're—fine. Make your call."

Thank goodness. My head pounded and I wasn't up for much more back and forth. The floor was eerily quiet as I punched in Kyle's number. Maybe they treated patients on another floor, or everyone was sleeping. A few staff wandered past the room that I hadn't seen when I'd peeked out earlier. They peered in as they passed. Was I the latest addition to a zoo that everyone had to check out? *Look at the crazy monkey.*

The man with the bowtie strolled past giving me a sideway glance that I would have missed if I hadn't been hyper-focused on the door. He hurried away like everyone else.

I gazed at Kyle's number but held back from hitting send, out of pride—a bit. He'd told me to be careful, and that fear that he'd see me as a danger seeker came crashing back. I also knew he was on a case and if Detective Enloe didn't like him on the phone, he wouldn't appreciate him running out to pick up his duped girlfriend. I would tell Kyle about the attack since it was a police matter, but not now.

I could always fake call someone…. I checked my pocket to make sure I had my car keys.

I lowered my head. My pocket was empty. I really had only one choice.

I cleared the screen and punched in the number for Arlene. She answered on the first ring.

I cleared the wedge in my throat. "Hey Arlene, is Hannah there?"

CHAPTER 15

Arlene didn't fuss or ask questions at my request. She did as I asked her. *Bless her.*

On my way down from the fourth floor, I couldn't avoid the scowl of Nurse Ratchet who escorted me from the premises. Or my reflection. I caught a glimpse of my flaming red eyes and rumpled clothes in the shiny elevator doors. My reek had only intensified. I looked like a psychiatric ward escapee. In truth, I'd felt like one with how they'd forced me to advocate for myself.

Hannah's hatchback glided to the curb across from the rehab center. Thirty minutes earlier when I'd called, I'd asked her to find the spare key for my car. My regular key was in the alley along with my mace and my dignity. After nearly losing Floyd she owed me. This made us even.

When I opened the passenger door, she dangled the spare set of keys in front of me before deep frown lines creased her forehead. I could only imagine the questions running through her brain.

"Don't ask." I dropped into the passenger seat and turned the heat vents my direction. The adrenalin had started it's slow seep out of my body, chilling me to the bone. It was two o'clock in the morning, and the rehab building had grown dark once again. I'd been somewhere on the fourth floor in an interior room. In the time I'd been inside, and on my way out as we trudged through corridors, passed the nurse's station, and I peered through pebbled glass into vacant rooms, I hadn't come across any other patients. The only activity I'd ever seen in this whole building seemed to happen on the fourth floor. My getting myself into the rehab center to check things out had only raised more questions about where everyone else was at.

Hannah looked me over from head to toe, her eyes wide with judgment. "Not going to say a word. Where're you parked?"

I rested my head back. "A block down, opposite side, near a dumpster."

We drove the short distance in silence and she pulled behind my car, her headlights reflecting on my bumper and catching glistens of glass on the ground and illuminating the busted back and driver's side windows. My car had been broken into.

I rolled out of Hannah's car. She kept it running and got out with me. A rock had gone through the back and driver's side windows. My backpack was gone. At least they hadn't tried to steal my car, or take my tires. I checked under the seat. My purse was there along with Robyn's journal.

A wave of relief ran through me, but it was short lived as my headache was back with a vengeance. Tonight had taken its toll, and I was exhausted. I bent at the waist and then back up, taking a long breath, which started a coughing fit.

Hannah rested her hand on my back. "Want to talk about it?"

I didn't look at her. "About what?"

"You can start by telling me if this is what you really do for a living? Because girlfriend, you might seriously want to rethink professions. You look like hell right now."

"It's not generally like this." How many times had I used that line in the past year? Hannah knew about the time I'd been shot, but I didn't intend to share about the time I'd been beaten up and nearly barbecued. Those events I kept compartmentalized so not to walk around in a constant state of PTSD. Although tonight's assault brought them back up. Because I had to call it for what it was—I'd been attacked. Again. "I was following someone and they got a jump on me." I gave her the Cliff Note version of what had led me to this point. Although talking did little to ease the tension headache between my eyes.

Hannah shook her head as she listened. At the end, she wrapped her arms around herself. "Hope you're getting paid well for this then." She gave me a hard look.

A lump formed in my throat when I chortled.

"Sorry if you don't want to hear it, but someone's got to tell you straight," she said.

"It's not that. I'm not getting a dime." I'd gotten the bit between my teeth and money had apparently ceased to matter.

"Seems kind of dumb then to put yourself through it. And Arlene."

"What about her?"

She shrugged. "Not that I want to butt into your business, but Arlene's a wreck right now."

Arlene? A wreck? Uh, no, that wasn't how Arlene rolled. "Arlene's upset because I called you out here? I asked you not to tell her any details."

"You're the one who called the house, remember? And the fact you need picking up in the middle of the night is reason enough. She genuinely worries about you. Do you really not realize that?"

My stomach squeezed. I did know that and I felt bad for having called— for putting myself in a situation where I had to call. "Will you follow me to the alley where I got hit?" I rubbed my eyes, causing the burning pain to return. I was brimming with smart moves. "I dropped my mace, and my keys, neither of which I want to have someone else find."

"Only if you're going home right after?"

Is this what it was like having a kid sister? I'd said I didn't want one, but at this moment, it was nice that someone had my back. I was too spent to argue or chase down any leads anyway. "Yes. I'm going home."

Hannah followed me to the street where LuAnn had gotten the better of me—at least, I was pretty sure it had to be LuAnn. With her as my prime suspect, I wouldn't be ringing her bell and confronting her in my current state. Going home and crawling into bed were the only things on my agenda. The house I'd seen her go into was dark. She'd likely run off after attacking me anyway. I would.

With Hannah's headlights shining down the length of the alley, I found my mace sitting on top of the garbage can, but my keys were covered in old coffee grinds and eggshells. It could be worse. I shook the keys off, but couldn't do the same with feeling dumb. It was more than that—my dad would have pulled himself up and gotten right back at it, beating the streets until daylight—pretend nothing happened. Being strong and in control was the only way I knew back from being violated.

Despite the storm of emotions rumbling through me, I stood tall and headed back to my car, lifting the items to show Hannah, when the glimmer of a clear cellophane wrapper, about two inches squared, reflected in the grass. I bent down to inspect it, using the light on my phone. I could make out the words Fentanyl 100mcg. Another wrapper had blown a few feet away from the other.

The envelope LuAnn had taken from Mr. Bow-Tie had been flat. I had thought it was money. But what if the envelope had been full of these fentanyl patches?

The nurse from the rehab center had mentioned that the drug could be extracted for shooting up. Maria had died of exactly that. I searched my jacket pockets and pulled out the plastic that had once contained a peanut butter cracker. I used that to grab the fentanyl wrapper and stuffed them into my pocket, zipping them in. Kyle might be able to get information off them.

Maybe LuAnn was selling the patches. Or she was supplying them for Gordon to sell. But if so, how did Amber fit into the picture? Was she involved, as Katherine had suggested?

Same thoughts, same day—I was desperate for a break from all this. There was nothing fresh except for my burning eyes and bruises.

Hannah tapped her horn to get my attention and my stomach nose-dived. I whipped around to see if any lights went on in the house. *Nothing*. The attack had done more than chip at my tough girl exterior, my nerves were shot.

I dragged myself back to the street and slid into my car. I pulled up beside Hannah. I didn't need to roll down the windows to talk to her because there were no windows. Score two for me. I was a damned winner. "Stay close, would you?"

"Sure thing."

"And Hannah?"

"Yeah?"

"Thank you."

She smiled and nodded as I pulled out and drove under the speed limit with Hannah behind me. My mind was swirling. What bothered me the most was how easily the attack had happened. One minute I was skulking down an alley, next thing I was blinded by mace, clawing my way out of a pile of garbage, and gasping for air.

My brain was too fuzzy to connect any dots. When I pulled into my driveway, Hannah passed. By the time I had parked, she was already by Arlene's door, waving.

I waved back. She'd done more than pay her dues. She'd done me a solid. She'd acted like a sister. I trudged up the stairs, texted Kyle a "Home and goodnight," and collapsed on my bed.

CHAPTER 16

The smell of coffee and dishes clinking in my kitchen downstairs pulled me out of the fog my brain was caught in. I'd barely slept and while the irritating effects of mace shouldn't last more than twenty-four hours, it hadn't been that long—and I hadn't only been maced. I'd been run down. I shifted to my side, my back muscles protesting with sharp aches. I was getting too old to be crashing into garbage cans without some serious payback. Even the ordinary clatter of dishes made my head hurt.

Floyd was lying next to me, his warm body snuggled against my arm. He wasn't barking, which meant two things: Hannah had brought him home early or Kyle was downstairs having retrieved him from Arlene's place. Kyle was an inevitable but unsettling prospect since I wasn't ready to tell him about last night's adventure even though I would have to, soon. I glanced at the unrumpled side of my bed. I'd go with Hannah.

There was only one way to confirm, but I wasn't concerned. If someone wanted to cause me more harm, they wouldn't be frying bacon, the scent of which had made its way up the stairs making my mouth water.

Arlene and Mitz stood in my kitchen working side by side. Floyd had gone down ahead and anchored himself in the center. Mitz hadn't seen me, her full attention on the sizzling bacon in the pan. Arlene stood at the sink, wrist deep in dishwater.

"Morning sleepy head," Arlene said, without turning in my direction.

"Morning." I stood behind Mitz and nuzzled her neck excited to see her and glad I'd taken a few minutes before coming downstairs to rinse my mouth, wash my face—the red around my eyes had faded, not disappeared—and pulled my hair into a ponytail. I didn't want to scare her or Arlene. Mitz set down the tongs and gave me a full-on hug. My heart skipped a few beats. How much I'd missed my ladybug, even though I'd hugged her a couple of days ago.

Coughing, Mitz stepped back. Next to her eyes, she had her thumb and index finger squeezed closed at the fingertips and then opened them fast to form L's. "Surprise."

I signed and said, "I guess. And a pleasant one. Are you sick?" Although I could tell she was by the red of her nose and the flush on her cheeks.

"Just a cold," she signed.

That had come on fast. I pulled her back in for another hug and she coughed some more. Candy's daughter Morgan had said her child was sick. There must be some flu-like crud going around.

"Hope you don't mind," Arlene said. "It was Mitz's idea. When she suggested it, Hannah agreed you could use the extra TLC. Rough night?"

Bless Arlene for not mentioning the red circles under my eyes, the fact I was moving around like a tortoise, or my late-night call. "Hannah told you I had a rough night? Is she joining us?" She was clearly taking this sister thing seriously.

"No, only the TLC part. I surmised the rest. If you need help of any kind it's because your case is consuming you."

There had been a time when I would have been upset at her presence in my house uninvited, but not today, and not after Hannah had told me how worried Arlene had been last night. "Thank you."

Arlene looked up from the dishes, a small smile crossing her lips. "You're welcome."

I leaned against the counter for support.

"I like being able to do things for my girls. I understand Hannah was a surprise, but she needs someone reliable in her life. If I can provide that, why shouldn't I?" She rinsed a plate and popped it onto the drainer. "And before you say it, no I'm not meddling in your business. I'm here for breakfast with you and Mitz."

My heart hurt in ways good and bad. I'd been so busy pushing Arlene off all those years after my mom died—only ever seen her as interfering in my life—it had never dawned on me that she truly viewed me as one of her girls, or how much she enjoyed that I lived right next door. Had I not wanted to see it because of my "stubborn streak" which she regularly reminded me about?

I hugged her from behind and put my head on the back of her shoulder, gathering strength in her presence. LuAnn's attack had done a number on me, to say nothing about learning of my mom on the fringes of this case. That alone had been enough to topple me. I ignored Arlene's little gasp and let her go, grabbing the plate of bacon and English muffins on my way into the dining room before she could say anything.

Arlene followed a few minutes later with the scrambled eggs in a bowl. We spent the next thirty minutes eating, catching up with Mitz, and talking and signing about how fourth graders could be mean. Admittedly, I was happy not to hear about vacation plans with Mommy Linda and full house renovations. But as I listened, it struck me, suddenly, that Arlene was a superb grandmother. She had learned to sign for Mitz, acted as a regular babysitter, took her to Junior Yoga and swimming, but best of all she listened and laughed and dissed all the girls who Mitz said were bullies.

I had trouble keeping my composure. She wasn't cold like Katherine, money-grubbing like Candy, or a bully like LuAnn. She was a widow with a grown son, a granddaughter she adored, and a stick-in-the-mud idiot ex-daughter-in-law who had only begun to truly get how lucky she had it. I'd been so hard on her all these years when in fact she'd always done her best, better than most, better than so many of the women I'd been around in the last forty-eight hours.

That wasn't fair. I didn't know their stories. I only knew that we were lucky, lucky, lucky sitting as we were in a dining room filled with love and bacon.

Once we finished, Arlene picked up her dishes. Mitz and I followed with ours.

"What do you have planned for your day?" she asked.

"Work." I didn't want to elaborate. "How about you girls? Anything fun?"

Arlene smiled. "Absolutely. Since Mitz isn't running a fever, we're going for a facial. Hannah's coming with, and then we're off to have lunch before we drop her back at Jeff's. I'm seeing Detective Kuni over the weekend, so prettying myself up. You're welcome to join us."

A girl's day—what were those like? My jaw tensed at the thought of Hannah being part of it again, instead of me. But it was starting to be clear why Arlene had let her come to live with her. She was lonely. She wanted a daughter. I could be that person. All I had to do was say yes.

Every minute I wasn't trying to find Robyn, the chance of me finding her or Amber diminished. And with the extra day of Mitz with Jeff, I had to take advantage. My quest might be madness. I knew that. I wasn't being paid for the job. There was no guarantee I'd succeed. People who were trained in the social work field had dropped out because it hurt to be surrounded by so much heartache, but I couldn't give up. These were motherless girls, adrift in the world.

I had so many questions. Who was dealing? Were the girls being "disappeared" when they knew too much? Why was Bernie keeping me at an arm's length? More to the point, why hadn't he gotten the police involved?

If I failed at getting those answers, how many other girls would disappear? How many other girls would be found with needles in their arm at some park?

Meanwhile, my daughter would be surrounded by the love of her grandmother and aunty, all three of them out on the town having a wonderful day.

"Thank you," I said. "I have a few things to wrap up on this case before I can rest."

Arlene nodded and went back to the dishes. She didn't say she was disappointed, but with the lack of a comment and the slump of her shoulders, she didn't have to.

If I did what the dead required of me, was I abandoning the living? Why couldn't I do both—please my dad's hard work and honor my mom's kind heart? Couldn't I just clear the case, then join the girls for a real celebration?

CHAPTER 17

While the girls were off getting facials, I'd get a face to face with Bernie Sokol. The man had lied to me, withheld evidence, and I'd been attacked because of whatever it was he was covering up. He owed me.

I dialed Carla. She picked up on the third ring. "Yes?!" That wasn't how she answered the phone.

"Carla?"

"Yes? Who is this?"

An argument raged in the background: one man, one woman. No prizes for guessing who they were. I strained to hear the conversation, but Carla must have had her hand over the mouthpiece.

"I have to go," she said. "Things are crazy around here."

"Carla. Give me one second. I need time on Bernie's calendar."

She snorted. "Not going to happen. You're persona non grata around here."

What? I was the outcast? When did that happen? "He has to listen to me..."

"Oh, he listened all right and now there's hell to pay." She dropped her voice down to a whisper. "He fired Gordon."

"He did?"

There were more raised voices in the background. "Gotta go." Carla hung up before I had the chance to say another word.

Bernie fired Gordon. I had a rush of adrenalin before my headache redoubled its efforts to knock me back. *No rest for the weary*. The drug dealer was out on his ear. Fantastic—it was exactly the break I'd been waiting for.

The image of Gordon running his hand down that woman's arm kept replaying in my mind. I was eighty-percent certain Gordon was the dealer; just had to nail down a few details to be sure. That being the case I should probably get Kyle in on the interrogation. He wouldn't want me to go in there swinging and questioning a suspected drug dealer by myself, especially if I was right and the scum bucket had been involved in the death and disappearance of those young women.

I scrolled through my contacts list. My finger hovered over *Hot Stuff's* number, then carried on down to google. Problem was, I didn't have any solid evidence, only scraps of data and the occasional stolen glance. Kyle was in training and busy. If I brought him in about Gordon, I'd have to tell him the rest of what happened last night…which I would. Perhaps his words that I was a danger seeker still stung. I didn't want to prove him right even now, but I could take care of Gordon if I had to. I'd gather more info and then give Kyle that call.

But damn…what was Gordon's last name? I tapped my foot while I racked my brain. Ah… I didn't need it. There would be a directory on Loving Grace's website. Surely he'd have a friendly headshot and some PR BS about how much he cared about the homeless women of Portland and why he'd dedicated his life to dealing drugs and making a quick buck off them.

With a few keystrokes on my phone, I was proven right. There he was, grinning like the proverbial cat: Gordon Stradlock. I hopped over to the White Pages and did a quick search: lots of Stradlocks—they must have moved here en masse and settled—but only two Gordons and only one who had the sad sack profile I was looking for: 52, single, living over off North Willis. This was my man.

I flung my front door open to find an envelope jammed into the letterbox. *Please, not more bad news.* I ripped it open and found a set of keys and a note. *"Took your car early to the dealership to get the windows replaced. Didn't want Arlene or Mitz to see it and start asking questions. Use my car, but don't get it busted up like yours."* She'd drawn a smiley face after that, but it didn't soften the blow. *"Love you, Sis. Keep yourself out of trouble today. -Hannah."*

I crumpled the envelope and threw it in the bin by my front door, found Hannah's car, packed Floyd into the passenger side footwell, and hot tailed it right over to Gordon's place—well, I sat in traffic and drummed my fingers on the steering wheel a bunch, but it was relatively plain sailing for Portland on a Friday. It wasn't until I was almost to Gordon's house that it struck me that him getting fired and me getting mugged might not be unrelated.

Great move, Kelly. Right into the lion's den. Again. You go, girl.

Gordon's neighborhood was an eclectic mix of newly built row homes in varying earth tones, and two-story homes built sometime around the early 1920s, with rickety fences covered in trailing flowerless rose bushes, framed in grassed yards.

Cyclone fencing surrounded Gordon's house. There was a square of wood that blocked the opening between the post and the gate. That meant a small dog. A cat would scale the fence. My boy, Floyd, would never make it through with his ears.

The gate protested with a high-pitched screech of metal on metal and I jumped. Anything that made me startle set my nerve endings to tingling. That attack had done a number on my psyche.

The front door was a faded putrid green desperate for a new coat of paint. I rang the bell twice before a woman north of eighty greeted me.

"Yes," she said, her hair a dandelion tuft and her translucent skin rosy pink. Her polyester pants hung off her skeletal frame, and her light blue floral rayon blouse had a scoop neck that hung low revealing a bony chest. Her thick lensed glasses made her eyes twice their normal size.

"Sorry to bother you. Does a Gordon Stradlock live here?"

"You one of his girlfriends?" She looked past me like I'd brought others.

I almost coughed, and not from the remnants of last night's chemicals in my lungs. "No ma'am. I know him from work."

"Oh, my boy's a hard worker. Day and night. Always working."

If Gordon didn't want to update his mom on his employment status, I wouldn't either. "Is he home?"

"What do you need him for? Boy needs a day off every now and then. Can't you give him that?"

"Yes, ma'am," I said, not wanting to go toe to toe with this lady. She looked frail, but plenty of fire resided behind those rheumy eyes. "But he's the go-to guy and I need his advice."

Her chin lifted. That seemed to appease her. "He has a separate entrance. Downstairs. Go around the side-yard."

"Thank you."

She cleared her throat and licked her lips. "Hope you're not planning to stay long. Don't like it when he has women friends around."

"That happen often?"

"Thought you just wanted his advice? You are looking for more aren't you?"

I smiled. "Your son is a very nice man, Mrs. Stradlock." I almost choked on the words. "But just advice."

"He is and handsome. The women who come by have no self-respect. They think he'll marry them if they hang out long enough." She gave me the once over. "But he's particular. Only the best for my son." She closed the door on me.

I guess I didn't meet her approval after all. A mother's love might blind you to many things, but she couldn't seriously believe he was top marriage material. I shuddered. It could have been PTSD jitters. More likely it was because Gordon didn't keep his scuzzy ways isolated to his place of work. Were some of the women who visited from the homeless shelter? Was he dealing drugs out of his mother's basement? There had to be something going on down there because no way the women were looking to Gordon for a win in the marriage department.

I rounded the house, following the narrow walkway, made narrower by encroaching bushes. A limb snagged on my jacket, and I stepped over a couple of rubber dog toys confirming my suspicion that a pint-sized dog roamed the premises.

I approached the dirty white door with caution. Even with his mom upstairs, dealers often weren't nice people. That fact was even more true if he'd been the one to assault me last night. But that part was unknown, and mafia types weren't nice either yet in my last case I'd managed to converse with them and even gain their assistance. I clutched the pepper spray in my pocket and knocked.

Gordon answered in his navy sweatpants and an open collared Izod shirt. His belly hung over the waistband. His dark hair stood on end like I'd woken him and his drooping eyes said he'd been sucking on a shot glass for much of the night. A yipping Chihuahua circled his feet, offering the occasional lunge at me, but the dog was all yip and no nip.

"Bobo hush," he commanded. When he looked up his eyes went wide before they became slits. "I've met you."

Um, like, yeah? Alley way? Mace? Running my ass over on your way out? I offered him my card. He didn't take it. "Kelly Pruett. I'm a private investigator. Got a minute?"

"A PI? What were you doing in my shelter looking like you'd been sleeping under a bridge?"

Gordon wasn't a smart man, but so far he gave off no *I mugged you* vibes. If he had been my attacker, I'd have expected sweating, evasion, not a straight-up admission that he knew me. He wasn't the alley way assailant.

"We need to talk," I said.

He stood straighter. "About?"

"A missing girl." More than one, and a dead chick, and a drug ring, and whatever your sleazy lingering hand on the shelter women meant. But I'd work my way up to that. "Robyn Baker has gone missing. No one has heard from her for over forty-eight hours." I'd get around to the question of Amber once I'd gotten him talking.

"Don't know nothing, and I'll know less now that I don't work at Loving Grace." His face turned red.

"If you could just answer a few questions? I have no one else to turn to and I'd value your expertise. With your experience, you have insight about their habits and preferences. Things I couldn't hope to know." Buttering him up seemed like my best option.

He worked his jaw, sizing me up. If he reached out his hand to touch me like he had that first time we'd met, he'd draw back a stump. He finally sniffed, turned, and left me standing at the door.

Bobo, who'd gone quiet, went into high gear. The little guy viewed himself as the protector of his universe. Floyd might get a kick out of him, but his yips made my already gnawing headache intensify. I didn't move.

"Bobo stop." Gordon shouted over his shoulder. "And you, come in already if you want to talk. Otherwise, go away."

Bobo went to find his bestie. I hadn't expected an invitation, but after Gordon's mother had mentioned women coming here, I had to see for myself. What if Amber and/or Robyn had been here...or Maria? There was only one way to find out.

I stepped inside his one-bedroom space. A kitchenette with a half-pot of coffee sat on the counter. There was a loaf of bread next to a toaster littered with crumbs. A jar of coins anchored the other end of the counter, along with empty clear glass sugar and flour canisters. A crumpled blanket covered the couch, along with a pillow. The place had the smell of foot fungus and a bathroom in need of a good scrubbing—what some would call a bachelor's pad.

If women lined up to get a piece of this squalor, it was only for drugs.

Gordon ran his hand over his hair, collected his cup of coffee from the kitchen counter, and eased into his recliner, popping the handle at the side so I had a good view of his hole-ridden socks. All he needed was a beer and a baseball cap and the picture would be complete—a slob, a lay about, a scum bucket. He was precisely who I thought he was.

"What's this about a girl named Robyn gone missing?" He seemed at least half-way interested. "From the shelter, yeah?" He didn't offer me a place to sit which was fine. I didn't want his cooties.

"Yes. The night I was checked in, she and I talked at length. She'd been at the shelter for about a month and showed concern that I was asking questions. The next morning, she's gone. Why?" Throw him a softball, see if he flinched or swung for the fences. If Gordon overreacted when I asked him the easy questions, he was hiding something.

"How would I know?" Bobo jumped on Gordon's lap, turned a couple of circles and settled.

"You were on duty and supposed to be in charge, right? Don't you have a locked door policy?" I kept my tone light even though being locked in a homeless shelter with him seemed like cruel and unusual punishment.

He slurped his coffee and smacked his lips like his mother. "You say you just met that girl but you became instant BFFs and had some long chat?"

"Yes." Not quite BFF's but she did confess she'd run away from home because of her alcoholic father, had a relationship with Trinity, and believed that the aforementioned girlfriend was cheating on her. That was a fair amount of confiding in my book. I couldn't remember the last time I'd shared that level of detail about my life.

Gordon nodded, his eyes narrowing. "What else did she say?"

"She told me to watch myself." I had to tread lightly. I wanted him to spill first.

"Watch yourself? What the hell does that mean?"

"She was scared of someone or something at the shelter. Which makes me wonder, how did you get her journal on your desk?"

"What journal? My office is lost and found. One of the ladies might have turned it in when I was out of my office. Wait…" He slammed his coffee down on the table next to him. Bobo didn't budge. He was used to Gordon's outbursts. "Mr. Sokol sent you down there to spy on me, didn't he?" He almost spat the words.

I stood my ground. Gordon had cracked sooner than I'd expected, but anger was good. It frees people up to talk.

"Unbelievable. I've never caused that son-of-a-bitch a problem. Then suddenly you show up, and I'm out of a job." He wiggled forward in his extended recliner, heaving over his belly to get up.

I took a step backwards.

"It was you, wasn't it? That night you ran from the shelter." His face turned from pink to puce. He had escalated fast. The man had a temper. "What the hell did you tell him about me?"

I cleared my throat, clutching my pepper spray. My temples pounded and my mouth had dried out in an instant. Coming here alone might have been a bad idea. But his mother was right above us and, sore from last night or not, I could run like hell if I had to. I didn't have any answers yet. My dad wouldn't have flinched. *Time to bite the bullet.* "I told him that you were dealing drugs and the women weren't safe with you near them."

He ground his teeth so hard I heard them across the room. "I'll sue that bastard for wrongful termination. I'm the victim here, not the women in the shelter."

My face heated up. He was the victim? Give me a break. He was a dealer. Maybe mid-level, but one hundred percent lowlife. "I saw you. With my own eyes. Handing out drugs."

He threw his head back and laughed. "Drugs? You think I'm dealing drugs? You must be high, lady."

I pulled my spray out of my pocket, finger on the buzzer, but didn't raise my arm. If he took one step I'd blast him from here into the next state. "That night. You were in the corridor. With a young woman. You handed her a packet..." Now that I thought about it, he was probably dealing fentanyl, which made everything ten times worse. If Mary-in-Farragut-Park had died from a fentanyl overdose... I shuddered, feeling lucky I'd only been maced in that alley. "You ran your hand down that woman's arm. The look on her face was one of deep disgust..."

"That night, you say?" He looked perplexed. Thinking. Then he cracked a smile. "Laundry tokens."

"Ha," I said, humorlessly. "Please." But he'd caught me off guard. Of all the lies he could have come up with, that one was at least tied to the Shelter. He was cleverer than I'd given him credit for.

Gordon jumped out of the recliner without any thought for Bobo. The dog dropped to the ground like no big whoop. I leapt back and raised my can of mace. He took four strides to the kitchen and grabbed the glass jar of coins at the end of the counter and thrust it at me.

I took it and turned the jar left and right. A lump formed in my throat. "Tokens?" The jar of metal coins had knocked the wind out of my sails. I couldn't find a smart response. It seemed so... So... Plausible. "Okay, let's say you're handing out laundry tokens. How come the woman I saw you with looked unhappy?" *Come on brain. Kick into gear.*

"She was crying because she and her old man had a falling out, he'd beaten her for the 'final time'—her words, not mine—and that's what landed her on the streets."

"She came crying to you?" That didn't sit right. I wouldn't go to Gordon Stradlock if my head had fallen off and he was the only man on the planet with a tube of glue.

"She was crying because all she had time to grab, before she left her home, was a bag of dirty laundry. She was desperate to wash her stuff and there were ten women ahead of her."

My muscles tightened. "What did she have to do to cut in front of that line?"

"A little housekeeping in my office. Place is dusty as hell."

I scanned his apartment, then ran my finger over the top of the television and presented him with the dust. "I can see the dust-free life is the life for you. In fact, I'd go as far as to say it's a real priority."

"I might have mentioned that my feet were killing me." He shifted and hooked his thumbs into the band of his sweats. "She said she'd studied as a masseuse and offered me a foot rub. How do you turn that down?"

"You say no." I put the spray back in my pocket. The man wasn't giving off a threatening vibe. His outburst of temper had flared and died down in an instant. Like Bobo, his yip was worse than his nip. The smile playing around his gross lips said he found this amusing.

"These women are in your care. They're not supposed to touch your stanky feet." I hadn't meant to say stanky, but I was tired.

"It was just the once." He flopped back down into his easy chair.

My eyebrow arched in full-on judgment. *Once. Sure.*

Gordon went on. "It's easy to sit on a pedestal and look down on me. You should see the things other people require. I only barter for laundry services. Outside our walls, women are forced to trade their bodies to survive. My 'foot rub for a laundry token' exchange is nothing in comparison. Now that I'm not there, there's no telling what will happen to those women."

"You mean they'll have to wait in line for their laundry?" I snapped. He wasn't smart enough to make up an elaborate lie. Did I believe him? Was he in the clear? I could barely keep the questions straight in my head. Sleep and peanut butter would help—perhaps the other way around. Gordon wasn't my attacker and he wasn't the drug dealer. Okay, so, who was? LuAnn was back to the top of the list.

"Where the hell did you get the idea that it was drugs anyway?" Bobo clambered back into his daddy's lap and snuggled down. At least one of them was enjoying Gordon's sudden retirement. "We don't allow drugs in Loving Grace. It's a clean house."

That was a crock. Amber had said as much when she left her message for Bernie. If the laundry token exchange program was real, who was to say it wasn't the tip of the iceberg? I wanted answers and I wanted them yesterday. "What about Maria Castro? Dead. Overdose. Needle in the arm. Farragut Park. Ring any bells?"

Gordon shook his head like I was the village idiot straying into territory I didn't understand. "Maria had her problems. They all do. Yes, she was turning it around, or so it seemed, but then she didn't." He held up his hand. "Before you say it, Amber told the same story. She said she was sober…for good this time. She'd been volunteering at the rehab center in hopes she could land a job there. She said old Bernie would take her seriously, quit listening to the poisonous witch, and let her back into the family if she could show she held down a job."

I hadn't heard that story; not from Bernie or Katherine or Carla. *So many secrets. So much convoluted bull.* "Which poisonous witch? Katherine? Did Katherine Sokol have something to do with Amber being on the streets this time?"

"Who knows. They all have their sob stories. Daddy did this. Hubby did that. Wah, wah, my mommy didn't love me…"

Gordon Stradlock: Night Manager, friend to the homeless women of Portland, showing his true colors.

"Gordon, sweetie, everything okay?" A small voice came through the air vent above our heads.

He glanced at me, concerned. I nodded. "Yes, Mom."

"You're not doing anything nasty down there I hope."

"No, Mom."

"Just checking. If you need me, hon."

Gordon closed his eyes and inhaled, a visible level of frustration building. When he opened his eyes, they were flat and devoid of all emotion. If he felt anything for those girls it was fleeting at best and colored by his feelings for his mother. He'd had a lifetime of being under a woman's thumb, and now he was literally living under her house. It made all kinds of sense that he exercised power over the women at the shelter.

"If there's nothing else, I've got things to do." He stood, letting Bobo fall to the floor again.

My brain raced to come up with another question. I needed more clarity, more answers, more anything. He was my only lead. He couldn't end the interview now. Who was the poisonous witch? Was it Katherine, LuAnn, who; WHO?

He walked me to the front door without saying another syllable and slammed the door in my face.

So much for my star witness. He'd given me nothing.

CHAPTER 18

I dropped into Hannah's car, kissed Floyd on the head and rummaged in the glove compartment for my peanut butter filled crackers. Of course, it wasn't my car so there was no peanut butter of any kind.

Gordon was scum. If nothing else came from my investigation at the shelter, I had at least gotten that piece of junk away from the women. Bernie might not want to hear from me, but I'd make sure Carla got the message to him that Gordon shouldn't be allowed to come back—ever. Not even if he was cleared of drug dealing, he didn't respect women at the most basic level. If I could figure out a way to warn people in other shelters, I would—perhaps Jessica could help there, too. I had wanted to touch base with her anyway.

I shot her off a text to see if she'd made any headway on flagging Amber or Robyn in the system.

I'd hit a brick wall. I could use some help—professional help. I needed Detective Hot Stuff. We were overdue for a conversation about my attack. He might not be happy and confirm his concerns, but it had to happen. In my coat pocket were the clear packages that had once contained fentanyl patches. They might have fingerprints on them. Maybe they'd tie to the envelope exchanged between LuAnn and Mr. Bow-Tie. Kyle could decide what he wanted to do with them.

Hey there, Hot Stuff. I typed. I immediately backed up over his jokey nickname. If I called him that, he'd sense there was something wrong. *Hi there,* I texted. *Got time for your favorite girl?*

He'd had a crazy night and was slammed, as I'd suspected, but after a few texts back and forth, I had him convinced to meet me in a little over an hour at one of our favorite spots.

I pulled into traffic, rehearsing what to say to him. "Hey, I was hit and maced last night." I grimaced. "Missed you. How was your night? Mine? Well, funny story…" Floyd listened to every word and approved all iterations of my confession of why I hadn't called Kyle right away.

We parked in the lot beside Common Grounds Coffee House and I took a minute to tidy myself up in the rearview mirror. Floyd and I did a circuit around the perimeter so he could mark every last blade of grass and claim it as his own, then I left him in the car with a chewy bone for company.

Inside the coffee shop, the fresh spring green walls made the tension in my shoulders ease. With its long communal table, gluten free options and tattooed employees, it read alternative Portland all over the place. My nose filled with the decadent smell of ground coffee and my mouth watered. My headache hadn't completely gone away, but it took a back seat to the anticipatory delight I felt at the prospect of a cup of coffee with my sweetie.

Kyle had already arrived and was seated in the red comfy chair across from the mustard-colored crushed velvet sofa in the corner. He had my mocha and a croissant waiting on the coffee table. If this were a blind date, I'd have proposed marriage on the spot—okay, maybe not. But he'd have me seriously considering it.

Unlike the last time we'd met up here, when he was in uniform, he was wearing pressed khakis and a button-down blue shirt with a down vest. He wore detective well.

I gave him a kiss on the cheek, then reached for his hand and squeezed it. He squeezed back—a good start. I slid onto the sofa and immediately grabbed at the mocha.

He eyed me over the top of his café latte. "You look a bit tired? I'd gotten your text when you got home. Long night."

"Stakeouts can be grueling," I started, but decided not to begin there. "Before we get too far, I saw Gordon today."

He stiffened. "He's still at the shelter?"

"Thankfully, no. Bernie did fire him and I went to his house." I ripped a piece of croissant. "Get this. He lives with his mother." I proceeded to tell him about our conversation and the laundry tokens.

"Do you believe him?" Kyle asked.

"Kind of. It's almost too weird not to be true, but I'm not convinced that's all there is to it."

"Is that it?"

"What do you mean?" I stuffed another chunk of croissant into my mouth. Buying time.

"Hon, I can't stay too long. We're knee deep into something and you wanted to talk."

I closed my eyes. Might as well yank off the Band Aid. I grabbed a napkin and reached into my pocket. I pulled out the two clear fentanyl patch wrappers and set them on the coffee table between us.

"What's that?"

"Evidence. Maybe."

He leaned in. "Fentanyl wrappers?"

I nodded.

"Where did you get them? Did Gordon have that?" He reached for the napkin, reluctant to touch them, like the good detective that he was.

"No. In an alleyway…. Close to Saving Grace." I continued to stall. I had to get over myself. I was human, and I had not sought out the attack. I could use his help with my case, but equally true I'd welcome my boyfriend's arms around me and telling me he was sorry and he wished no one had ever hurt me or would ever hurt me again.

But that wasn't what happened.

He retrieved an evidence baggie from his jacket pocket and bagged the evidence. "Out with it. From the beginning."

I gave him the bullet points rather than the fleshed in version of events: Loving Grace, Saving Grace, the package going from Mr. Bow-Tie to LuAnn, LuAnn having a home to go to…that I'd been sprayed with mace right before I'd been mowed over.

"Back up." Kyle had his hand in his pocket. "LuAnn Schroeder?"

"Not sure on her last name," I said, surprised he hadn't seized on the fact I'd been assaulted even a little. And the fact that he knew her name had me nervous. How did he know who she was? "She's a long-term shelter resident, but she lives…"

Kyle didn't even excuse himself. He left Common Grounds in ten long strides, his phone glued to his ear. I was desperate to find out why but knew better than to intrude on his "police" work and that's exactly what it felt like. He was in full on detective mode.

I finished my croissant with little nibbles to ensure I didn't throw up. I couldn't manage the coffee. My stomach was a swirl of acid.

When Kyle returned, his official face came back with him, not a trace of my boyfriend to be seen. "I need you to come down to the station with me."

"Me?"

"No, Floyd," he snapped. "Yes, you."

"Why?" I couldn't stand. My knees had turned to Jell-O and my brain a mass of blobby nothing.

Kyle took me by the elbow and steered me to the parking lot. "My car or yours?"

Floyd was in Hannah's car and I couldn't leave him there. I pointed to Hannah's car.

He grimaced but didn't ask where my car was. Instead, he fished in my bag and found the keys. "Are you safe to drive?" He stared at me as if we were perfect strangers, not like people who shared a bed. *Episodically.* When I could make time for him. *Between cases.*

"I am."

"Your eyes are red. Have you been drinking?"

"Jeez, Kyle, it's not even noon, of course I haven't been drinking. I told you, someone, probably Luann, sprayed me with mace."

"My car."

I collected Floyd, told him what a good boy he was, waited while he rewatered a couple of his grass-conquests, then joined Kyle in his ice-cold vehicle.

We didn't speak all the way to the station. I used the interlude in friendly relations to text Hannah and explain where her car was. I apologized for inconveniencing her but omitted the fact that my boyfriend had turned into, I don't know what, and was escorting me to the station under what could only be described as hostile conditions.

Kyle handed Floyd off to a very nice looking uniformed young woman, who was more than happy to do whatever Kyle asked her to. If her eyes had mooned at him any harder she'd have created her own orbit.

Kyle left me in the lobby and took the stairs three at a time. Within ten minutes I was in an interview room with him and his boss. *Fun times.* I was looking forward to this big time.

"Where were you last night?" Kyle's boss, Detective Enloe who I'd heard so much about, wore a stark white shirt and dress pants, his sleeves cuffed to the elbow. His suit jacket hung over the chair back across from the conference table where we sat.

I hadn't been at this table since Kyle had brought me a file on my first case.

"Why am I here?" I directed my questions to Enloe, seeing as Kyle wasn't making eye contact.

Enloe shot a look at Kyle. "Detective Jaeger hasn't updated you?"

I shook my head. Kyle hadn't told me squat.

"Would you like to tell me where you were last night, Miss Pruett?"

Like I had a choice. "As Kyle has clearly told you, I was outside the Loving Grace Women's Shelter."

"All night?"

Okay. This was a real interrogation. I'd already told Kyle that I wasn't in my car all night. Had he not shared that part either? Was Enloe trying to catch me in a lie? Sure would be nice if Kyle had filled me in—or cared for two seconds that I'd been attacked. "Can I have a glass of water?"

Kyle retrieved a glass of water from the table in the corner of the room and put it down in front of me gently. I tried to make eye contact with him, but that wasn't happening.

"If you'd like to start at the beginning, Miss Pruett?" Enloe clicked on the tape and waited.

"Kyle knows what I was doing there. I believe the Shelter is a hub for drugs. I also believe that two girls, formerly staying at the shelter, are missing and endangered. I went to the shelter to gather intelligence which I planned to bring to you to see if I couldn't get you to take this seriously." My temperature rose, and with it my voice.

"Where did you go when you left your car?" Enloe didn't bat an eyelid.

"I witnessed the potential exchange of drugs or money outside Saving Grace. I'm thinking drugs."

Enloe jotted a note on his pad.

"That's the pain and drug rehabilitation center," I said.

"We know what Saving Grace is, Miss Pruett. Continue."

"I followed LuAnn…"

"LuAnn Schroeder?"

Hell, they were really stuck on LuAnn. If they'd been tailing her, we might be getting somewhere. I nodded enthusiastically but then regretted it. I downed my water and pushed my glass towards Kyle. He got me another and sat back down beside his boss, serious as ever. They'd found something. What the hell was it? The girls were out there and vulnerable. LuAnn was dealing as far as I could tell. If I told them the whole sordid story I might get the lead I was so hungry for. "I followed LuAnn to a house, but was then accosted in the alleyway."

Kyle flushed at that information—finally. It was nice to see that he did care.

"You maintain you were attacked in that alleyway?" said Enloe.

"Yes," I said.

"What time was this alleged attack?" He was writing in his little notepad again.

"There is no alleged." I folded my arms over my chest. "Nine. Ten....I..."

"The problem we have, Miss Pruett," he said cutting me off, "is that you were in the vicinity of the victim's home."

Victim? I'm the victim.

"The deceased was found at the rear of her apartment. She was sprayed in the face with pepper spray, hit over the head, and strangled."

It took me several seconds to process what I'd heard. "Deceased?"

Enloe raised an eyebrow. "That is what I said. LuAnn Schroeder was murdered last night."

I checked in with Kyle. He couldn't possibly think I had anything to do with a murder, but it now made sense that he'd switched into his official role when he knew I'd been at her home. There couldn't be even the slightest hint of impropriety or he could lose his job.

But LuAnn? That threw everything out the window. I'd had her pegged as being in cahoots with Gordon but that looked flimsy at best. But Gordon was out of the picture and now LuAnn was dead. If neither of them was my dealer, what the hell was going on? Whatever was happening went deeper. Much, much deeper.

"We're waiting, Miss Pruett."

"I was heading toward the back of the house when I got attacked with mace, and that was right before I got shoved into a row of garbage cans. I didn't see by whom. But I did get myself over to Saving Grace for assistance."

Kyle's flush turned deep crimson.

I kept my eyes trained on my hands. I sensed his proclamation of loving a danger seeker was being seriously reassessed.

"You're off the case," he said, standing.

I glared at him. So much for Kyle evolving and fully respecting my job. But I hadn't taken orders from my first husband and I sure wasn't about to take them from a man with a badge who thought he knew better than me.

"Please sit down, Detective." Enloe's voice at least was calm and measured before he looked at me. "But Detective Jaeger is absolutely correct."

Kyle complied, but was back to not meeting my eye.

"Are these yours?" He pointed at the baggie of plastic squares.

"I found them outside of LuAnn's house. I can't honestly say who they belong to, but I wanted to bring them in."

Enloe didn't crack a smile or say thank you or do anything that made me think he appreciated my effort. "Do you own pepper spray, Miss Pruett?"

"Yes."

"Are you in possession of it at this time?"

"Of course."

"And were you all of last night?"

My throat locked down. "No. I dropped it when I was attacked and I wasn't in possession of it for a couple of hours I guess." I leaned back in my chair, the stress of the conversation soaking my armpits.

"Do I need to take you into custody, or will you turn that piece of evidence over to me voluntarily?"

Evidence? Custody? He didn't truly believe I was a suspect, did he? I thought of Mitz visiting me in prison, with Jeff nodding, having always expected it would come to this, and Arlene clucking her tongue in agreement with her son. "Voluntarily, of course. I have nothing to hide."

He tilted his head. "Good choice. You may be Detective Jaeger's girlfriend, but that doesn't pull weight with me. You've been at the scene of a brutal murder. And a weapon of the type in your possession was used to incapacitate the victim."

I emptied my bag on the table and pointed at the mace. My head was only now registering that LuAnn had been killed. I'd thought when I came back and found it sitting on the garbage can, that I really had been blinded. But what if it had been placed back there after being used? Was I being framed? "Who do you think did it?"

Detective Enloe stood. "Detective Jaeger, take that spray cannister into evidence and then join me. Miss Pruett is free to go. For now. But we're going to want your DNA."

My wall of resistance nearly crumbled at the prospect of leaving. If I was getting out of here, they could have whatever they wanted. "Take it. No problem. I didn't kill LuAnn. I didn't kill anybody." Although I sure as hell wondered who had. Had I been hit by the real killer on their way out? Or did they come back after I'd left? Maybe, if they'd used my pepper spray. Was it a drug deal gone wrong? Could I have ended up like LuAnn had I not forced myself up and gone to the rehab center?

Detective Enloe was saying something as he strode to the door.

"Excuse me?" I murmured.

"I said, don't go far. A tech will be in for the swab momentarily." The door slammed behind him.

Kyle hung out, silent and judging and sad and disappointed and all the things I didn't want to see that minute.

"Why do they need my DNA?"

"Skin was found underneath LuAnn's nails," he said.

My stomach roiled. She'd fought off her attacker. "You know I didn't do it. If you find my DNA on her, it's been planted."

He closed his eyes and nodded. "When you get released, please go home." He got up and left the room without another glance. It was like a gut to the knife—worse because it was delivered by someone I loved.

I wanted to crawl under the covers and sleep for a million years. This case had taken a turn for the worse. I never thought I'd ever be a suspect in a case—had my father? I was letting everyone down.

After having my mouth swabbed by a DNA tech, I collected Floyd and walked out onto Third Street. The park where my father and I used to sit in was empty. Floyd needed a break, but I couldn't bear to go in there. There were just too many memories.

My car was in the shop. Hannah's car was at Common Ground and I'd already inconvenienced her once today. And *Hot Stuff*, now decidedly cool stuff, wasn't talking to me.

That left Arlene. The thought of calling her and explaining why I was at the justice center was too much for me to handle right now. I scrolled through my phone and ordered an Uber "with dog." It would take longer to snag a ride, but it would give me alone time to lick my wounds and find a jar of peanut butter.

CHAPTER 19

When the Uber pulled up outside my house, Trinity was on my doorstep.

Floyd bounded up the steps, ears flapping in the wind, and made friends with his new friend.

"Hey." I tried to sound upbeat, even though I felt like I'd been to hell on a sandpaper carpet and come back with rug rash and skinned knees.

"Hey, yourself." She rubbed Floyd's head the way he liked.

I wasn't sure which way to go after hey. How had she found me? What was she doing here? Why hadn't she texted ahead?

"I called," she said, "It went straight to vm. You turned off?"

I was. I'd turned the ringer off at the police station.

"And no. I'm not stalking you." She smiled. "I've got a lead."

I turned the key in the lock, had a twinge about letting a homeless girl into my house, caught myself being a jerk, and invited her in. "Let me get Floyd a chewy-chew and you can tell me all about it."

She jiggled from foot to foot. Damn, was she high?

"We gotta go. She's been seen."

My heart leapt in my chest. "Amber?"

Trinity's face fell. "No, Robyn."

Ugh. Of course. Not 'ugh' ugh, but bad me for blurting out the wrong name.

"She's in a shelter in Oregon City."

"How did you…" I fished under the kitchen sink, Floyd butting his head against my ankles in excitement.

"That social worker lady. She told me she couldn't say how she knew, but she knew. She called me. Can you even believe that?"

127

Social worker lady. Did she mean Jessica?

"They never do that. I mean, maybe sometimes there's someone who's half-way decent, but mostly they're all like, 'We sympathize that you girls are good friends, but this information is for family only.'"

I smiled to myself. Jessica had come through. These young women hadn't had a single ally in their short lives, but one act of kindness and Trinity's face was lit like a Christmas tree.

"Ready?" She grabbed me and dragged me towards the front door.

I still ached from last night's attack and stung from my interaction at the police station. What I really wanted was a hot shower and three days in bed. "Give me one second." I plodded back to the kitchen, found a jar of emergency peanut butter, and snagged two spoons in case Trinity wanted some PB, too. "Ready when you are," I said.

I kissed Floyd and told him to be a good boy and locked the door behind me.

Trinity had run down the steps. "Where's your car?"

"In the shop."

"Got gas money?" She jingled her keys at me. "Coz if you do, I've got the rust bucket."

We gassed up as soon as we hit a station. I sucked down four teaspoons of peanut butter and Trinity talked all the way from Portland to Oregon City, a forty-five-minute drive.

Everything I'd read in Robyn's diary was backed up by Trinity's stream of hopes and dreams. They would get jobs and buy a house and live by the ocean and get a dog. Things would get better, you wait and see. "As long as we're together, everything will be fine."

I wished I believed that. It hadn't turned out 'fine' with Jeff, even though we'd given it our best shot. And I honestly thought Kyle was the one, but he was giving me the cold shoulder.

I adjusted my feet over the hole in the floor of her car while checking my phone. Jessica had tried calling—four times. She'd finally resorted to texting.

Robyn in system at Hope and Help in Oregon City. If you don't pick up, I'm going to call Trinity. Don't want Robyn there a minute longer than she needs to be. Call me when you're free and I'll fill you in.

I didn't want to stop Trinity's happy babble, but Jessica had details for me. "Just going to check in with Jessica," I said.

"You don't have to announce it." Trinity was like Mitz, hip to the rules of modern etiquette. You could talk to a friend and text at the same time and it wasn't considered rude. In a few short years everything I'd been taught about good manners had altered completely. You could talk to three people at once, electronically; exit a conversation without saying why or goodbye; screenshot a chat and humiliate your frenemies. It was a strange new world that Mitz was learning to navigate. I closed my eyes and said a prayer that my girl would always be safe.

I hit send.

Jessica picked up on the first ring. "You there already?"

"On our way." My stomach growled loud enough to make Trinity laugh. "What do I need to know?"

"Hope and Help is a church-run group. Salt of the Earth. They'd give you the shirt off their backs. They're totally legit, but they'll send Robyn for conversion therapy."

I frowned at my phone. Did people do that anymore? Hadn't the whole "you can alter your sexuality with aversion and talk-therapy" been debunked?

"I can read your thoughts on this topic, but they mean well."

Not well enough to stay out of other people's private lives, apparently.

"Get her out of there. She's been through enough." For a woman who was no longer involved in social work and wanted to guard her heart against too much pain, Jessica sure did care a lot. We said our goodbyes as Trinity pulled round back of the church.

"You go," she said.

"You don't want to come with me?" I had my hand on the door handle, ready.

"Robyn's mad at me. I don't want to make a scene. And anyway..." She pointed at her short hair and ear studs. "If they see me they might get ideas and lock her away forever."

Hope and Help's reputation preceded them.

"I won't be long." I eased myself out of the car. My head was doing better, but my muscles took that as a sign to start complaining about the battering they'd taken in the alley. I hadn't had time to process the fact that LuAnn was dead and I'd been assaulted by someone whose goal was to incapacitate me, at minimum. I was running on peanut butter fumes and adrenaline.

A woman met me at the front door. "I'm Mrs. Oppenheimer. You are?"

"Kelly Pruett," I said, offering my business card to the thin, waif-like woman. Her wire-rimmed glasses that barely stayed on her small bulbous nose gave her a serious look that said she ran things around here without a lot of hassle. But her eyes were warm like a school counselor whose mission was to get you to college, but who likewise understood the angst of growing up.

"I'm looking for a friend of mine. Robyn. Small girl, around eighteen, strawberry blonde."

"Someone called ahead and said you were coming." I owed Jessica more than coffee next time I saw her. "Your young friend was sweet, but very shy. I remember her because she asked me if there was a store nearby to purchase paper items. When I asked what she needed them for, she said she liked to write and was working on a novel. When I was her age, I had aspirations to do that, too." She had a far-off look in her eye. "Then I got married, children, life. Now with keeping the homeless fed and sheltered, there's no time."

The description she provided left no doubt that it was Robyn. "Could I see her?"

"Oh, she's not here," said Mrs. Oppenheimer. "She wrote for hours…" She pointed towards a room to our right. "Over in that corner. Then, this morning, she simply walked out. Not even a goodbye or hint of where she might be headed."

Damn. Had she worked out that Hope and Help wanted to help her shuck her sexuality? "Did anyone say anything to her?"

"Say anything?" Mrs. Oppenheimer smiled.

I didn't want to get into Jessica's theory. I wanted to find Robyn. "Did she leave anything behind?"

The matron shook her head. "Not that I saw."

"Mind if I take a look?"

She walked me into the main room with its long couches, a TV stationed at one end and round tables with games strewn on top. It looked like a Parks and Rec center, but a cot room off to the side said it served a different purpose.

A couple of women played cards at the corner table. An elderly woman dozed on the loveseat that had seen more than a few afternoon naps. I inspected the chair where Robyn had spent time—lifted the cushion, felt down the sides, peered underneath—unsure of what I'd thought I'd find. There was nothing.

"I'm sorry you missed her," Mrs. Oppenheimer said from behind me.

"You said she seemed in a hurry to leave. Did you get any indications that she might be upset?"

She nodded. "When she first arrived. She insisted on sleeping where she could see the door and only went out if there were several women going at the same time."

"Did she have to be on a list to get in here?"

"No, we take walk-ins when we can. Especially this time of year when it's so cold outside, we try not to turn anyone away. But I added her to the list in the databank." Her face grew stoic. "She mentioned she was concerned about someone finding her. I assume since your social worker friend called, that person wasn't you."

I met her gaze. "Absolutely not. We are friends." An exaggeration, but I was on her side. And desperate to understand why she'd run. It could very well have something to do with the drugs and/or fentanyl patches—or LuAnn. It most definitely had to do with whatever was happening in the shelter—or the rehab center. Only Robyn would be able to fill in that blank.

"She was concerned about staying in one spot too long, but she didn't have much money. Have you checked on the edge of the city near the water?"

"What's there?"

"Shantytown."

My muscles tightened. "A tent city?"

She nodded. "I told her it wouldn't be safe. It is, however, a place to blend in if you don't want to be found. It's bigger than a couple of city blocks. I was there once and it's not good." She shuddered, which made me do so involuntarily.

I thanked her and was on my way.

Trinity was as anxious to get to the tent city as I was.

"Shantytown" was an understatement—more like a barely-repurposed dump. The cyclone fence that ran along the entry was hung with grey mesh, a rudimentary, but effective blind against nosy neighbors, though they weren't close to any standard residences. A small unmanned green shed sat at one side of a large opening in the fence. From that entry point, I had a view of the makeshift city. Pop-up tents speckled the grounds. Blue tarps were either draped over the tents or strung between trees. Garbage piled at one end gave the place a landfill vibe. Grocery carts littered every available space and were stacked high with leaf bag-size plastic bags probably filled with people's possessions. The smell that blew off the river and over the camp was a mixture of sewage, sweat, and grime.

A few residents of the city milled about, none glancing our direction. Outside many of the tents, people used concrete blocks as chairs. A woman swept her "stoop." Another hung a T-shirt on the back of a chair, presumably to dry. In the coolness of the day, that might never happen.

Wrapping my jacket around me a little closer, I smoothed the bump of Robyn's journal underneath. I had a feeling I might need it. The kid was running scared. I was on the verge of finding out why and the excitement knocked my body ache down from a six to a four. I also had more focus than I'd had in hours.

Trinity trotted on ahead of me, chatting to people and getting her bearings. They talked to her in a way they'd never talk to me.

I moved further into the makeshift city, unnoticed. A group of men gathered around a table, cards in their hands. A fire crackled in a nearby pit, the smoke wafting over them. The men looked harmless enough, playing their games, a bottle of lager next to each of them. But my momma-bear genes kicked in and my stomach tightened. They looked like they wouldn't hurt a fly, but what lurked underneath? Gordon was a grinning fool with a gut that hung over his trousers. He was also a low-grade predator who took what he could from vulnerable women without any qualms.

I approached the woman sweeping. "Excuse me."

She froze in mid sweep, the whites of her eyes growing.

"Didn't mean to startle you, I was hoping...."

She turned her back and disappeared into her tent without uttering a word.

Trust no one. That motto permeated the entire community.

I turned and, just like that, spotted Robyn. Bundled in a couple of layers of coats and scarves, she could have been anyone, but her strawberry blonde hair peeked out of a skull cap and framed her small face. She was walking toward an area where the tents were huddled closer together; next to a tarp-covered communal area with another roaring firepit in the middle.

"Robyn," I called.

She took one look at me, turned, and ran.

I hadn't expected her to take off. It took me a few seconds before I kicked it into gear and followed. She had youth on her side and was fast as she beelined it for the rear of the city. Trinity was obliviously talking to someone. I was on my own.

There must be a way out back there. As I grew closer to the cyclone fence, I saw it—a small opening. Robyn went through it with a simple sideways twist. My exit from the premises wouldn't be nearly as graceful. I had to slow and squeeze through, lamenting my lack of a workout routine every second. The pocket on my jeans caught on a piece of jagged metal which dug into my skin. Thankfully, my tetanus had been updated when I got shot.

By the time I'd unhooked myself, she'd disappeared off the well-used path. Low-growing brush crowded the walkway and a rut had formed down the center either from bikes or grocery carts being wheeled back and forth. In a slow jog, I traversed the dips trying not to sprain an ankle.

"Robyn, it's me Kelly," I hollered, in case she'd ducked off the route to hide.

A couple of tents had been pitched a few yards from the pathway. A shirtless old man—his sunken chest dotted with a few, wiry grey hairs—came to the edge of the path to inspect the commotion. "Hey there, we don't allow strangers through here. This is private property. You have to be a sworn in member of the family."

I turned my head and raised my hand in a *hello* and *nothing to worry about here* gesture and ran directly into a wall of muscle. I bounced back and onto my butt. "What the?"

"Did you hear the man?" Goliath said. "Stop."

I scrambled to my feet. "I'm looking for a young woman. Blonde, about this tall..."

His eyes narrowed to slits. "What do you want with her?"

Both feet planted in a defense position, I put my hands on my hips, ready for anything. "What are you, the welcoming committee?" Poking the bear might not be a great idea, but I was beyond tired and so close. I couldn't let Robyn slip away again.

He opened his mouth, no doubt to offer me a sarcastic response, but I stepped around him and took off in a full run. As I'd hoped, he was more bark than bite and I didn't hear any footfalls behind me.

I'd made it another hundred yards further when the rapid pounding of my heart made me slow, having always been more of a sprint versus long distance runner. The path ended in a clearing. The flat grass took a steep drop off on the other side of the rutted road. I walked to the end of the line, watching for movement. The cliff sat above the highway system. Cars whipped past, at least a few stories below. Looking across the roadway to the industrial district, there were no indicators Robyn had gone that far. Even with her speed, she wouldn't have had time to traverse that dangerous hill and cross the highway.

I turned and scoped out the bushes surrounding the greenspace. They were large enough to hide a small person.

"Whatever you're running from Robyn, I'm here to help." Hopefully, I wasn't talking to a bunch of bushes, but if it turned out I was, then so be it. There's only so much a woman can put up with before she stops caring about appearances.

The last week had me beat. I'd been bullied by a woman who was then murdered, infested with bug bites, lost my dog, dealt with my long-lost sister, now apparently favorite "girl" to my ex-mother-in-law. I had my daughter going off to Disneyland and my former home about to be renovated, and I accidentally found out my mother was involved with Saving Grace.

But that wasn't all. I'd been lied to by my client, fired by my client, told not to find a missing girl, by my client—and, the icing on the cake, someone who was possibly involved with that missing girl had attacked me, which had the police wondering what my role was and my boyfriend more than a bit miffed at me.

I was tired, wrung out, and pissed. I didn't have any leads. People were dropping around me. No one seemed to care about the homeless women, especially not the most vulnerable of their sad and sorry sorority—and they were in peril, as in deadly peril. I needed to find Robyn like a ten-peanut-butter spoon session. It was serious, as serious as anything I had ever taken on.

I doubled over and put my hands on my knees. I couldn't break down now—not when so many motherless girls depended on me. The tears rose at the realization. That was why I couldn't walk away.

Maria, motherless since she was a kid, was dead. Amber, orphaned when she was 13, was missing. And Robyn, who had run away from home because her dad couldn't deal with his wife's death, was hiding out close by. All of them had run from Loving Grace and I had to find out why. Drugs? It had to be connected to the drugs, but how? Robyn was my only real connection to that world.

My goal was simple: to find Robyn and restart my case. I stood and brushed my hair from my face. I had to sound positive, upbeat, reliable. She'd been let down by so many people she had no reason to trust me.

"I'm Kelly Pruett. We met at Loving Grace a few nights ago. Remember?" *No sound.* "I was there undercover. That's why I told you my last name was Robertson. I was hired by Bernie Sokol, the man who founded the shelter. His granddaughter Amber went missing."

My speech was met with continued silence. "I thought I had it figured out. But I need your help." I'd hoped that honesty would gain her trust. Not even a branch moved.

"I understand you're scared. Whatever it is though, I can help. I've spoken to Trinity. She was at the shelter looking for you." Best not say that Trinity was with me since they were estranged. "She said you called the night you left, but never showed up to meet her. She's worried, Robyn. I'm not sure what happened between you two, but I don't think it's what you believe it is."

Still nothing. I saved my best card for last.

"I have your journal with me."

A rustling in the bushes. "You have my journal?" A small voice came from somewhere around me, but I couldn't tell which direction.

"I do." I patted my jacket.

Goliath appeared at the end of the pathway. "You need to go." He shoved a giant-sized finger in my general direction.

"Robyn, please." I ignored him, talking into the wind. "Come out."

Goliath made two steps my way before Robyn popped up from one of the bushes near him and touched his arm. "It's okay." She grinned at him. "She's fine."

He glared at me then smiled at her. "You sure?"

"Positive. Thank you, George."

A Beauty and the Beast moment. Robyn apparently inspired those around her to protect her—a useful skill in this setting.

He snorted in my direction, probably ticked that I'd outmaneuvered him earlier. "Just holler if you change your mind."

"I will."

When he was out of sight she walked my direction. "Where is it?"

I slid the journal out from under my warmup jacket and handed it to her.

She yanked it out of my hands and pulled it into her chest like it was a lost child. I understood the feeling, I wanted to do that to her right now. Her face was dirty and gaunt. Had she eaten the past few days? Her skin was pale and her lips had a blue tinge.

"You're cold. I'm starved. Can we go get something to eat?" I used my mom voice because I was a mom and a damned good one. I knew when a kid was struggling.

She shook her head. "It's safer here."

"Safer from what?" I didn't want to tell her I had waltzed straight into the encampment and side-stepped George to find her. If someone had really meant her harm, they wouldn't meet much resistance.

"I can't say."

"You have to, Robyn. Things have changed since you left Loving Grace." Things I didn't add: LuAnn has been murdered and someone took a run at me, whoever's running drugs is panicking and lashing out, we need to get you to a safe house.

She shook her head. "Thank you for the journal. But you need to go. They don't like strangers here."

"Robyn, I'm not leaving without you. I was serious about Trinity. She's freaked out that you called her."

"I don't want to see anyone get hurt."

"Have you seen someone get hurt?"

She nodded, her brow creased with worry, grief, I couldn't tell. "Who?"

"Amber," she whispered.

The bottom dropped out of my world. I'd been chasing shadows all this time, but some part of me had always believed I'd find her.

CHAPTER 20

Robyn clutched her journal closer.

"Where's Amber, Robyn?"

"I don't know." She looked down at her shoes and back up at me. "And we're safer that way." Her eyes were wide and her shoulders hunched. The kid was as scared as anyone I'd ever seen and I'd seen scared.

"I get it." I took a step in her direction.

She took a step back.

"Why don't we go to my place and talk about it?"

"I'm not leaving. They're serving beans for dinner."

I summoned my most convincing mother-knows-best voice. "I have left-over lasagna, French bread and a salad." I hadn't made any of the food that was on offer, but that wasn't the point. From there, I could keep her safe and get the information I was desperate for. Two birds, one stone.

Robyn shrugged.

Oh, come on. Who doesn't go for lasagna? What had her so scared she'd turn down a home-cooked meal? Well, a home-heated-up meal. I thought of what else I had left over from the last weekend with Mitz. I dug deep, conjuring all the times I'd had to convince my Ladybug to do something she didn't want to; her homework on a Sunday night, the dishes after a movie, taking Floyd out for a last pee when it was raining. Wow, my girl had it so good. And it would stay that way. I would have moved the galaxy with a single roar if someone had her so terrified she'd be willing stay in a place like this.

A flash of inspiration landed in the middle of my fuzzy brain. "And fudge bars. I've got half a box of fudge bars left."

Robyn's eyes lightened, like Mitz's did when she was excited. "Fudge bars?"

I nodded. "You'll be safe. I'm a PI. I carry a gun. I live next to my family." I almost added and my boyfriend's a cop, but after Jessica's stories of the things some police did to the homeless person's belongings, that might not be a plus. "I promise, you'll be okay. You can clean up and we'll have dinner and talk. The only thing I ask is you tell me why you ran. Deal?"

She shook her head again but didn't run when I stepped closer.

I put my hand on her arm. "I'm not one of those people that are making you promises they can't keep."

Her wall crumbled as her eyes filled with tears. "All I want to do is sleep."

The downside of being out on your own. How did one rest with real abandon when danger lurked everywhere? You'd always have one eye open. *That* I could help with. "My daughter has the most comfortable bed."

She closed her eyes. A tear trickled down her face and her chin trembled. The decision to trust or run waged inside of her. She opened her eyes. "Okay." She stepped onto the path, leading us out of the camp. "But no questions. Just sleep?"

I believed I could keep her safe. At least I felt like she'd be safer with me than she was out here. And I was anxious to hear what she knew about Amber. We only had one hurdle to breach: Trinity.

We ducked through the fence and into the camp.

I needn't have worried. The second she saw Trinity, Robyn set off running, shouting her name. "Trin! Trinity!"

They stood in the center of the camp, their arms wrapped around each other, while the men by the fire clapped and cheered—not in a creepy way. They weren't making fun of the girls. They were cheering them on. The lump in my throat grew so huge I almost couldn't swallow.

Robyn and Trinity were wrapped in their private world all the way back to the car, arms around each other's shoulders, whispering and nodding and playing with each other's hair.

Trinity handed me the car keys and opened the door for Robyn. The two of them climbed into the backseat, continuing to whisper.

"Anyone going to clue me in on the story?" I turned the keys in the ignition.

Neither of them answered.

"Right. Would you prefer drive through instead of lasagna? Burgers, milkshakes, and fries? Then home?"

"Thanks," said Trinity. "But we're good. We'll take you home and drop you, then we'll be on our way."

Don't trust anyone. Not even someone who's pulled your girlfriend out of a tent city and reunited you.

I pulled onto the freeway, weaving in and out of traffic, trying to figure out how to convince them to stay at my place where they'd be safe. Oh, who was I kidding. I wanted them safe, but I had to get them to talk to me. I turned the radio on, but there was only static.

Robyn and Trinity giggled in the backseat, lost in their own world.

Despite the win of finding Robyn, I was gloomy and feeling sorry for myself. I'd done all the right things and gotten all the wrong answers. Now I needed to pull one out of the fire and get Robyn to spill what she knew about Loving Grace, Saving Grace, Maria's death, and Amber's disappearance.

We cruised off the highway and into my neighborhood, but my usual jolt of happiness—being close to the beautiful house my dad had left me—wasn't there.

Instead, Hannah sat on the bottom step, ruffling Floyd's ears. She'd worked out my boy was home alone, gotten a key from Arlene, let herself in, and taken Floyd for a walk…without losing him. She was learning.

I pulled up and heaved myself out of the car.

"Hey, Sis."

I had two homeless girls in the back of the car. Hannah had been cool when I left the rehab center, hadn't asked too many questions, but she'd been around Arlene for a few days now. She was going to catch the, "Your sister, Kelly, takes too many risks. Mitz shouldn't be exposed to the PI lifestyle" vibe.

Robyn was out of the car fast, descending on Floyd like a ten-year-old. She squealed and kissed his head as if they were old friends. That probably meant she'd left a dog behind. These women lost so much when they took to the streets.

"Is this your dog?" Robyn looked to Hannah for answers.

Hannah smiled. "I wish. This spoiled pooch belongs to my sister." She looped her arm through Robyn's and walked her up the steps. "When I'm reincarnated I'm coming back as her dog because he has the best life. Sleeps on her bed, farts in her face, but she doesn't complain a bit. If I farted on her it would be a Federal offense."

Trinity stood at the bottom of the stairs as Hannah charmed her girlfriend. "We'll stay for an hour so Robyn can get her dog fix. She misses Bella."

I nodded. I was right. Robyn had a dog back home. Man, it would kill me to have to abandon Floyd. We trudged into the house.

Hannah took Robyn and Trinity into the front room, all of them loving on Floyd, while I headed into the kitchen and grabbed the lasagna from the fridge. I slid a slab onto a plate and popped it into the microwave then cut the French bread into hearty slices.

My phone chimed with Mitz's ringtone. I left the lasagna and headed for the back door where I might have some privacy, then pulled up the video. There was the thing I needed, Mitz's strawberry curls and smiling face, staring up at me.

"Ladybug," I signed.

"Mama," she answered.

"How are you doing, baby?"

Mitz stuck out her tongue. I wasn't supposed to call her baby anymore. But she'd always be, no matter what.

"We're definitely going to Disneyland and Mommy Linda has all kinds of fun things planned," she signed. Her face was lit up from the inside.

I'd put that out of my mind almost as soon as Linda had mentioned it and Jeff had confirmed it. I wasn't thrilled, but he and I could work out the details later. That's why our arrangement worked. We put our daughter's welfare before our own differences.

"You'll have to get some Minnie Mouse ears," I chirped, hands over my head in our private sign for Minnie. She loved that mouse and I knew that would make her beam. I needed Mitz-beams more than ever. "Hey, do you mind if I have a friend sleep in your room for a few days?" I signed.

"Kyle?" she said and spelled out with her fingers.

"No," I said, holding back a chuckle. I didn't tell her that Kyle and mommy shared a bed when he was here. Even though we'd been dating for over a year, I never had him spend the night when Mitz was home. I wasn't sure why. Clearly Jeff and Linda hadn't hidden that part of their relationship from her.

"Not, Kyle," I signed. "It's a young girl that I'm helping."

"Okay. She can play with my things if she wants." My Mitz was so good. What wouldn't I give to have a hug from her right this minute or run my fingers through her curls? *Tomorrow.* "That's so cool of you, sweetie, but she's actually bigger than that."

"Like Aunty Hannah?"

"Kind of."

"Can I meet her when I come over?"

"Maybe," I said. Wow. Was Robyn and Trinity going to be here all weekend? I hadn't thought it through. "Sweetie, Mommy has to go."

"I love you. Kiss Floyd for me."

I choked back a sob. What had I done to deserve such a beautiful soul in my life? "Love you too, Ladybug."

She laughed and disappeared from my screen.

"You good?" Hannah stood in the kitchen doorway.

"All good," I said, even though it wasn't.

"The girls are going to stay the night." She hooked a thumb towards the front room.

My mouth fell open. She'd managed to convince them I was safe in under five minutes. "How?"

"I told them I lived next door and if they needed me to beat anyone up for them, I would." She wiggled her eyebrows at me like it was the best joke in the world.

I stuck another plate of lasagna in the microwave, hit the buttons and waited.

"You really okay?" Her tone was gentle and I had to look away so she wouldn't see that she'd landed right in the tender spot when my defenses were down. I was fried and I knew it but with Amber remaining out there and a killer on the loose, I couldn't go to bed and sleep my way through.

The lasagna dinged and I swapped it out for a third plate. "I need to ask a favor."

"Name it." She didn't hesitate.

"Would you sit with me while I talk to the girls? I need another set of ears in case I miss something."

"You betcha. Let me pop next door and tell Arly I'll be awhile."

I held out my cell phone. "Call her."

Hannah shook her head. "She doesn't like the phone. She needs people, you know?" She jogged towards the front door right as the microwave dinged again.

"Dinner," I shouted.

Robyn and Trinity came into the kitchen, hand in hand.

"Your sister's cool," said Trinity. "She gets it."

Huh? Got what? I mean, I guess she was cool, objectively speaking, but what did she have that I didn't?

"She's lived on the streets." Trinity pulled out a chair, sat, and helped herself to a slice of bread. "She understands why you've got to play it safe."

In my short time as a PI, I'd had quite a few near misses and head on impacts with bad guys. I kept thinking I was playing it safe, but apparently, I was a slow learner.

Hannah was back before I'd heated her lasagna and she fell into chatting with the girls like she had known them all her life. I let them chatter on and on, even though I itched to get to the investigation. They talked about softball, dogs, school, hair dye, the music of Billie Eilish, the comedy of Hannah Gadsby, and the awesomeness of Lizzo. For three-quarters of the conversation, I had no idea what they were talking about.

Hannah smiled across the table as she wiped her plate with her bread. "Kelly's a PI, did you ladies know that?"

The room fell silent. They did. They didn't like it, but they knew.

"I don't know much about what she does, so perhaps you can help me interrogate her?" Hannah said.

Trinity smiled.

"I'll start," said Hannah. "Do you have a gun?"

I laughed. I mean, yes, but what did that have to do with the price of bread? I nodded.

Hannah nudged Robyn with her elbow. "Your turn."

"Have you ever killed anyone?"

"Whoa," I gasped. "I'm a private investigator, not a hit man."

"Trinity?" My sister smiled at her new best friend. She was good. She'd gotten them talking and then she'd turned them on me…brilliant.

Trinity reached for Robyn's hand. "Why were you really at the shelter?"

I leaned on the table. "Bernie Sokol, who is Amber's grandfather, hired me to find out whether drugs were being dealt at Loving Grace."

Both girls fell over laughing. Floyd was particularly interested in them flopping around and snuffled around under the chairs hoping for some dropped food.

"He didn't need to hire you to find that out." Trinity snorted. "The old man could have come down any day and hung by the back door and seen it for himself."

"Was that what Amber did? Hang around the back door and watch?"

The laughter leaked out of the room. I'd blown it. We'd been doing so well.

"She means well," Hannah said, "but sometimes she goes in with a sledgehammer when what you need is a banana."

Trinity laughed, but Robyn didn't crack a smile. "Amber is safe," she said. "I already told you that."

My heart raced so fast I thought I might fall off my chair and join Floyd under the table. If I opened my mouth I'd get it wrong. I kept it closed.

"You can tell her." Hannah patted Robyn's arm. "She looks like a scary detective-type and she charges in when she shouldn't, but her heart is in the right place. If she told you she will keep you safe, she will."

Heck, Hannah Hanson: PR representative for Kelly Pruett Investigative Services. My skin tingled at the sound of that.

Robyn took a sip of water. "There's this black car that comes by. Not every night, but I've seen it a few times in the month I've been there."

"To the shelter?" I asked.

"No. The rehab center. I'd seen it before, but I hadn't paid any attention to be honest. There are plenty of girls walking the streets and the curb crawlers trawl for dates…" The way she said it made it all sound so normal. Girls sold flesh. Men bought it. It was the way of the world outside Loving Grace.

"What made you notice it this time?" I asked.

"There was an argument. In the car. The person in the back said, 'I'll kill you if you don't get a handle on the situation.'"

A black car had pulled into Katherine's place as I was leaving a couple of days ago. But there were a thousand black cars in and around Portland. It wasn't likely she was talking about the car Katherine had been waiting for. They were all looking at me…waiting. I had to drag my brain back to the table, rewind the tape, and connect to the last thing Robyn had said. There had been a fight; words, a threat, there. "Like a figure of speech – 'I'm going to kill you if you don't finish your lunch?' That kind of thing?"

"I know the difference," she said, a bit too defensive.

"I'm sure you do. Sorry. Go on."

"It was like *you either get this shit pulled together right now, or I'll kill you and make sure they don't find your body*." She shuddered and reached for her girlfriend's hand again. Trinity took it, her eyes fixed on Robyn. A tear ran down her face. "They saw me. When they pulled away, they rolled down the window and looked right at me."

"Man or woman?"

She closed her eyes and shook her head. "They had a tattoo." She ran her hand down her arm. "Like a sleeve."

That could help narrow it down. "What kind of tattoo? Flowers? Tribal?"

She shook her head.

I thought of the sheath Katherine had on when I saw her. She had a printed long sleeve underneath her flowy dress. At a glance, that might look like a sleeve tattoo.

Robyn pulled her journal out and flipped the pages towards the back where she had done some sketching. My focus saw for the first time the big eye and long lashes she'd been drawing that first night we met. I thought back to Amber's picture—wide eyes and long lashes. Had she been hinting right then she knew who I was talking about when I asked?

I cleared my throat at the missed opportunity from the beginning and watched as she flipped to a dog-eared page and handed it to me. "I drew this the first time I saw the car."

The picture was of a black sedan. I'd seen it when I went through her journal the second time but had discounted it. Now the drawing struck me hard because it looked *just* like the car I'd seen at Katherine's place that day. *Damn it.* I should have stopped to see who got out of that car. What had I been thinking? What kind of detective was I, anyway?

My attention turned back to the page. Robyn was an excellent sketcher and had shaded the car perfectly. But the picture had the back end angled away with no plate showing. While my brain tried to work out how I could track down the car, Hannah had cracked a bottle of wine and gotten four tumblers from the cupboard. When I raised an eyebrow, she raised hers right back.

"Get real, sis. If you think these two ladies don't deserve a glass of wine, you're on the wrong planet."

They were, what 17? 18? Then again, if we'd been in Europe they'd have been allowed to go into a pub with us. One glass wouldn't hurt them.

Robyn took a sip and went right back to her story. "When I came back in, LuAnn was at the backdoor of the laundry room. She was irate. She asked me what I was doing out there. I told her I'd been smoking, but she ignored me and raced outside. She must have seen the sedan too because she came back real fast and came at me like a freight train. I mean, she had her hands on my coat collar and demanded to know what I saw and if I was the stupidest person on the planet."

"She was that angry?"

"No. She was terrified. The sedan frightened her."

I had no idea what it meant, but the fact that LuAnn was scared—scared then and dead now—felt important.

"She told me to get the hell out of there and don't look back."

I let that surprising information sink in. "And you did, right then?"

"I didn't have a choice. She wanted me gone and I already had my backpack with me. My journal must have fallen out at some point, but I didn't realize it until later."

"When you left, was the sedan gone?"

"Yeah. LuAnn watched for it and gave me the *all clear* and led me out the front and to the bus stop. I texted Trinity to meet me at the park, but LuAnn said no way. I had to get on a bus and go to a shelter in Oregon City where she knew I could get in with no hassles. So, I did."

"LuAnn wanted to protect you." Trinity was awed. Gentle. "When this is all over, we'll take her some smokes. You know, say thank you."

There was no easy way to break the news and, in any case, according to my sister, I was a bull in a china shop, even on a good day. I needed to tell them; now.

I gathered all my strength and blurted out the news. "LuAnn was murdered yesterday."

CHAPTER 21

Robyn's face crumpled, her hands flying to her mouth to cover her sob. "It's all my fault."

The three of us chimed in immediately with a chorus of "no" and "of course not" and "don't be ridiculous."

I knew for a fact it had nothing to do with her. I'd seen LuAnn in action. "I think the fact that she was dealing drugs probably lead to her death…"

Robyn's head jerked up. "No way. I already told you she was a good person." She wiped her face on her sleeve. Hannah was already there, tissues at the ready.

Robyn might want to believe the best about the dead linebacker, but I believed what I'd seen. "LuAnn went to the rehab center and collected an envelope from Mr. Bow-Tie."

"Did you see what was in the envelope?" Trinity bristled. "You people are very quick to judge us. If you only saw an envelope, perhaps it was money."

I didn't get it. Why were they defending her? I could use help understanding where they were coming from, but Hannah didn't look in my direction. She had her "listening" face on and had her eyes trained on Robyn. I needed a listening face but I wasn't sure I could pull it off. I was used to asking questions and evaluating the answers, not waiting…and waiting…and waiting.

Trinity leaned over and whispered, "Tell her."

"Really?" Robyn fidgeted with her fork, stabbing the remnants of her lasagna.

Trinity nodded. "How else can we stop this?"

Robyn sat up straight. "LuAnn would never do drugs. She'd been in NA for years. She was a card-carrying member of the 'don't go down that road' crowd.' She was tough because she had to be. She'd learned it the hard way. The street isn't kind to junkies. It's the fastest way to go under. She told me more than once *don't get sucked in. You can get out of here if you keep your nose clean and your head high.* She had hopes for us. Like, she cared. She wanted our lives to be better than hers. Her mom kicked her out when she found out…"

Hannah shook her head. "I don't get it. If I had a kid and they told me they loved someone, my first response would be 'WOOHOO! Good for you!' Not, 'get out of my house.'"

Robyn and Trinity beamed at her, gratitude oozing out of their pores.

I should have said that. I meant it. I'd gotten rusty at the "soft" things you were supposed to say to all the people you cared about. Mitz was easy to love, but everyone else was tricky, tricky, tricky. They all had opinions about how I should live my life and I wasn't cool with that. Although I had to admit it had gotten better…

Trinity leaned on the table with her elbows to get closer to me. "Are you hearing what Robyn is saying? LuAnn was one of the good guys."

Robyn jumped in, breathy and excited. "Gordon was a slimeball. Nettie is a pushover. Most of the women are so broken they don't bother with anyone. It's the outsiders you need to worry about."

"Okay. Back up." I tapped my finger on the edge of my plate, realizing too late that it sounded like I was shutting them down, when I was actually centering myself. "Let's say Trinity is right and it wasn't drugs in that envelope…"

"I am right. One-thousand percent." Trinity sat back and gave me a fake smile and a curt nod.

"And let's also say that Robyn is right and LuAnn was vehemently against drugs. What was she doing at Saving Grace?"

"Signing people up," said Robyn.

I squinted at her, my version of a listening face, but I was pretty sure it came off as exactly what I meant, which was, 'What the hell are you talking about?'

Robyn turned back to Hannah, the good sister, the better listener, the kinder person.

"I went there once when I needed antibiotics. They do stuff like that for Loving Grace residents sometimes. I had an ear infection that wouldn't go away. LuAnn took me over and introduced me to the nurse. I was like the only person in there. They were so great." She smiled, her tears a thing of the past. "They ran a bunch of tests to make sure my iron levels were okay and I didn't have any deficiencies. They gave me meds for my ears and a bottle of multivitamins." She dug in her backpack and found her vitamins. A rubber band held a couple of scraps of paper to the outside of the bottle.

"Huh." Hannah looked at me, "Sounds like a great operation. Helping people get back on their feet. What do we have to say about that, sis?" Underneath the innocent sentence I could hear what she meant. They'd taken me in when they thought I could use detoxing, and released me, which meant I shouldn't have a beef with them.

"There aren't many places you can go for help when you're homeless." Trinity's tone said she believed I didn't understand their lives the way Hannah did.

That might be true. But I did understand some things perfectly. Amber had gone missing, Maria was dead, and LuAnn had been killed *for a reason*. All this "lovey-dovey, Saving Grace is heaven" stuff might be true on the surface, but they were missing the point. "Something bad is going on in there. I know it. LuAnn wasn't going there for her health. She had a fight. It was a…"

"You're barking up the wrong tree," Robyn said, sure of herself. "Saving Grace is squeaky clean. If you want to look anywhere, look at the shelter, not the rehab center. There are deals going on at Loving Grace all the time."

Robyn had started to share but was holding off on telling me everything. I could feel it. How to get her to talk, though? It wasn't like I could ply them with liquor and interrogate them and….

"Shall we move to the front room?" Hannah cut into my thoughts. "Get comfy? This chair is making my butt go numb." She topped up our glasses. It wasn't much wine per cup, but I had a mom moment which I had to crush hard.

The three of them moved out of the kitchen in a little clump of babble and chatter, repeating what they'd already said. Even Floyd abandoned me for the excitement of the living room.

I followed along and lowered myself into the easy chair. I'd been going at this the wrong way. If I took my foot off the gas, and let the conversation unfold naturally, it might work better. Not my forte, but I kept my mouth shut and my ears open.

Hannah listened to the laundry room stories: The Gordon is a creep tales, the pointless locked-door policy, when everyone knew you could get in and out of the place a million ways. Nettie was a chump. Judy was a harmless nutjob. LuAnn the favorite inmate. In my line of work, I spent more time talking to men than women. Most of them said what they were going to say, then moved on. These three women kept circling back, adding more details, asking each other questions, mirroring facts back to each other. It was giddying...and a little annoying.

Every few sentences Robyn snuck a look in my direction. It took every ounce of discipline not to leap on the opportunity and shout, *WHAT AREN'T YOU TELLING ME?*

"Back in the Cowlick Saloon..." Hannah laughed. "No, really that's what it was called. Middle of a cow town, nothing but farms and cowhands as far as the eye could see, they thought no one knew they were dealing out of the bathroom, but I tell you." She whistled. "We wouldn't have had a bar to run if the drug dealers hadn't been there. Traffic in and out those doors like crazy."

The girls nodded. "The produce guy who comes to Loving Grace deals E," said Robyn. "Drops off the veggies on a Tuesday then hangs out down at Farragut Park until he's sold whatever stash he's brought."

Trinity nodded, her face serious. "You can get anything in Farragut. Addies. Meow-meow. Crush. Whizz. Brown sugar. Kit kat..."

I'd gotten so many things wrong in this case-that-wasn't-a-case I wondered if I shouldn't hang up my PI badge and take up macrame or car detailing. "Nothing goes on at Saving Grace? Really?"

"How does that make sense, Sis? They're a pain and rehab center. The opposite of..."

Robyn broke in. "They help. Not just with meds and vitamins, but the forms and the agencies and all the places you can get help. It's super hard to navigate." She leaned forward in her chair. "When I had my earache, I went to a doctor's office, yeah? But I couldn't pay. They told me I was eligible, but I didn't know where to go or how to apply."

"Eligible?"

"For benefits." She hopped out of her chair and dashed to the kitchen. When she returned she had her vitamins in one hand and a small card in the other. She handed it to me. "Know what that is?"

It was an Oregon Health Plan Medicaid card.

"That's freedom. That gets you the help you need. You show this card and your medication is free. Saving Grace helped me get this." She tucked it back under the rubber band. "It's worth thousands of dollars."

It was like getting hit by a two-by-four of sense. "Say that again."

All three of them stared at me. I must have used that tone my sister had mentioned. The one that scared people off.

"It's worth thousands of dollars?" Robyn cocked her head. "But, like it is. I can't afford meds..."

Alarm bells went off all over the place in my head. It was late, too late to call a colleague? Who was I kidding? I was calling. "I'll be right back." I grabbed my phone and stepped out the back door.

Back to the old contacts list. "Yeah, *Hot Stuff*," I muttered, "I'm going to have a hot tip for you. I'll keep you posted." *Huh*. I was having a bit of a delayed reaction of him escorting me to the police station without telling me what he was doing.

I had Carla's cell number for those "just in case" times when we had to serve papers in a hurry. Not every case runs on a day clock and only during working hours. Sometimes we had to interrupt a judge during dinner or track down a villain in the middle of the night.

It rang twice before she picked up. "Hello."

"Carla, hey. It's Kelly. Sorry to disturb you."

"It's fine. Just got home and was catching up on my recorded shows. You much of a mystery fan? You must be in your line of work. If you haven't already seen it, *How To Get Away With Murder* is a great drama." She paused. "I'm sorry. You're probably not calling to chit chat. What's up?"

"Any chance you could meet me for a drink? I've stumbled onto something that might help me find Amber and I want to pick your brain. I'd rather not do it over the phone." What I meant was, I didn't want two homeless girls and my sister listening in, but I didn't share that with Carla.

"Why not? I haven't been out on the town for, oh, days." She laughed. She had a great laugh. Infectious. "You familiar with *Backwoods in the Pearl*?"

I wasn't, but that's what google was for. "I'll be there in," I looked at my watch. "Half an hour?"

I didn't have a vehicle, which meant I had to go begging again. Trinity gave me her keys as soon as I asked, but Hannah waved her down and gave me hers instead. "Don't leave it there, this time." She smiled as she told me off. It was a friendly admonition. I'd have to get used to her style.

Traffic was light. Parking was a cinch. Carla was nowhere to be seen.

I found a stool at the end of the bar where I had a view of the front door. The barman was right there—hair back in a neat bun, tattoos up and down both arms, very Pearl District—asking me what I wanted. What I wanted was Amber back home and Kyle snuggling with me after dinner, and my world back to its regular grind. But that wasn't on the menu. I picked the beer with the lowest alcohol content and asked for a glass of water.

The place had a cabin-y vibe with plenty of highly polished wood. The corners of the tables had the outline of a pine tree burned into them, making for an artsy vibe. My drink arrived before Carla, but only just.

"Sorry." She unwound her scarf and took off her coat. "Parking was a bitch."

That's the way with Portland traffic. If you hit it just right, there are three spaces available. If you get stuck at the wrong light and arrive ten minutes later, forget about it.

The friendly barman returned, Carla's drink in hand. She must be a regular.

It was a foo-foo drink with a whipped cream top and a frosted rim. "Caramel hot toddy," she said. "To die for."

I sipped my water while she ordered some food: a loaded burger and a side of onion rings.

I wasn't hungry, but I didn't want to stiff the waiter when it came to tips so I ordered a small bowl of chili.

"How can I help you?" Carla said, all business.

I felt the ease of familiar conversational patterns warm my bones. How wonderful to be talking to someone who spoke my language—no "listening faces," no "warm up" chat, no asking the same question a million times. She was busy, I was busy, the most respectful thing we could do for each other was get right to the point, stay there, and conclude our business.

"It's about Saving Grace," I said.

She nodded, a sly smile on her lips. "Wondered when you'd get there."

I slapped my leg. I knew my gut wasn't wrong. There was some bad juju in that place. "So?" I waited.

"What do you want to know?"

"Where to start?" I backed up and told her how enthusiastic Robyn and Trinity were about Saving Grace being a "haven" of some kind, free from all taint, a true beacon in the community—on their side.

Carla laughed. "That's what they're supposed to think."

My food arrived, but nothing could have been less inviting. I pushed it aside and held onto my glass of water. "Are you going to tell me or do I have to beg?"

"Depends. Can you promise that I'm kept out of it?"

"Absolutely." It sounded good already and she hadn't said a thing.

"Because I could lose my job for what I'm about to tell you."

I put up two fingers in a salute. "Scout's honor. I will never tell another living soul."

"It's about the old witch…"

I sat, riveted, and listened to her incredible story. By the time she'd finished, my gut instinct had been totally validated and I had my marching orders. But one thing didn't quite sit right. "Why haven't you said anything before to Bernie, to the authorities, to anyone?"

She looked away. "I tried. Once. But he was so busy that he didn't want to hear it. Plus, he's always defensive of his family. And honestly Kelly, what would I do if I got fired? My job is all I have. You can understand that I'm sure?"

That I did. "But still…"

"At the end of the day, I reasoned that it isn't something that affects me or even the law firm directly, and there are a million balls to be juggled on any given day. Maybe I should have but let's face it, I'm a bottom rung. I have a feeling he'll actually take it seriously if it comes from you."

So far, Bernie hadn't taken me as serious as I'd hoped. But if what Carla said panned out, he'd have no choice. "I can't thank you enough." I pushed her hand away from the bill and forced my credit card into our waiter's hand. "It's the least I can do."

Carla finished her fancy cocktail and ordered another. "I'm going to hang here," she said. "You have places to go and people to see."

I left her chatting to our favorite barman and put the pedal to the metal, my mind in a whirl. Katherine was at the center of the whole rotten business and I would prove it beyond a reasonable doubt.

* * *

It was misting and pitch black by the time I turned onto Belmont and I could tell even from the distance my house was dark. When Mitz visited, you could land an airplane by the amount of illumination coming from the windows. Hopefully, no lights didn't mean that Robyn and Trinity were asleep. They'd be interested in what Carla had said.

When I pulled into my drive, the garage door was open. It had been closed when I left. Robyn or Trinity might have done some laundry or come outside for a smoke. Given the events surrounding this case—dead and missing women all over the place—it was not cool. Doors should be closed and locked…at all times. End of debate.

I glanced up at Arlene's quiet, dark house. Seven thirty was too early for her to be in bed. She and Detective Kuni were supposed to be going out on a date but that wasn't until tomorrow night.

I held my breath listening hard, but only heard distant traffic. My heart pounded. LuAnn's murder and my attack had me on a knife's edge.

I went in through the garage, hitting the down button for the door, and calling for Floyd. No floppy-eared galumphing came to meet me. The house was silent, with no TV, no music, no sounds of nails clicking on hardwood floors.

"Hannah?" I called. No answer. "Robyn? Trinity?"

My heartbeat quickened. I opened and closed the fridge door. That usually got Floyd's attention. Nothing.

The hairs on my arms stood straight up. "Floyd." My voice raised a couple of notches. "Come, boy."

If they had gone out, why hadn't Hannah texted me? I did some breathing exercises—in through the nose, out through the mouth—trying not to get ahead of myself. They could be upstairs, engrossed in something at the computer.

I crept into the living room and stopped. The cushions on the couch were askew. Not so strange, given that three young women had been hanging out in here, but the whole room was wrong: off, messed with. Books had been taken off the shelf and put back on their sides. Was I adding two and two and getting five? No, there were all kinds of little things that didn't simply say, "Hannah, Robyn, and Trinity were here."

It was as if an intruder had been through the place quickly, trying not to make it seem like anyone had been here. The blinds were parted, like someone had peeked through them. Floyd's bed was turned sideways. The drawer to my side table was ever-so-slightly open.

My heart crashed in my chest. It had been doing a lot of that lately. Was this how my dad had lived his life or had he taken it in stride? Because it sucked to be riding wave after wave of adrenaline highs.

I bolted upstairs. "Floyd?" *More silence.* The door to my dad's room was open. At first glance, nothing looked touched. My gun safe was locked and secure in the closet. If someone was in the house, I should be armed. Fingers shaking, I punched Mitz's birthday into the gun safe keypad and retrieved my Glock, my breath ragged.

Gun in hand, I slunk out of the bedroom and strode to Mitz's room. There was a book on the floor and her games box had been pulled out from under her bed—little tells everywhere.

Where the hell was everybody?

I fumbled in my jacket pocket and found my phone, punched in Arlene's number, praying for an answer. I got voicemail instead.

A shiver ran through me from cold and nerves. Maybe Arlene wasn't answering because she couldn't.

Zipping my gun in my jacket pocket, I ran down the stairs and right to Arlene's place. I pounded on the door and hollered. "Arlene, are you in there?" *Nothing.* "Damn it Arlene? Where the hell…"

CHAPTER 22

Arlene's front door banged open. "Lord almighty, child, what's wrong?" Arlene, dressed in a navy velour leisure suit, held a wine glass in front of her, as if she had not a care in the world.

"Are you okay? I thought…" Tears sprang into my eyes. "Why aren't your lights on? You didn't answer your phone. Have you seen Robyn and Trinity and Hannah? And Floyd?"

She stepped aside to let me in. "Everyone's here. I guess the time got away from us. I forgot to put the porch light on. Not that I thought you noticed these things, with the hours you keep. We're back in the kitchen. The moment you left, they were bored at your place and I'd just made cookies. I had them come here to keep me company." She squinted at me. "Didn't mean to scare you. Are you okay?"

I gulped under the forced back tears and nodded. They were fine. Everything was fine. Except for the niggling feeling that someone had been in my house. If Arlene had invited them over right after I left, they wouldn't have been knocking down books on shelves. But it wasn't something I could call the police about. There were no signs of forced entry—nothing but my gut saying someone had been in there.

"Did you forget to close the garage door?"

She thought about it for a second, sipping her wine. "I guess I did. I'm sorry."

She and I'd had words about unlocked doors in the past. I was too grateful that everyone was safe to remind her of that. It was time to switch gears and be less of a bulldozer. "Do you have more of those cookies?" They might help me charm my way into the next phase of my plan.

155

"I do."

Floyd trotted to the door as soon as he heard me. I bent down, ruffling the top of his head before burying my face in his fur for a few beats too long. He wiggled out of my grasp and sauntered back into Arlene's kitchen where the action was…and no doubt the food.

Hannah, Trinity, and Robyn were at the dining table playing dominoes, the tiles strewn out in front of them.

"Hey," Hannah said.

Robyn looked up and nodded at me with a small smile. A plate of cookies sat next to her elbow, her journal next to that. She'd showered and changed into a pair of jeans and a sweatshirt I recognized as Hannah's as it was from her job, Casa Diablo. She looked far more rested than when I'd left her a couple of hours ago.

Trinity had borrowed some of Hannah's stylish gear, too. She was jammed up next to Robyn, counting her tiles and studying what was already on the table.

"Pull up a seat," Hannah said. "You can help me beat these cheaters."

The girls laughed. There was already an in-joke that I was outside of.

"Just wished you'd have texted me," I whispered.

She eyed me. "Ah, was big sis worried when she got home and didn't find us there?"

I smiled. "Something like that." I went to the counter and took a cookie. No nibbling for me this time, I popped the whole thing in my mouth.

Behind me, four women laughed and joked and shuffled domino tiles on Arlene's kitchen table. If I told them what I knew that would all change. They'd be somber, serious, worried. They didn't need that.

I had to go it alone. Or did I? Perhaps taking one accomplice for safe measure would be smarter.

"Can I borrow Hannah for a bit?" I leaned against the kitchen counter, hoping I was signaling a nonchalance I didn't feel.

"What do you mean, borrow?" Arlene squeezed Hannah's shoulder and I surprised myself with another pang of jealousy.

"I'll have her back before her carriage turns into a pumpkin." The room didn't respond with the laugh I'd hoped for. "I won't…"

Arlene lifted her hand to silence me. "I've seen that face before. You're about to do something questionable. I realize I can't stop you, but I'll be damned if you'll go alone."

I took a couple of steps in her direction, wrapped my arms around her and squeezed hard. I was as shocked as she was—twice in one day. Things had taken a strange turn between us.

"I wouldn't ask, but I have to check something out." And I don't want to end up like LuAnn or, for that matter, like myself with more chemicals in my face. Having a lookout could help me avoid that. The things I wasn't saying were multiplying. Wasn't that always the way when I got deep into a case? I was onto something, I knew it. Arlene would stop me if she knew what it was…ditto Kyle. Only Hannah would roll with my hairbrained idea.

"I'll be back." Hannah did a passable Schwarzenegger impersonation, making the girls laugh in a way I never could. She excused herself, ran upstairs for her 'investigative outfit,' leaving me with a faintly hostile room.

"You going to tell us where you've been?" Trinity folded her arms.

"Tracking down leads." I popped another cookie. I needed peanut butter, but Arlene didn't keep any in the house because, she said, 'You eat too much of it as it is. Your father had problems with his cholesterol.'

Robyn took Trinity's hand. It was good to see they'd mended their fences. "What kind of leads?"

I'd thought to share with them what I'd learned from Carla. But how could I tell them they were in great danger without freaking them all out? "What I've learned in my years working with my PI father, and being one for a couple of them, was that most leads are dead ends. You find scraps of information—LuAnn was scared, Saving Grace is 'clean,' that kind of thing—and you form a hypothesis."

Arlene topped up her glass, not that it needed a refill.

"I talked to a colleague about Loving Grace and the possible drug problem…" That was a lie, but only a tiny one. The less they knew the better.

"You're not going to go down to the druggie park, are you?" Arlene gasped.

Robyn and Trinity burst out laughing. "It's not a druggie park, Arly. It's just where you go to score. It's fine as long as you know how to carry yourself." Trinity gave a sideways look which said she didn't believe I could pass as a dealer or a customer—which was fine because I wasn't headed to Farragut Park.

Hannah threw her arms out in a TA-DA gesture as she entered the kitchen. She was dressed in black from head to toe and had on a balaclava. A bit overkill, but I smiled despite myself.

I ruffled Floyd's ears. "Be a good boy. I won't be long."

Robyn dropped her arm and Floyd waddled in her direction. "He's the best boy, aren't you, Floyd." He had a pal and he soaked up the love like a tubby little dog sponge.

We said our goodbyes and headed out to the car. It was cool enough that we needed the heater, but Hannah's car didn't have holes in the floor, so we were good on that score.

"Want to tell me where we're going?" she said.

"Before we begin…" I owed her this much. She needed to make an informed decision. "What I'm about to do could be seen as skirting the law."

She turned the key in the ignition. "Cool."

"I don't want to get you into trouble. I get it if you'd rather not."

"Sis…" She grinned. "I've seen more trouble than you've had hot dinners. It's all cooler than a hothouse full of cucumbers. We're doing stuff. Together. I've waited my whole life for a sister I could do this with."

Hannah appeared to have the same bulldog DNA that I'd gotten from my dad. We were sisters. It turned out that today was a day for developing lumps in my throat. I stared out the window until the feeling subsided, then gave her directions to Baumgartner & Sokol.

"Back to my original question. Are you gonna fill me in?" Hannah wove through traffic like we were on the set of *Speed* and she was Sandra Bullock.

"I already told you that Bernie Sokol hired me to find out whether drugs were being sold at Loving Grace Women's Homeless Shelter."

She leaned on her horn and swore at a driver who wasn't doing what she wanted him to do. "Yes, and Arly has filled me in on everything she knows. Women's shelter. Undercover op. Drugs. Missing girls."

"Right."

"I didn't tell her about your attack, by the way. That can be our little secret." She sounded pleased with herself…and why not? She had a new family, new friends. Everybody loved her. And she'd done me a solid… no, more than one. She'd done me a couple of favors and didn't seem to begrudge me her time or energy. It was time to reassess my opinion of my half-sister. She was turning out to be okay.

She leaned on the horn a dozen times and flipped a driver off.

I grabbed the handle over the door to stabilize myself. She was weaving a bit hard for my taste. "I appreciate that. What I didn't tell the girls back at Arlene's though was when I got inside, the hospital suites were empty— which doesn't add up. I've seen a van of patients dropped off there." More than once, but it hadn't really sunk in.

"Outpatient?" She swore at another driver who, as far as I could tell, was doing 70 in a 60 MPH lane.

"Maybe, but if Carla's info is right, there's another—far more nefarious side—to Saving Grace's operation."

"You have my full attention," she said.

"It's a pill mill."

Hannah leaned on the horn for so long I had to cover my ears. "Okay. So, it's a pill mill."

"If Amber found out and planned to blow the whistle, it's no surprise that she went into hiding."

She was silent for a couple of seconds, though her concentration on the road never wavered. "You think someone murdered that LuAnn chick because of a pill mill?" She didn't sound convinced.

I double checked my seatbelt for the third time.

"That's what we're going to find out. There's always a trail. People never think to look at the bills, but there's an evidentiary trail right under our noses."

Hannah took the exit ramp at speeds no one in Portland was used to and squealed to a halt when we hit the light. Moments later we were a block from Bernie's offices and plotting our break in.

"Carla says Katherine Sokol—Bernie's first wife—has known about the pill mill for years. She's at the center of this. If I can prove that, then I can take it to Bernie and convince him to take it to the police." Or I will if he won't, but I could decide that later. Either way, I waited for Hannah to tell me what an amazing twist it was, to have learned that Katherine Sokol was so evil she'd threaten her own granddaughter, but there was no such wave of approval from her. She was too busy futzing with her ski mask. "Did you hear what I said?"

"The grandmother is the wicked witch of the west and you're going to prove it?"

That about summed it up.

"Do we know why?"

"Carla said it had to do with Katherine's life being ruined. First by their adoptive daughter, Amber's mother. Then Amber." I continued filling her in on the rest of what Carla had said—about Candy and Morgan and the stream of women who had gotten between Katherine and Bernie. Katherine Sokol was the ice queen because she'd had her heart broken a hundred times and her way of getting back at all of them was to bring Bernie down with the very thing that had ruined their lives: drugs. But not just any old drugs—drugs in the very place he'd built to honor the sister who'd taken her own life. This whole mess was built on a foundation of ancient history. Katherine was enacting her revenge against Bernie's sister, Grace.

Hannah pulled her mask over her face. "Whew. People are screwy and families are the screwiest. Unless you actively work at maintaining your friendships—including friendships with family members—they sour. Like everything else. If you don't tend to it, it dies."

She might have well as punched me in the gut. In an instant, I thought of all of my relationships and how I hadn't done so well over the years with them. I had been improving a lot on most of them. But one in particular had weighed on me these past few days. Even if she wasn't family…yet. I couldn't talk, so I didn't. Instead, I turned my attention back to Bernie's offices where the answer to this puzzle was packed away in a box of papers on the second floor.

I could have gone through the front of the offices and gone up from there, but I didn't want to implicate Carla by having a record of entering Bernie's offices after hours. She'd been nice enough to give me her building and office key to the upstairs suites and directions on how to reach their floor by first going underground.

We found the little-known grate that covered the entrance to the Shanghai Tunnels and slid it away from the opening enough to jump through. We dropped into the dark which was when I realized I hadn't brought a flashlight. My phone would have to do. At least my gun was safely tucked in my jacket.

I tripped not once, not twice, but four times before I got the hang of swinging my phone down to the floor, where the occasional bucket or brick lay in wait. I was a walking-talking trip-and-fall hazard.

We picked our way through the dank, dark space—me counting the side tunnels the way Carla had told me to—until we reached a set of iron stairs. It was nothing fancy, just rungs slotted into the wall.

"Your job is beyond nuts, sis." Hannah sounded impressed. I didn't have the heart to tell her that this was precisely the point in the proceedings when things tended to go off script. We were breaking and entering and we were about to go in for some grand larceny. This was "felony" level activity, rather than "misdemeanor." Or at least it would be if Carla was right about the goings-on in Saving Grace. And on that note, I guess my activity simply mirrored their activity—seemed fair to me.

My partner in crime was fit enough to race up the ladder, hand over hand, and pop the grate at the top.

I took slightly longer but did my best not to pant when I breached the hole at the top of the tunnel. "Put the grate back, just in case Security does a sweep." If Carla was to be believed, there was a patrol guy who came nightly. She insisted they were donut-eating former-cops and there "wasn't a cat in hell's chance" that they would cause us a problem as long as we didn't draw attention to ourselves.

My new favorite person had given me a key to the backdoor of Baumgartner & Sokol and gained us access to the storage room upstairs. We were so close to breaking this case wide open that I could hardly stand it. I had a tremor in my hands and a severe case of dry mouth.

Inside the room, a light from the courtyard illuminated the space. The boxes were exactly where Carla had said they would be: Loving Grace in one stack, Saving Grace in the other. There had to be a paper trail. That's what thieves and fraudsters always forgot: the paper trail. All I had to do was connect the dots. Since I suspected the rehab center was at the core of the pill mill—they were the suppliers, Loving Grace simply offered a solid stream of customers—I selected a box from the top of Saving Grace and set it on the floor.

"Stand guard, okay?" I whispered. "If you hear anything, we have to get out of here."

She stood near the door, looking out into the hall. "Where would we go exactly?"

I didn't have an answer. Jumping out the window would get us killed. Hiding under a table would get us caught. I had a gun that I'd never shoot at a security guard, or anyone else for that matter, for doing their job. With no good options, I hurried.

I plopped on the ground, popped open the lid and stared inside for a beat.

"What are you looking for?" Hannah asked.

"Not sure yet, but I'll know when I see it," I said. Truthfully, it could be many things: an invoice, a ledger. It would be too much to hope for check stubs, deposits in accounts other than the center's. I wasn't entirely sure what would be the smoking gun, but I dug in and fingered the papers for anything that looked suspicious.

The first few files I came across were Medicaid information files: how to make claims, requirements, compensation schedules. Perusing the pages educated me to the fact that detoxing a patient paid well. Short-term treatment was lucrative. Long-term harder to get approved, but there was plenty of money involved when it did. Although seeing as they weren't keeping patients more than a few hours, if that, any such claims were a complete fraud. Other than hundreds of sheets of insurance papers relating directly to Medicaid, nothing struck me as outside the normal scope of a rehab center's business though.

Jessica had told me that they rotated patients in and out of Saving Grace without a "step down program." It was to their benefit not to have those services. The more people came through the doors, the more money they made. It was cold and calculating, but healthcare paid big bucks. To say nothing of the fact that they could pad their pill orders if they had a steady stream of patients.

The next box showed registered patients for the past couple of years. It was a list of sorts. The other boxes might contain actual patient files, but they weren't in the box with the patient list.

There were hundreds of people registered into the beds of Saving Grace all on the same date. Were there a hundred beds or patients in Saving Grace? Not that I'd seen. Except for the van full of people that were dropped off here and there. And where did they come from?

I found the patient records in another box with hundreds of names. I would have thought HIPAA would have prohibited records from being thrown into a box and left in a law office. But if Saving Grace was doing something irregular, HIPAA rules were the least of their concerns.

Near the back of the records, I recognized one of the names on the file label—Ruth Comfrey—the Ruth who had thought I was my mother.

I pulled out the file and scanned the contents. She'd been in for detox several times: quaaludes to mushrooms, to everything in between. That poor woman had done some serious self-medicating in her time. Given our interaction, I didn't doubt the damage to her mind had been severe. I tucked the file back in and went to the next box.

There were accounting records of money in and money out. They were dated fifteen to eighteen years ago.

I pulled out the pages and read. Even back then, they reported hundreds of beds at the rehab center with more patient names, and dates of birth, addresses. But unlike the earlier documents, the Medicaid records were attached, as were insurance papers for submission for reimbursement to Saving Grace. The records back then were much more organized. I hadn't found a record of their medication orders, but was there such a thing? Did they keep duplicates? They had to, somewhere. This might prove a little trickier than I had thought. *Keep looking, Kelly. It's in here. You know it. Carla wouldn't have sent you here if she didn't believe you'd crack the case.*

I scanned the papers but my eye got snagged on a signature. While Katherine's name was on the bulk of paperwork, Barbara Pruett had signed a few of the original documents. My mother's smooth handwriting was on several of the insurance requests. I couldn't stop staring at her handwriting. The way she crossed her T's, and flipped up the end of her S's, the roundness in her Es. They looked so familiar, and in a flash I understood why. I did something similar with my letters. I'd never realized until now.

It also answered why Ruth might have mistaken me for my mother. Ruth was being treated at the rehab center at the same time as my mother was working as a bookkeeper. Perhaps at some point they'd crossed paths, whether Carla had been aware of that or not.

Hannah hissed. "You almost done there, sis?"

"Someone coming?" My hand went to the pocket of my jacket where my gun was stashed, but withdrew my hand just as quick.

"The elevator dinged. It was phantom, but it freaked me out. Hurry, will you."

"I am," I said at the same time I thought I saw a pattern. Saving Grace needed the patients' particulars so they could order the meds.

I grabbed out some more ledgers. These were financial and more current, precisely what I'd been looking for. Buried in these line items would be concrete proof that they were ordering more meds than they were prescribing. I didn't have time to go through them all. Laying out pages from the past year, I turned on the night camera on my phone and took pictures of the different pages to peruse later.

A flash of light came through the back window. I hunkered down on the floor, inhaling carpet fumes, and waited. Car lights swept over the ceiling and down the wall, then disappeared. We were fine for another minute or so. I swallowed the lump in my throat and set the lid back on and pulled another box.

This one contained more current check registers and patient files. That's when I spotted medical files for Maria Castro, Amber Moore, and Robyn Baker. I cracked Robyn's file first. Inside were several billings for detoxing, one for severe status. Pain medications were not only for treating various pain issues among the patients, but also to detox slowly. Except I was certain of one thing after having spent time with Robyn: she wasn't an addict, nor did she have pain issues.

These medical records had been falsified, the charges bogus: smoking gun.

If they'd done the same with Amber and she'd found out…Or had seen someone's file she recognized…like Maria and Robyn…

It was coming together. No wonder Amber was so scared. Katherine was running a pill mill. That could include fentanyl, like what had taken Maria's life—so not just pills, but meds of all kinds. Amber had found out. Katherine had threatened her granddaughter, forcing her into hiding. That all hung together. *Amazing.* All it took was the right person pointing me in the right direction and the case was solved.

I pulled out Amber's records and flipped through them. There was a pattern: chronic detox, then more drugs prescribed. This was it—another smoking-hot gun. I'd have a cabinet stacked with them by the time I finished. Kyle would be impressed when he saw this data. I had her. Katherine Sokol would go down for creating a prescription drug empire.

A crash sounded from the courtyard, sending my heart into overtime.

"What the hell was that?" Hannah tiptoed to the window where I'd seen the light earlier and looked out. "Damn. It's security again."

I shoved the three files inside my jacket and zipped it up. "We need to go." *Nothing like stating the obvious when you're under pressure, Kelly.* The security guard was making his rounds, checking gates—and probably grates into the tunnels. We had about a minute, two at the most. "I suggest we run."

After securing the office door, we made our way back through the tunnel, getting out and securing the grate before the security guard got that far. We sprinted to Hannah's car. Adrenaline bolted through me and my heartbeat pounded in my ears. Somehow we made it undetected.

Hannah tossed me the keys and she slumped in her seat, staying low. I did the same, started the car and drove.

"Did you at least find what you were looking for?" she said once we were clear of the offices.

"Oh, yeah." I gripped the steering wheel. "That and much more."

CHAPTER 23

I dropped Hannah back at Arly's house with strict instructions not to alarm anyone—no saying where we'd been, no talking about what I'd found—nothing. She agreed to all my demands with her usual good cheer.

"Thanks, Hannah." I was on the verge of giving her a hug when she lunged and wrapped her arms around me.

"My pleasure," she said. "I knew one day you'd need me. I'm glad it was sooner, rather than later."

"Give Floyd a big kiss." I raced down the steps to my house just in case she was about to lay some more sisterly love on me. I'd had quite enough for one day.

Once inside, I closed the door. First things first, I had to call Bernie. I finally had concrete proof. He'd fired Gordon which meant he at least part-ways believed me. Now he had to dig out the rest of the cancerous weasels eating his charitable organizations so Amber could come out of hiding. I hit his cell phone number and waited...straight to voicemail. I tried again...same. Did I remain persona non grata as Carla had phrased it? Well, that had to stop. If he wasn't taking my calls, I had to take the news to him—personally.

What I had on my phone proved that Saving Grace was a pill mill with his former wife pulling the strings. An operation like that required more than just a few in the organization to be in on the fraud, or at least the doctor writing the scripts and the person doing the ordering and anyone with half a brain and eyes to see.

Had my mother been aware of what was happening at the time? I'd been mulling that idea over since I'd seen her signature. It had only been on a few documents and I couldn't imagine she did, or she would have told my father, right? Dad, though, was always out investigating, and I was far too young to talk to about things like that—and of course I was always hanging out with my dad. One thing I was certain of, she wouldn't have been complicit and I hope the same could be said for Bernie. Everything I knew about him said he was a good man, including and probably most importantly, that my father had liked him and worked for him. Kyle had suggested otherwise, but he didn't have the history with Bernie and his firm like my family did.

Despite that, there was that one-in-a-million chance that he only looked like a decent human being but belonged to the scammers and liars, and cutthroat grabbers of the world. I had to take a chance on him. What choice did I have? He loved Amber, that much I knew for certain. Once he learned that Katherine had orchestrated this horror and threatened his granddaughter when she rumbled the whole operation, surely he'd go to the police. Like Carla said, maybe he would take me seriously when presented with the reality.

Amber was only a few phone calls away before she'd come out of hiding. I could feel it.

* * *

I had just one more call before I headed out to deliver the good/bad news.

I sat in my comfy chair—the one Mitz was used to seeing me in; I didn't want to alarm her—and dialed. It was a little later than our usual call, but even if she'd spent the evening meeting Linda's parents on my normal schedule, I had no intention of missing a "goodnight" unless we absolutely had to.

"Ladybug," I signed as we went into video chat. Every cell in my body exhaled when my curly red-haired girl filled the screen. "How was your night?"

She was sitting on her bed, cross-legged. "Good, mama. Guess what?"

"What?" I expected a run through of her facial with Grandma Arlene and what Linda's parents had served for dinner, even an update on her friends.

"Mommy Linda and I picked out new colors for my bedroom today."

Jeff had mentioned Linda wanting to renovate the house. He'd said nothing about Mitz's room, the room that she and I had decorated. My only tell was my eye, which twitched, but I smiled hoping she hadn't seen me freak out. "Well, it's just paint, right? Paint always needs to be freshened up. What color did you choose?"

"Yellow, and white stripes."

Ugh. "Nice. But you're keeping the furniture I hope?"

"No. She says out with the old and in with the new." Mitz smiled, oblivious to what that truly meant, or at least what it certainly sounded like it meant to me.

I was the old mommy, and Linda was the new one. My jaw tightened. "But you've always loved your white bed and dresser, haven't you?"

She frowned. "Yes, but Mommy Linda says I can't stay little forever. I said we should ask you, but she said you would just want to keep it the way it was. And it was her house now too."

"She said that, huh?" I smiled, my jaw aching.

"We're going to buy a bunch of cool stuff, Mommy, and start from scratch," Mitz signed.

I looked down so Mitz wouldn't see my response. Linda was trying to remove me from Mitz's daily world and last I checked, my name was on the mortgage for that house until Jeff could refinance. "I see. What did Daddy say about all this?"

"He wasn't home yet, but I think she was planning to tell him."

The word *tell* was really getting under my skin, but I refused to show any of that to Mitz. "You seem really excited, Ladybug."

"It's going to be fun."

"Sure it is." My mind reeled. Linda had told me they were "going to Disneyland," fine. But this change without discussing it with Jeff or me, not okay. The emotion lodged in my throat and I kept it there, hidden from my precious daughter.

I hadn't called to get into this conversation. It deserved more than signing over a telephone screen. "I definitely want to hear more about the plans, but let's talk about it later, okay? Just wanted to say I love you and goodnight."

Mitz flopped onto her belly. "I love you too. Where's Floyd?"

"Nana has him until morning."

"Sleepover," she signed and giggled. "Like us tomorrow night. Aunty Hannah-banana's going to be there, right? Maybe I can go hang with her at Nana's and Floyd can come over then, so he can sleep with me if you're working."

Dagger to the already-compromised heart. I hadn't been working weekends in a long while, but even she'd seen I was engrossed in this case.

But I was almost there and had even more incentive to get it wrapped up tight, and quick. "Let's play it by ear. Okay sweetie, got to go. I'll see you soon. Love you."

We signed goodbye, and I crushed the off button until my finger turned white.

My brain was a mass of buzzing flies and red-hot rage. I'd tried to be amiable to Linda—despite our history. But her actions as it came to redoing Mitz's room, and not talking to Jeff about it, felt underhanded, even for her. Or did he know... he'd told me about the renovation. Maybe he'd held back, certain that I'd respond poorly...and I definitely was responding.

One thing was certain; he and I had to talk it out...and we would, but not at this very moment.

Once again, Hannah had left her car keys with me, so I had wheels. I grabbed my purse and stomped out to Hannah's car. I leaned on the horn as I pulled onto the freeway. I wasn't in the habit of honking at other drivers, but I could learn. It was satisfying in a bitter-sweet way. I was mimicking my sister with none of the benefits I truly wanted.

The climb up to Bernie's place up on Council Crest was dark and windy, but this time his massive gates didn't come up on me in surprise. I hit the buzzer. When the gate didn't budge, I buzzed again. *Silence.* I could see lights on in the house, but the gates remained shut and locked.

Going home was tempting after this day, but no sleep for me. I had a pill mill to close. And I wasn't in the mood to take no for an answer.

I pulled my car off to the side so not to block the gate and grabbed my warmup jacket from the backseat, zipping it up as I stepped into the frosty air. The space between the gate's bars was too narrow, but the large, emblazoned S was curvy enough for me to contort through to the other side—minus one belt loop that caught on the curve, reminding me of the bruise I'd sustained last time I crawled through a space not designed for my mom bod.

By the time I'd unhinged myself, and reached the portico, I was covered in sweat and was winded. Swearing off peanut butter for the umpteenth time, I knocked and rubbed my hands together waiting. The house was lit up bright, but there was no answer.

"Bernie? You in there?" I hollered and pressed my ear against the door, listening. No sounds came from the other side—including no moans or pleas for help. The memory of my dad lying on the floor after his stroke flashed in my head. I checked the doorknob. It turned easily, making my muscles tighten, and the door opened. "Bernie? Everything okay?" *Silence.* "It's Kelly. I'm coming in."

I hustled through the two living room portions and through the kitchen to make sure he wasn't downstairs.

I ran up the carpeted marble steps and stood on the landing. "Bernie?" I projected my voice loud enough that someone outside could hear.

Bernie's office door was closed, but a muffled thunk, thunk, thunk came through. I rolled my eyes and put my hand on my chest. He must be on his treadmill and hadn't even heard my calls. I could wait downstairs until he was done so not to scare him—except I didn't want to spend all night waiting for a guy with an exercise obsession. I tapped the door with my knuckles and opened it at the same time. "Hey Bernie, it's me, Kelly."

The door swung wide and my throat closed. Bernie wasn't on his treadmill, at his desk, or anywhere to be seen. My mouth hung open.

Candy's limp body hung from the overhead fan, her face and limbs blue, her feet catching on the back of Bernie's chair with each rotation.

CHAPTER 24

"No," I whispered. The horror of Candy hanging washed over me like a rogue wave. I found the wall switch and flipped off the fan with my elbow. It looked like suicide, but I'd learned enough from my last two cases not to disturb possible evidence. The fan creaked with a high pitch squeal to a stop. Candy's body swung side to side. Her face was blue and her tongue bulged from between her lips, leaving no doubt she was dead. Acid shot up from my stomach.

I dialed 9-1-1 on my cell and reported the situation. When I hung up, I couldn't move, frozen to the floor.

Where the hell was Bernie? I stared at the phone in my hand. It was a communication device, I knew that. I could hit a key and talk to a person. I knew that, too. But how was I supposed to find Bernie Sokol's number?

Candy's foot tapped the top of her husband's chair, snapping me back into reality. I scrolled through "recents" and stabbed Bernie's number… straight to voicemail. "Call me. I…" Her face was more than I could bear to look at. I turned my back on her. "Just call me. Now. It's urgent. There has been a death." It was vague, but alarming enough that he might get over himself and return my call.

I needed to do my job: assess the scene, take mental notes, and look for anything that might tell me what the hell had happened. Three deaths in three weeks: Maria in Farragut Park, LuAnn in her apartment, and now Candy in her own home. The danger was closing in and it centered around Bernie and his charitable interests. Katherine must be running scared. Was avenging herself against her husband so important she'd kill for it? I mean clearly…my brain twisted around the facts at hand and while I knew

170

what I knew, I was having a hard time adding up the columns and making emotional sense of this mess.

I scanned the area, careful not to touch a thing. My prints would already be around the guest chair from our first meeting. No sense adding to my problems by touching anything else.

The room looked neat and tidy. On the credenza were pictures of Candy alive and well on her wedding day. Next to it was Amber's childhood picture. Then there was Bernie serving food at the shelter, then Candy and Bernie in Hawaii, lei's around their necks, cocktails in hand. He had a Mai Tai and she had a Blue Hawaiian. My chest gripped in grief. They looked very much in love.

Katherine had said Candy was a money-grubbing little slut, but she was the ex-wife, so she would say things like that. Oh, hell, where was Morgan? She needed to know her mother was dead. At least someone had to tell her.

Come on, Bernie. Call me.

There were no obvious signs of struggle. The door downstairs had been unlocked—not broken down. Other than the body, no indicators of foul play were evident. Considerable strength would have been required to hoist a full-grown woman up to a ceiling fan, even one as scrawny as she was.

Avoiding the body, I scanned Bernie's desk. The position of the desk mat bothered me. With my jacket sleeve covering my finger, I shifted it to the side revealing a file labeled *Amber and others.*

Curious what *others* meant, I slid it out from under the blotter and opened the file. A picture of Amber was on top. Her wavy brown hair was tucked behind her ears, and a straight toothed smile revealing deep dimples. Below the photo was handwritten notes on Maria Castro. Bernie had been listening to me. If it hadn't been for the dead woman hanging from the ceiling, I would have been relieved.

The 9-1-1 operator called back to inform me that the police were at the gate. I ran downstairs and pushed the remote button near the front door. A few minutes later, a uniformed officer came in. I handed him my business card and gave him the quick rundown. He was grilling me about turning the fan off when the Deputy District Attorney and ME arrived. They ordered me to remain downstairs while they investigated.

I made my way to the traditional living room, dialing Kyle as I crossed the threshold.

"What's up?" he answered.

Just hearing his voice eased some of my muscle-freezing tension. Even when he wasn't thrilled with me, I realized, I loved him. "Needed to hear your voice."

He didn't say anything. Not even a grunt of recognition. I remained under a cloud of suspicion.

"How's your night going?"

"Fine." He wouldn't relent. He was annoyed and he planned to stay that way. "What do you want, Kelly?"

Finally, an in—the dam burst, words falling out of me as if I had no control. "I broke the case, but then I talked to Mitz and Linda is planning to take my place." The tears came readily now, the exhaustion of the last two days overpowering my desire to remain stoic. "I came to tell Bernie about the pill mill but when I got here, she was dead."

"Kel, slow down. What's going on?"

I closed my eyes. "She's..."

"Kelly? What's happening? Where are you? Who's dead?" His voice was taut.

"Candy Sokol. Well, not Sokol. Appleton. She didn't take his name, but she's Bernie's wife. And she's dead."

He cleared his throat. "How do you know that?"

I pushed the palm of my hand above my heart to quell the heaviness in my chest. "I found her."

A few seconds of silence followed. "Of course you did." We'd had one second of a cease fire, when I'd allowed myself to imagine he'd forgiven me for being near the LuAnn situation, and now we were back at square one.

"I didn't plan this. Like I said, I broke the case and came here to give Bernie a full report." Yay, me. I had solved the case without having to fight off the culprit and nearly getting killed myself this time—well, almost. I had walked myself out of that alley after being maced. My dad would be proud. But there were a lot of dead bodies and it had taken me forever to get to the bottom of the corruption at Saving Grace. I hadn't solved the case so much as had it handed to me. Kyle didn't need to hear that right now. "The police and medical examiner are already here."

A beep came from his end of the phone. "Where did you say you were at?" Kyle had silenced the high pitch noise.

I gave him the address. "It's on Council Crest. Why?"

"I just got a page. Looks like I'm on my way."

"Definitely homicide?"

He didn't confirm or deny.

I dropped onto the sofa and put my head between my knees. I'd immediately suspected it, but the ME must have found something to indicate that Candy's death looked suspicious.

Kyle hung up without saying goodbye and I was left to watch Bernie's house fill up with the cast of characters who accompanied a suspicious death. They trailed up and down the stairs in their white suits and shoe gloves, ignoring me over in the corner.

It seemed like ages until Kyle turned up, but my phone told me it had only been half an hour since we talked. Behind him was my not-so-favorite detective, his boss, Detective Enloe.

Seeing Kyle immediately grounded me. I wanted to fling my arms around him—for warmth and comfort, and reassurance that everything would be alright between us. But that wasn't possible with Enloe nearby.

Enloe nodded on his way up the stairs. "Going to need you to stay right where you are, Miss Pruett, until we've assessed the situation."

No way I was a suspect in this murder, too.

Kyle steered me back to the couch. "How do you get involved in these things?" His voice was hushed.

"I told you." I wanted to lean into him so bad, but that wouldn't do either of us any good. "I came here to tell Bernie what I'd learned about Saving Grace. When no one answered the door, I let myself in."

"Closed door means don't come in." He wasn't as stoic anymore, but I wasn't sure if I could handle him being cold to me a minute longer.

"There's a girl missing, Kyle. I'm not capable of sitting back. It's just not in my nature."

Kyle took my hand, nodding, and his eyes softened. "Before we do anything, we need to notify Ms. Appleton's family," he said. "Any idea where we can find them?"

Right on cue, the front door swung open. A whiff of floral perfume blasted in before Morgan rushed through the door, her kid in a car seat and a diaper bag slung over her shoulder.

CHAPTER 25

Morgan's apple-red face was blotched with white patches and she had a look of panic in her eyes, a normal response to coming home to find police cars and a meat wagon in your driveway. She looked put together in her black yoga pants and red sweater. She set the car seat down on the sofa in the modern living room and joined us in the foyer, her eyes darting towards the stairs and back.

"Where's my mom?" she demanded.

"Who are you?" Kyle asked, his demeanor professional, not demanding or defensive. He was in work mode and I admired that he knew how to handle himself.

"This is my home and I'm her daughter, who do you think I am? And what's she doing here?"

"Miss...?" Kyle began.

She didn't fill in the blank for him. "Where's my mom? Is she hurt? Answer my question."

"Let's go into the living room."

Her face crumpled as she followed Kyle into the traditional side to avoid disturbing the baby...but she knew. How could she not? The house was swarming with cops. It was interesting that she thought something had happened to her mom, though, and not Bernie. She hadn't asked about him. Not once.

"Miss Pruett came to talk business with your father and..."

"He's not my father," she said.

"Kelly came to talk to Bernie Sokol on a matter of business."

"I know all about her business," Morgan said. "She gets into everyone else's. She makes trouble. Makes people fight. You did this, didn't you? You made them fight? This is your fault."

I wanted to tell her that it wasn't me. It was Katherine, but this was neither the time nor the place.

Kyle didn't break stride. He remained composed, professional, impassive. "Ms. Pruett entered Mr. Sokol's office where she found Mrs. Sokol unresponsive."

"Mrs. Sokol?" Her head whipped between us. "You mean my mom or Bernie's ex?"

"I'm sorry to tell you that your mother was pronounced dead by the medical examiner about twenty minutes ago."

Morgan's legs buckled and she collapsed into a pile on the floor. Her sobs came in loud gasps.

Kyle helped her to her feet and escorted her to the couch.

I ran to get a box of Kleenex and returned shoving several tissues at her. I understood grief. My dad had fallen apart when my mom died, lying on their bed for days just saying her name. That had made it impossible for me to grieve as I had a father to take care of. By the time he'd surfaced and threw himself into his work, I'd shut down my feelings about my mother's death. I'd experienced that combo of crushing grief and denial all over again when I lost my dad, forcing myself to work harder and harder to honor his memory.

I reached for Morgan's hand, but she snatched it away.

"What happened?" she finally asked through shaky breaths.

"At this time, we believe your mother's death might have occurred under suspicious circumstances." Kyle was perfect for the role.

Morgan's eyes flew open. "What? Why? Oh my God. How?"

"That will be determined during the autopsy." Kyle retrieved a notepad from his back pocket.

"Where were you this evening?" All eyes shot to the stairs where Detective Enloe was descending with a cell phone wrapped in a sparkly protective case, already in an evidence bag.

"At the beach…" Morgan jumped up and met the senior detective at the foot of the stairs. "Holy crap. You found it. She's been looking for that everywhere. Where was it?"

"In Mr. Sokol's office, under his desk."

"Under his desk?" Morgan said, her voice small. She wanted to know and she didn't want to know in equal measure. "What was it doing there?"

"Why don't you tell me?" he said.

"I have no idea."

Kyle held out a small trash can for the mountain of tissues she'd created. "You said you went to the beach with your mother?"

Morgan nodded. "A couple of days ago and we wanted to stay longer..."

"But you just came back. Alone. Why is that?"

Morgan burst into tears. It took several minutes for her to calm herself enough to talk. "It's all my fault. She came back for the humidifier. It's a special one. I put a vapor rub in it, and when I plug it in, it reflects stars onto the ceiling. It calms my son and he'd had a rough night last night. As I said, we wanted to stay longer, but we needed that so she volunteered to come back for it." A fresh wave of tears rolled down her face.

Detective Enloe's eyes narrowed. "Let me get this straight. You wanted a humidifier at the beach? Outside?"

He was missing the point. Morgan was telling the truth. I'd heard the baby coughing. It made sense that Candy had come home to collect the machine and...

And what...what could I tell him had happened here? If Katherine was behind the murders, why had she killed Candy? Bernie's new wife had nothing to do with the shelter or the rehab center.

Morgan sniffled, blotting her nose with a tissue. "We were staying at the Stephanie Inn. You can verify we'd checked into the Carriage House. The humidifier is a special kind."

The front door flew open, crashing against the plaster wall. Bernie stood, gasping, his face pouring with sweat. "Will someone tell me what the hell is going on here?" His earphones dangled in his fists. He stuffed them in his track suit pocket and wiped his face with his sleeve. In classic Bernie style, he'd been for a run.

Morgan ran to him and he welcomed her into the biggest bear hug I'd ever seen. She sobbed into his chest, muttering, and mumbling incoherent sentences. I hadn't seen that coming. I'd thought of their relationship as cooler, more "at an arm's length." You never know what goes on behind closed doors. They'd looked like adversaries when I first saw them, but there was a natural warmth in that hug.

Unless...

No, that wasn't what was happening. My PI brain saw shades and shadows where there weren't any. Morgan had just lost her mother, of course she'd throw herself at the man who'd loved her.

Finally, she raised her face to his. "She's dead, Bernie. Mom's dead."

Bernie's jaw fell slack and the color drained from his face. If he was acting, he deserved an Oscar. Although I didn't think he was—I forced myself to stay neutral and observe rather than jump to conclusions. He broke from Morgan and charged the stairs, knocking Enloe to one side like they were in a rugby match and the goal post was at the top. The trail of police tape and number of white-suited professionals told him which way to run. Or did he already know where she was hanging? My mind slid effortlessly out of "post-shock muddle" into my best "PI-analysis-tracking mode."

If Bernie had killed Candy and strung her up then left the house, it wouldn't take a master planner to work out when to return. There were plenty of places around his property where he could have hidden, waiting. But motives…what reason did he have to kill his present wife—well, past wife, now?

Enloe pointed at the officer outside Bernie's office. "Don't let him in."

Bernie bashed into the waiting officer like a battering ram. "Let me see her. You've got to let me see her."

Morgan sank to the floor, wailing. "Mommmm." She buckled and curled, ending in the fetal position. You could not have written this to be more textbook-dramatic in terms of their responses.

I waited to see who pointed the finger first.

"Who did this?" Bernie clenched the bannister outside his office, spitting into the stairwell below. "Who killed my wife?" He charged back down the stairs and went chest to chest with Detective Enloe. "I want a proper investigation. Not some brush off. I don't want this buried in some report. I want answers. I want you to find who did this." He spotted Morgan on the floor and went to her aid. He was gentle, cautious, solicitous. "Let's get you over to the couch. Do you think you can stand? Let me help you…"

I pulled Kyle back into the living room while the family drama unfolded. He didn't take his eyes of Bernie, but he allowed me to move him a few feet away so we could talk.

"I think I know who did it."

That got his attention. Not that I was looking for that—I wanted to help. Because I really did know this time.

"Katherine Sokol has been running a drug ring," I said.

Kyle had his professional mask fixed to his face. "Go on."

I pulled out my phone and scrolled through the paperwork I'd photographed just hours earlier. "She wants to hurt Bernie…"

"Back up…" He frowned as he took my phone from me. "What am I looking at?"

I tried to explain as quickly and simply as I could. He listened intently and left me for Enloe when I was done with my tale of drugs, murder, fraud, and revenge. Enloe shot a couple of killer looks in my direction while Kyle downloaded my theory for his boss. Enloe hadn't ruled me out of the picture but he had nothing to rule me in because I hadn't done anything…other than get attacked and solve a major crime. I was feeling pretty good about myself. There was only one thing left to do. I had to talk to Bernie so he could close the pill mill down at Saving Grace and Amber could come out of hiding.

Enloe had made a decision. I could see it from all the hustle and bustle of the officers as they went about their duties. Bagged evidence went out the doors. Forensics made an entrance. They went about their jobs with clockwork precision.

Everything stopped when Candy made an appearance on a stretcher, the body bag underlining the horror of what had transpired. We stood to attention, our heads bowed, Morgan's wails the soundtrack to the devastating procession, and when Candy was out the door and in the ME's van, the baby woke coughing and spluttering.

Bernie and I would not have a chance to talk about Saving Grace tonight.

Kyle turned to me, his face a mix of police detective and boyfriend. "We might need you down at the station, but you should go home and get some rest now. We've got this."

I had zero pushback in me, not because of the exhaustion, but because he was right. The case was littered with dead bodies. Katherine Sokol had gone way off the rails, killing everyone in her path. I didn't need that kind of threat to my life. I'd tell Kyle more about my frustration with Linda later. He had bigger fish to fry, as my dad would have said. And in all fairness, Jeff and I needed a chat before anyone else.

"Later?" I wanted to stand on my tippytoes and kiss him leaving him with no doubt that we were right for each other. But his boss was still in the picture somewhere.

"I'll do my best." He let his hand rest on my arm for a few seconds longer than was necessary.

We were going to be alright. I wanted to dance—which wouldn't be appropriate at the scene of a murder. I smiled and nodded instead. "Whenever you can, Hot Stuff. I'll be waiting."

He laughed. It was just a small huff of air, but all I needed.

In spite of the sobbing daughter, the colicky baby and the dead body, I'd done my best and deserved a rest. I floated out to my car and breezed home.

* * *

By the time I turned onto my street I could barely keep my eyes open. The house was dark and the girls were nowhere to be found, but they'd been so happy at Arlene's. Maybe they'd decided to stay next door after a raucous night of dominoes and laughter with Grandma Arly and Aunty Hannah. That was good. I didn't want them in my house with a psychopath on the loose.

I checked my watch. Although they should have Katherine in custody by now. Things were all working out great. With the wicked witch under lock and key, perhaps I could convince Robyn to tell me where Amber was.

I secured the files I'd taken from the offices upstairs in my dad's gun safe and crashed on the couch. On the fringes of consciousness, I felt a wrinkle in my sleep. The wrinkle became a crackle, then a pop. I'd heard that noise before, felt it before—an acrid smell. My eyes flew open. *Smoke.*

Hannah was snoring in the overstuffed chair across from me. She'd snuck in with Floyd while I was sleeping. It was a bit alarming that I hadn't heard her.

Floyd sounded the alarm, his deep woofs indicating he smelled it, too. "Hannah," I yelled. "Fire."

I glanced upstairs. Had they all come back? Were Robyn and Trinity in my room or Mitz's? Had Robyn been smoking and fallen asleep? I leapt up the stairs. The smell receded. The bedroom doorknob was cold—no fire in there. I burst open the door. Robyn and Trinity were fast asleep. "Get up. Get dressed. Now."

I hoped the tone in my voice was enough to rouse them. Both girls were out of bed and on their feet in a single bound. It struck me that living on the streets means you never get REM sleep, you're always one disaster away from a life-threatening tragedy. As I turned away they were grabbing clothes and backpacks and heading for the stairs. Mitz would have taken her time, been hard to wake, since she had the luxury of feeling safe when she slept. The mixture of gratitude and sadness was an unfamiliar combo. I was happy for my daughter and sad for these girls.

I got to my dad's gun safe and pulled out the files, tucking them under my shirt.

Hannah was already in the kitchen. She nodded towards the stairs which led to the garage and the laundry room below. The smoke was coming up the stairwell. "Get outside with Floyd. I'll call 9-1-1," she said.

Good advice that I should follow. But this was an old house, built with very few of the safety measures of new builds. This place was a matchbox waiting to explode into flames. I couldn't let that happen. It was the last thing I had of my dad's, and it wouldn't be going anywhere.

Curling smoke, black as night, filled the stairwell. I thrust the files at Hannah. "Please don't lose these." I grabbed the fire extinguisher from under the sink and a dish towel which I put over my nose and mouth as I barged past her. I ignored her yelling my name and sprinted down the stairs.

The smoke was coming from the laundry room. My dryer was engulfed in flames, smoke pouring out of the front glass door. Robyn was suddenly behind me, Hannah behind her. "Get back," I hollered as I aimed the nozzle at the dryer and blasted it with foam. The smoke kept coming, and the flames licked the wall. I'd seen enough fire in my previous case to last a lifetime and I had no intention of losing my dad's house, my house, to it now.

"Fire Department's on its way," Trinity hollered, coming up from behind Hannah and Robyn. She stepped past me to open the dryer using a wet towel over her hands as protection. Whatever the source, the fire had started inside. "Aim above the flames and blast it," she ordered.

Willing it to work, I aimed the nozzle where she directed and squeezed the trigger. Foam shot out. Robyn and Trinity coughed. "Get Floyd on his leash and out the front," I barked. They hesitated. "Now," I demanded as black smoke consumed the small room, but the fire was almost out.

My trio of helpers pounded up the stairs, yelling for Floyd. He'd never had so many saviors.

A few more shots of foam did the trick. I stumbled outside the garage as the sound of sirens filled the air. Robyn, Trinity and Floyd were standing at the stairs that led to Arlene's house. Hannah handed me the files and went over to the firemen.

Arlene hustled down her stairs and chivvied the girls back to her place. She wasn't lonely anymore—not with Hannah firmly ensconced and a couple of teenage runaways to look after.

Hannah returned to my side. "What the hell?" she said. "You think the security guard saw us last night and this is retaliation?"

"This wasn't done by any security guard." Or did Katherine have a network of killers and saboteurs working for her? Even my sleep-deprived brain had a good laugh at that one. Katherine was in custody. The case was over. We were safe. My house was old, the washer and dryer set were almost as old as me. Faulty wiring had played a part. I had to think about the most likely causes, not what my weary, paranoid brain coughed up.

The Fire Chief lumbered in our direction, his flame-resistant uniform making a monster out of a giant. "You have a habit of drying oily rags in your dryer?"

"Oily rags? No, sir." Where would oily rags have come from? I tried to think of who'd been where but all I could come up with was laundry tokens and the girls having dirty clothes I knew nothing about. "But the dryer wasn't even on."

"It's called spontaneous combustion. The oil from the rags generates its own heat, essentially. They should be disposed of properly. Never put those into a dryer."

My stomach hurt. I had seen rags in the last couple of days. They'd stood out. "When you say oil, you don't mean deck stain, do you?"

"That's exactly what I mean. Next time you do a household project, be more careful on how you dispose of the supplies." He strode away, directing firefighters, shooing the lookie-loo neighbors who'd come out for some late-night, or was it early morning, entertainment.

"Katherine was staining her deck." It sent shivers down my spine. I'd discounted the idea that she was working with an accomplice, but she couldn't have set the fire personally. She was in custody. *Right?*

Kyle. I texted. *Is she under arrest? Do you have Katherine Sokol in custody?*

If he didn't, we were all still in danger. My phone remaining silent meant he was in an interrogation or wrestling a madwoman into the back of a police vehicle. How insane did you have to be to kill this many people, stalk an investigator, rifle through her house, then come back and set the place on fire?

I didn't have a handle on her psychology. She'd struck me as cold and calculating, not given to outbursts of passion. But the pieces added up, even if she didn't. She was on the Board of Loving Grace and Saving Grace. She'd been the accountant for a billion years. She understood the paperwork and how to obfuscate a trail—and she hated Bernie. Creating a pill mill in a rehab center was a work of genius. Killing everyone when you got caught the actions of a deranged mind. Thank goodness we'd stopped her before she got to Amber—I mean, Rest in Peace, Maria and LuAnn. Oh, gosh, and Candy—but at least one girl had been spared...I thought, anyway. God, I didn't even know that for sure.

Hannah steered me to the stairs and into Arlene's place, Floyd trotting dutifully at our feet.

"I need you to help me with Robyn," I whispered. "She knows where Amber is. We have to tell her it's safe to come out of hiding."

"Whatever you need, sis." She squeezed my shoulders and pushed me into the kitchen.

"Robyn?" Hannah went directly to the table and joined the girls. "We can let Amber know that the wicked witch has been apprehended."

'We,' she had said. 'We can let her know...' Hannah thought of herself as one of them, just as they did, and perhaps she was. She'd been a fatherless daughter, just as I'd been unmothered too soon.

Robyn shoved her chair back as she began texting, then stepped into the yard for privacy. Even now she didn't trust me to see what she was doing.

We all waited, eyes glued to her back. When she returned, she shook her head. "Not until Katherine's booked and behind bars."

"But she's alive?" I could barely breathe I was so relieved. "Amber's alive?"

Robyn nodded. "I told you she was safe before."

Trinity snorted. "We take care of ourselves, Kelly. If one of us needs to go to ground, we can do it."

Maria's death said they couldn't. LuAnn had been a fully grown woman, not a green girl, and she hadn't made it. Candy was safely in her own home, insulated by high gates and a cushion of wealth. That hadn't made any difference. Katherine had access and motive. There was nowhere she couldn't go and no corner of the city out of her reach. Money opens doors. If she put her mind to it—or had more time—she would find Amber eventually.

Arlene already had the coffee on. As soon as I was seated, she handed me a small jar of peanut butter—organic, low sodium, the "healthy" kind, but nonetheless PB. "Just this once," she said, "on account of the fire."

With a jar of PB in one hand and spoon in the other, I fought back tears of gratitude and got up and hugged her. "Thank you. Arly."

CHAPTER 26

I had the whole day ahead of me and things to move from my house and into Arlene's. Arlene had let Jeff know of the situation, and he'd keep Mitz with him for part of the day. With the smoke damage in the laundry room, black streaks up the stairway and the fancy charcoal swirls on the kitchen ceiling, not to mention the entire house having a barbeque gone wrong kind of odor in it, we wouldn't be staying at my place for a few days anyway.

An insurance adjuster would be out and he'd make a determination on what the true damage turned out to be. The insurance would be enough to put me up in a hotel, but with Floyd's need to stretch and Mitz staying with me for the next couple of nights, it made more sense to be at grandma's house.

Arlene was busy in the kitchen, humming away to herself. She'd already put out bagels and cream cheese, some jam and last night's peanut butter, along with a plate of ham and cheese for anyone who wanted to "go European" as Hannah called it. It was the first time Arlene and I had been alone since Trinity and Robyn had arrived. I grabbed a mug from the cup tree and sat myself down at the breakfast table. "Got a minute?"

"For you? Always." She took off her apron and joined me at the table, coffee in hand. She reached for a bagel and set about buttering it.

"Have you heard anything about Linda's desire to redo Jeff's house?"

She put down her knife. "Jeff said something about it recently. I am so glad you decided to talk to me about it. I know you don't like me getting in the middle of things between the two of you, but he did ask what I thought about it. And I have a feeling it wasn't the house you're taking issue with."

"You're right. It's redoing Mitz's room. How do you feel about it?"

"Well, Jeff is trying to make all of the women in his life happy at the moment. And that's no easy task."

He was balancing two worlds and I did feel for him on that level. "I do get that, but I get this weird sense that Linda is trying to take my place with Mitz." I grimaced. "I mean, it's just paint, but..."

"I understand what you're saying. But Linda is part of our lives now, whether we like it or not. Maybe she's just trying to fit in. Mitz does talk about you all the time. Whether it's rational on her part or not, Linda might feel threatened by that, too."

"I am Mitz's mother."

"Hmmm... Mothers take all kinds of forms. But I'll always have your back." She winked.

I looked at her as she took a bite of bagel. Mothers absolutely did come in all forms. Arlene had taken me under her wing, whether I'd embraced it or not, and now she was there for Hannah. She'd always be there for Mitz. She'd blossomed. She seemed less harsh, less judgmental, more in touch with her happy side—or was that me? Was I seeing her in a new light?

Jeff and I would need to have that talk, but Arlene had given me something to think about.

"Thanks, Arly," I said through a mouth full of bagel. "I appreciate your insight and your support."

We decided to let the girls sleep, but at nine I woke Hannah and the two of us hustled over to my smoke-damaged home to get some clothes. She was her usual, happy self. She was like my ex-mother-in-law that way—and me, I guess—we all wanted to feel wanted, useful, like we were doing something that made a difference.

"You taking *all* your shoes over to Arly's, I mean Arlene's?" Hannah said, standing with her hands on her hips staring inside my closet.

"Only a couple. I'll take those with me to the shelter."

"Nice." She tossed in a pair of boots I hadn't worn in a couple of years. "So, the case is wrapped?"

I yanked a couple of shirts out of the drawer to donate, and then put a couple in my overnight bag to take to Arlene's. "Maybe? I think so. I hope so. I'm not sure."

"What's left to do on it?"

My phone dinged. It was Hot Stuff.

YEO—that meant for your eyes only—*Her fingerprints were on Candy's phone. She's in custody. Can't say more at the moment.*

"Wow." I was allowed to tell Hannah, surely. She wasn't tied to the case or involved in law enforcement in any way. "They've got her dead to rights. Katherine Sokol has been arrested." I couldn't have been any happier if I had won the lottery. They'd cornered the wicked witch with concrete proof she'd been in Bernie's study around the time Candy had lost her phone. A good attorney would be able to throw all kinds of shade on that, but it was a start. It meant they'd investigate her at a minimum. "We've got to tell the girls."

We left the clothes and shoes and grime of my house and booked it back to Arlene's.

Robyn and Trinity were at the breakfast table, being waited on by a very smiley Arly.

"I have news." I plunked myself down at the table. "Katherine Sokol is now in police custody."

If they were happy it didn't show on their faces.

"Have they brought charges?" Robyn asked.

I had no idea, but was that really the point here? Amber could come out of hiding. "They have enough evidence to lock her up and throw away the key for a long time."

"She's rich," said Trinity. "She'll have lawyers. Good lawyers. Rich chicks like her don't do time."

I wanted to argue. But, Leona Helmsley and Martha Stewart notwithstanding, she was right, the rich often got a slap on the wrist rather than real time. "Can we tell Amber anyway?"

We all looked to Robyn—who only had eyes for Trinity. "What do you think? Shall we text her?"

Trinity shrugged. "We can't make the decision for her. Text her what we know and see what she says."

Once again, Robyn excused herself and went out back. I nibbled a slice of cheese while Hannah helped herself to a bagel with raspberry jam.

The back door opened. "She's asking who else has been arrested."

No one was, as far as I knew. It was day one, hour one, in terms of the investigation proper. I shook my head.

The back door closed and Robyn went back to tapping on her phone. There was some comfort in the fact that Amber was alive and well, but what information did she have that kept her hidden away? Teenagers weren't known for being savvy in that way. She had to be scared out of her wits to stay hidden for this long.

My stomach was a pit of knots, which could only be calmed by a spoon of PB. Before I'd even touched the lid, Arlene handed me a teaspoon. "Just a small one, okay?"

I put the spoon down on the table as a concession to her worries about my cholesterol and set to kneading Floyd's ears instead.

Robyn tapped on the window and beckoned Trinity outside.

It was worse than waiting for exam results back in high school, hoping against hope that we got the grades we needed to start the rest of our lives right.

Robyn and Trinity returned to the kitchen table, somber and silent.

"Well?" The jar of peanut butter was within reach. Not even Arlene frowning at me could stop me if I needed an emergency dose.

"She says to check the van. If it's still arriving, she can't come back."

"The van?" Floyd registered the change in my energy, his tail stiffening and his nose jutting up in the air.

"The one that brings the patients to Saving Grace."

I grabbed a jacket from the hall rack and made a beeline for Hannah's car. "Come, if you're coming," I shouted. I'd seen the van Amber was talking about that first day I'd emerged from the shelter and a few times since. She was telling me I'd missed a clue.

No one had joined me at the car by the time I had the keys in the ignition, which I took to be a no. I revved the engine and hit the gas.

I parked a good distance from the shelter and grabbed my backpack. My timing was perfect. About a block from Loving Grace, at the corner near the crosswalk, a van full of people passed. I was about to step out to go across the street when a hand gripped my bicep, sending my stomach to my feet.

"Barb," Ruth's screechy voice pierced my ear. I had no time to turn to the voice before she was at my shoulder, holding on tight. "They know, Barb. They know."

"Ruth," I said, stepping away to ease her grip. She held firm, digging into the meat. At least she hadn't attached herself to the arm that had taken the bullet in my first case. It had healed, but any pressure reminded me that the scar ran deep.

Panic was etched into her tired and lined face. Her graying black hair was greasy and stringy. "You have to go. Don't you see. If you don't, they'll hurt you. They'll hurt you like they do. Red, white and blue."

The phrase snagged in my brain. Robyn had written the same thing in her diary. Who said it first, the madwoman or the poet?

She might be mentally unbalanced, or downright crazy, but she clearly believed what she was telling me. "I do see."

The muscles around her eyes quickly relaxed, taking her from mad to sad. She released me and ran her rough fingers through my hair, her dry skin catching on the strands. Her hands smelled of roses and dirt. Her fingernails were yellow. "I missed you, Barb. Where have you been?"

She had to be seeing me as my mother. "I've been around, Ruth. Were you looking for me?"

As long as she kept talking I had the perfect cover. We looked like a couple of broads catching up.

The van had stopped in front of the rehab center and its occupants filed out and moved toward the front door. In the entranceway, where LuAnn had done her deal, a man in a white coat shepherded the beat and broken of Portland into the gloom of the detox center. I couldn't tell if it was Bow-Tie man, but I would have bet a fair amount on him being involved.

Were they getting the help Robyn boasted was available in Saving Grace or were they shipped in to boost numbers for the mill—or both? The paperwork would tell us. Bernie had all the proof he needed in his offices. All he had to do was read and the truth would be made clear.

Ruth's eyes filled with tears. "I tried to warn you before. Before you got in that car. You didn't listen. Why didn't you listen?"

My blood ran cold. News of my mother's death hadn't even made the five o'clock news eighteen years ago. But my mom must have at least passed through the shelter, despite Carla claiming ignorance and Katherine's claim that she didn't remember her. Or did she remember her and lie about it? My mother had processed that paperwork I'd found at the law firm... And Ruth was telling her/me that we needed to go... Had my mother stirred up trouble? Ruth sure seemed to think so. There was so much I didn't know about my mom.

"I was wrong not to listen," I said.

"You were." She shook her head. "But this time you have to. You have to go. Please don't ignore me."

"I won't."

She leaned in close and whispered. "I'm not what they look for. But you keep looking. And they see you looking."

She was more observant than she'd appeared. Had she seen me poking around? Or did she mean Barb? She must have. Had my mother been investigating something? Had the rehab center been a pill mill for decades? The hundreds of beds suggested it. "What do you mean you're not what they look for?"

She shook her head with vigor. "You know. I'm just a number. They don't see me. They see you, though."

I had to be careful not to lose her in case she could tell me more. "We used to spend time together, didn't we, Ruth?"

"Barb, enough already. We both know what's going on here. You tried to help me learn how to do things, but I'm not you. I can't see, no matter how hard I look. You're smart." She tapped her fingers against my temple. "I'm not smart."

"Yes, you are," I said. "You definitely are."

"You always say that." A small smile played at her lips.

It almost sounded like my mom had tried to teach her a skill. "Who is the *they* that is watching me?" I asked, refocusing her.

"She's on the board of direction..."

The blood froze in my veins. Even scattered, scrambled Barb knew that Katherine Sokol was the wicked witch.

"Ruth!" Nettie's voice, even from the other side of the road, made Ruth jump. She wrapped her arms around her torso and ran towards the shelter, even though it wasn't open for "guests." Perhaps Nettie was kind and let Ruth hide out there from time to time. I could hope for some small mercies, right?

I followed Ruth to the doors of Loving Grace. It was strange to think how little I'd understood about these women's lives just days ago.

"Oh, it's you." Nettie wasn't glad to see me—not one bit. "What are you doing here?"

"Could you spare me a minute?"

Nettie sneered. "I was busy before you butted your nose into our business, but now you've gone and got Gordon canned, I have to do it all myself. So, no, I don't have a minute."

I waited. She hadn't walked away. Curiosity killed the cat and while I didn't want to see anyone else die, it wouldn't hurt if Nettie was intrigued by what I had to ask her.

"Thirty seconds." She tucked her clipboard under her arm and fixed me with a stony stare.

"Amber..."

"Not you as well? I told the officer already. She was here. She ran away. We don't lock them in and throw away the key."

I hoped she meant *my* officer. If Kyle had been down here asking questions, we were headed in the right direction.

"Amber told her grandfather she knew something."

Nettie leaned on the doors to Loving Grace, waiting.

I picked my words carefully. If Nettie was involved with the pill mill, she would be even less inclined to tell me anything now that we'd started making arrests. "Amber was clean and sober."

Nettie nodded. Was that a smile I saw playing on her lips?

"She had gotten herself a job," I said.

"At Saving Grace, yes. She was proud of herself. She didn't just get sober, she got a life. Thought her grandfather would be proud of her at last. Made it worse when she took off."

"But why did she take off?"

Nettie shook her head. "They do. It just happens."

Her phone buzzed at her waist. "If there's nothing else?"

Time to gamble. "What's going on inside Saving Grace?"

Nettie's face folded in on itself. "No idea what you're talking about." She turned and let herself into Loving Grace where Ruth stood huddled by the doors.

I'd hit a nerve but had no idea whether it was a major hit or a small nick. Was she afraid or guilty, involved or merely suspicious? I needed someone who knew the ins and outs of the organization but whom I could trust. I knew just the woman. As I had a million times before, I scrolled through contacts and sent a text.

Any chance we could meet? I need to lean on you for info, if you don't mind. Backwoods in the Pearl, again?

I watched the dots pulse while she wrote her answer. *Crazy day with what's been going on. I'm putting some time in at work. How about offices at 6 PM?*

You're a peach, I said. And I meant it. It's good to have connections in the right places. It's even better to have friends.

CHAPTER 27

I texted Hannah, so she and Arlene wouldn't worry about me. There's a first time for everything.

Doing some surveillance at SG. Hannah was a smart cookie. She'd work out what the abbreviation meant. *Want to see if I can ID some of the other players Amber is afraid of so I can help Kyle nail Katherine.*

Kyle hadn't asked for my help, but he'd understand when I delivered it—bad enough that there were strangers who would do these women harm, but the fact that their own families had it in for them really got me.

Hannah wrote right back. *Smiley face. Heart. Heart. Rose. Evil face.* Whatever that meant. Emoji was another language, one I had begun to learn for my daughter's sake, but which I'd have to perfect if I planned on having a relationship with my half-sister...and I did. She'd arrived and made herself part of the family. I caught myself. She was family and had been all along. I just hadn't known for the first thirty years of my life and once I learned of her, I'd fought against it. I'd batted her back and downplayed her efforts but the truth of the matter was, she'd lost Floyd on accident. Anyone could have done that—even me. And without her, Robyn and Trinity wouldn't have stayed and talked to me. They'd have been in the wind. Hannah wasn't only a half-sister I had to learn to put up with, she was a friend I could rely on.

I stared at the emoji's for far too long then tapped in a couple I could get behind. *Heart. Dog.* Wishing there was a guide for these things, I lobbed another heart in there and hoped I was sending the message I wanted to send.

I hung around outside the rehab center for a couple of hours, taking notes. I spotted Bow-Tie man at a window, and Nurse Ratchet who'd treated me. There were a couple more faces that came and went, but it was clear the center itself wasn't where people went to get their fix. In all the time I'd been staking out this street, I'd never seen junkies heading for the front or back doors, just the van, delivering people. Based on what I knew, Katherine Sokol had set up a scam which required registered patients and once she had those, her people could order as many meds as they needed. I hadn't dug into the street value of a single dose of methadone, but it couldn't be cheap.

I'd forgotten to grab a bottle of water and Hannah's car didn't have a secret jar of peanut butter, which meant I was hungry, thirsty, and cranky by the time the van pulled around front and collected the "patients." I hadn't counted them going in, but given how crowded the van was once they'd taken their seats, no one had checked in for the night.

I snapped a couple of pictures and sent them to Kyle. *This is who they use. Street people are brought in, registered, maybe given a jar of vitamins, then driven back to their regular corners and shopping carts and city parks.*

He didn't answer and I didn't expect him to. He was in full homicide detective mode, which gave me the warm fuzzies.

My phone rang. Who rang anymore? Weren't we all about the texting? Well, Hannah, it seemed hadn't gotten that memo. "Yep?" I said.

"You'd better come home."

I squeezed my eyes shut. I'd only just gotten my head around the idea that I wasn't mad at her for losing my dog. "Floyd?"

"Um, no," she whispered. "Jeff's here. And Arlene is shouting at him. I think you need to get back here."

* * *

I used Hannah's Guide to Weaving Through Portland Traffic all the way to Arlene's and while I could never do that with anyone else in the car, swearing and swerving helped me blow off enough steam that by the time I got home, I was almost calm.

"Ladybug!" I signed as Mitz threw herself into my arms.

Her nose was still red, but she didn't have a fever. "I like your new friends, Mom," she signed. "Trinity showed me her tattoos."

Great. Just what I needed—my nine-year-old asking me if she could have a tribal tattoo around her bicep. "I'm glad you're having fun, Bug. Want to take Floyd for a walk with the girls?"

Mitz frowned. "Which girls?"

"Trinity and Robyn. They'd love to see Floyd's favorite places."

Mitz pulled a face. "They're not girls, Mama. They're women."

I laughed. She was right, of course. "Want to…"

Trinity stepped in, hands waving for 'I want to say something' and signed, "Mitz wants to know how to build a cardboard fort."

There was much I'd missed, including that Trinity knew sign language. How had they gotten to fort-building already?

"Grandma Arlene has some boxes in the basement, so if it's okay by you, Kelly, we'll head down there."

"Of course." I signed back. "I'll come join you after I've talked to Daddy." I signed to Mitz.

Mitz hugged me hard and bolted to the basement door with her new besties, Floyd flopping along behind them like he was in heaven.

Jeff and I took one look at each other and wordlessly decided to move our discussion next door.

* * *

"Homeless women?" he said, incredulous. He didn't even ask a question about who they were or why they were at his mom's place.

My jaw twitched. "Homeless, yes. But they're good girls. Women, I mean. They've fallen on hard times. It happens."

He bristled. "This is what I'm always concerned about with you. Linda said she thought it was better to remove some of your influence from our home, and I'm starting to think she's right."

My hackles went up with such lightning speed that my body felt like an electric jolt had raced through it.

"You're insane if you think this is okay," he continued. "They're *homeless*, Kelly. They could be into drugs, prostitution, and a dozen other criminal activities."

"You know nothing about them." I'd thought those same things only days earlier, but I'd already learned so much about my own preconceptions.

"I know you should have thought twice about bringing homeless people into our child's environment."

"These young women need a break. They're not criminals. They're not going to murder us in our beds or steal everything in the gun cabinet. We've given them a place to stay and something to eat. That's all."

"What about the fire at your place? You're going to tell me that wasn't their doing?"

It wasn't, but I didn't want to tell him that Katherine Sokol had hired someone to frighten me. The less he knew about this case, the better.

He wasn't done with me, though. He went on, detailing my failures. "How about the time you had an intruder in the backyard? Or the attack you had in your office? I don't even want to get started on how your case nearly killed my mother. All high risk and dangerous."

My head was dizzy from his list of my epic failures. And there was that insinuation again that I sought danger out. I had to admit, when the items I'd dealt with in the last couple of years were listed off like that, they made me look bad. They would look even worse if he knew the latest installment. "I get it, I do, but you changing paint and letting Linda run rough shod as my dad would say over everything I did in Mitz's room, is hardly the answer."

He blew out a breath. "I hadn't actually heard about that part. But my mom was none too happy."

Arlene wasn't kidding when she said she had my back, despite her call for me to see both sides. I stifled a small smile. "Well, I do get that Linda is the woman of your house now. I do. I just think Mitz needs to know I'm there too."

He sighed, relenting. "I agree. It's just—she's insecure and jealous of you."

His shoulders slumped. God we'd come so far in our ability to communicate these last couple of years.

His near confession had me taking pause. "I don't know why she'd be jealous. You and I have been over that one. We are far better friends...don't you think?"

"Of course, but try telling her that and I don't think it's entirely about us. It's just good old jealous, period."

It was such a weird place for me to be in; talking to my ex-husband about his girlfriend who had been my friend until she slept with my ex-husband. I should be the one having all the issues. Okay, I had plenty of my own. "Look, I'm clueless on what to say about all of this. Kyle probably gets jealous of you too sometimes. But we're going to have to figure it out. Mitz deserves that."

He didn't say anything after that. He sighed and walked out of the front door.

I followed him out as far as the driveway, but only watched him climb the stairs. Mrs. Galway, across the road, waved and smiled and went back to sweeping the sidewalk outside her house. We weren't all that different to the people in the Shantytown, gathering in our kitchens, sweeping our porches, navigating our lives.

I stepped back into my blackened house to take stock. Jeff wasn't wrong, but he wasn't right, either. My profession was dangerous. I took risks. Sometimes I paid a price for that, but not because of me. That's what he didn't understand. I was placed in dangerous situations because of *them*: the wicked people who were out for themselves, the selfish people who didn't extend their good fortune outside their tiny circle, the heartless people who would hound their own granddaughter to her grave to protect their own business empire. If someone didn't take a stand against evil, where would it end?

I had to set an example for Mitz and show her I was on the side of good. I'd never stop trying to do what was right.

Feeling both agitated and good about myself and my life choices, I decided to take a gamble and text Bernie. They had to have let him go by now.

Kelly Pruett, checking in. Got time to talk?

As I waited for a reply, I watched from the shadows as Jeff left Arlene's and made his way to his car. It sounded like Arlene had given him an earful. I knew what it meant to be on the wrong end of a tongue lashing from her.

My house. One hour. Bernie wasn't messing around.

I trotted next door and told Arlene where I was headed, how long I'd be, and what I was up to. This was followed by a text to Kyle with most of the same information so he didn't think I was stepping on his toes. Even this old dog could learn new tricks. Then I ran down the basement steps to update Mitz and Hannah and Trinity and Robyn about where I was headed. But they were far too happy to interrupt. It seemed the fort was going to be more of a castle than a box and a blanket and two chairs. Trinity had an Exacto knife and was making crenelations for the walkway next to the portcullis, apparently.

The drive to Bernie's place was somber. He'd just lost his wife. Not, not "just." He'd recently lost his wife to homicide and not some random killing that you might put down to drugs or alcohol or misadventure, but a calculated murder perpetrated by his ex-wife.

The gates to the property were wide open as was the front door.

"Bernie?" I didn't shout. That didn't seem respectful. I tiptoed into the foyer and spotted him on the modern side of the room, hugging Morgan's baby boy to his chest.

"He's barely said a word." Morgan appeared in the corridor that led to the kitchen. She had a bottle of milk in her hand. She tested it on her wrist.

I remembered those days. They went by so fast. How terrible that baby Thomas's life would be overshadowed by the death of his grandmother. He'd never know Candy, with her garish lipstick and tarantula hairdo and love of expensive jewelry. She was more than that and I knew it, but my mind was short-circuiting. I hadn't known the woman. I'd met her twice and in passing. She was probably a lovely human being who'd adored her grandchild.

"Grandpa," she said, loud enough to get his attention, but gently enough that I knew that something new had started in this household. Morgan had made her peace with her mother's husband. "Want to give Thomas his bottle?"

Bernie spotted me over Morgan's shoulder. "I don't want the little man to hear this." He stood and handed his grandson to Morgan. "You feed him and I'll be back as soon as I can."

I followed Bernie to the other side of the house, but he didn't enter the formal living room. They'd thrown sheets over Katherine's furniture, declaring an end to her reign.

"She's denying everything," he said. "Katherine insists that she doesn't run a pill mill. Never harmed Amber. Doesn't know where she is." He rubbed his face.

"There's proof, Bernie. It's all there in the paperwork. She's not going to be able to wiggle out of this one, no matter how hard she tries."

He looked at me with such hope and despair that I wanted to wrap my arms around him and squeeze some love into those tired bones of his. But I had good news. "Amber's alive."

He broke. He cupped his hand over his mouth and wept as if he were the baby and not Thomas. "You're sure?" he said when he gained his composure.

All I knew was what Robyn had told me, but she wouldn't lie.

"Where is she?" he asked.

That was the million-dollar question. Where was she? "She's waiting until everyone involved has been caught and put behind bars."

"I didn't keep her safe. I couldn't. I..." Bernie slid into a dining chair, inconsolable. He'd lost his sister to drugs, his wife to violence, and his granddaughter didn't believe he could protect her from her own grandmother. He was right to grieve.

I waved at Morgan on my way out and snuck to my car, my heart heavy and my mind buzzing with questions. How you lived your life had consequences. Bernie had built a charitable empire, but lost touch with his own granddaughter. He'd lost the one while trying to save the many.

I sat in the driveway for a few minutes, my own life flashing in front of my eyes. Was I Mitz's safe place or was Jeff right, was I only a hazard where she was concerned? Did I bring stability or chaos? Was her world safer because I was out here crusading for other people's lives?

An hour ago, I'd been certain of the answer to those questions, but the truth was, I wasn't sure. Once this case was over, I'd have to do some serious thinking.

CHAPTER 28

At five minutes to six, I parked a block away from the law offices of Baumgartner & Sokol.

The building was quiet but the door was locked when I arrived. I used the key Carla had loaned me to go in. The reception area was deserted and all the lights were out.

"Carla," I hollered, but didn't get a response. I peeked down the hall. Her office was illuminated. I headed that direction. "It's Kelly."

I'd been in these offices at least a hundred times over the years. But the only time I'd seen it this quiet was when I'd engaged in a little felonious action myself. The silence had a skitter going across my skin.

My nerves weren't calmed when I reached Carla's office. It looked like a hurricane had blown through. There were files and papers everywhere. She'd said it was nuts at Baumgartner & Sokol and this backed her claim. Looked like Kyle and Enloe had been here and done a blitz raid on her office. I could only imagine what upstairs looked like where all the boxes relating to Loving Grace and Saving Grace were located.

I had a warm sense of accomplishment that started in my belly and spread far and fast. I'd made that happen. I'd broken a major drug ring, albeit over the counter and borderline white collar. If Amber hadn't gone missing and Bernie hadn't hired me, that dirty business could have gone on for decades longer. The debate about whether I was a force for good or bad waged inside me, but I was tipping heavily towards "good."

Carla had handwritten notes everywhere. I focused the light on one where she had signed her name: long strong strokes, loops, a flip at the end of her T, and a quasi-Elizabethan swirl for the final L. I moved the paper to one side. She had a notepad covered in signatures. She'd been practicing. She needed to get that downstroke just right. The flip at the end of the T was distinctive. She'd been signing documents. The T was for Tony, Bernie's business partner, but it was the L at the end of Sokol that was the giveaway. She'd been signing Bernie's name, but way at the back of the pad was where I discovered the shocker. Katherine's name appeared on page after page of practice signatures. They'd arrested the wrong woman. I fumbled for my phone, brought up "favorites" and chose Hot Stuff.

I'm at Baumgartner's office and I need you here now.

That knowledge hit me in my gut. I did need him. For the first time since I'd taken on the PI gig I knew I needed Kyle. Real bad. I'd often felt adamant about going it alone and proving my metal and being one of the boys and measuring up to the memory of my father. Even though I'd made vast improvements by including him in this case, and even Hannah, I'd swallowed the theory that "doing it alone" was the true measure of strength. Sometimes real strength was realizing you needed help and you consciously chose not to be a one-woman band.

"Hey?" Carla stood in the doorway, grinning. She was glassy eyed and swaying. Was she drunk, high, both? "How you doing?"

"Great." The sweat had already gathered under my armpits and spread down my shirt.

She chuckled, low and steady. "You never were good at acting."

"Acting?"

She grimaced. "We both know why you're here."

My heartbeat quickened. "Yeah. Remember, we had an appointment to talk? Let's go for coffee. My treat."

She pulled a small revolver out of her cross-over bag. "I don't think so."

"What the hell? What's wrong with you? Carla? Tell me what's going on."

Her hand shook, but that didn't do me much good. It was a small room and we were at close quarters. If she decided to take me out, I was a goner.

"Hand me your purse."

OMG, I had trusted her. She'd told me to go after Katherine and I'd done it. Whatever line of BS she was selling, I'd been buying because of our professional relationship all those years.

"Your purse. Now. I know you carry. Hand it over."

She was aware of my history and should be concerned that I wouldn't go down quietly. I gathered my thoughts. I had to figure a way out of here. I put my bag on the desk, wishing I hadn't taken my gun out of my jacket earlier, but didn't slide it her way. "Wow. Okay. You want to tell me what this is about?"

I'd never seen such a cold look in her eyes before, but it left no doubt she would pull the trigger. "Stop with the bullshit, please."

I gulped. We were beyond lies and pretense now. "You set Katherine up. You're the one running the pill mill. You sent me after Katherine so you could…" What did she want? What was her end game? "So you could get away. You're wrapping this up and…" My brain scrambled for answers. If she'd been doing this for decades, she was a very rich woman. She could go wherever she wanted. Then again, if she'd been doing this for decades, she'd been rich for a long time, too. Why run now? Why implode and go on a killing spree? What had changed? "Why, Carla? Tell me why. I want to understand."

She shook her head. "You really have no idea, do you?"

"I know you were sending homeless women to the shelter to line the pockets of the rehab center. You also recruited people from the parks and streets and drove them directly to Saving Grace. You registered them and used their details to allow Mr. Bow-Tie to order meds. I've seen this all myself…"

She laughed and aimed her piece at me. "Wrong track, chick. Sorry. Wrong track, wrong train, wrong carriage. And this is the end of the line."

"All you need is some names and social security numbers, right? And a doctor who'll prescribe stuff. Did Katherine even know? Did Bernie?"

"Oh please, Bernie's in his own world. He thinks everything revolves around his pain. Typical man. Woe is me, my sister died. Woe is me, my marriage ended. Woe is me, Amber's in trouble. Boo hoo. Cry me a river." She waved me away from her desk with the barrel of her gun. "Of course, Katherine is a different matter altogether. Katherine is a very smart lady."

They were in it *together*? Then why had she sold Katherine out? Had they had a fight?

"So, it's you and Katherine?"

She waved the gun in the air. "Was. Past tense. I loved Katherine like a mother. She got me off the streets, helped me get sober, and got me a job. She was the one who inspired me to stay on the straight and narrow. Said I was like the daughter she'd never had. Kept an eye on my career." Her lip curled. "All bull, of course. When former-hubby Bernie went begging, she folded. Couldn't even keep her mouth shut for one more week. That's all we needed. If that bitch granddaughter of hers hadn't…"

"Amber?" I yelped. "You threatened Amber? She's in hiding because of you?"

Carla wiped the beads of sweat off her forehead. *High. Definitely high.*
"I never had to. Once Maria bit the big one, Amber got the message."

The woman was insane. She'd killed Maria to warn Amber off whatever
she'd uncovered. "What did Amber do anyway. Work out what you were
doing when she was working at Saving Grace?"

She shrugged.

For years I'd worked alongside Carla. But right under my nose, and
those of everyone around her, she'd been plotting and stealing and lining
her own pockets. She'd been sizing us all up for what she could take from
us. "What now? You planning to shoot me?"

"Oh hon, no. You were so cut up about the case, you hung yourself."

"Like Candy?"

She chuckled. "Except you, my dear, foolish friend, are going to
voluntarily put that noose around your neck in the bathroom. I've already
taken the liberty of writing out your suicide note."

My jaw clenched with images of Candy blue and rotating from the fan.
"You really believe some would buy that?"

"You've been a lone ranger for so long, and with the grief of your father
dying and all these poor girls dropping like flies, they'll buy it." Her pupils
were blown. I had no idea what kind of drugs she'd taken, but she was so
high she barely knew what she was doing.

"No one will believe for one minute that I would take my own life. I
love Mitz too much."

"Ohhh...." Her smile was crooked and broken, her breath ragged and
stuttering. "Mommy loves her baby." She took a step closer her voice rising
as she did. "She loves her so much she works all the hours god sends and
never sees her. You're out on the town, talking to criminals and tracking
down leads, when you should be reading her a bedtime story." She slammed
the butt of her gun into the wall making me jump.

I didn't waver from my conviction. Despite my profession, no one
could ever question my love for my Ladybug above all other things. I'd
never kill myself. Never. "They won't believe you, Carla. You might be
someone no one cares about, but I have people who love me and know
how I tick. If I am found hanged and you leave some cheesy note in your
forged handwriting—nice calligraphy, by the way—they'll hunt you to the
ends of the Earth and string you up like a pinata."

Her eye twitched and she hesitated. Thinking. "You could be right.
Hanging you might not be the best option. Too similar. Move. Out the
door." I walked past her, the tip of her gun brushing my ribs. I'd have

grabbed it if I thought I could survive a gunshot to my stomach. I stood in the hallway. She waved the gun to the right.

I walked down the hallway. We were going to the Shanghai tunnels. "How much did my mother figure out?" I asked. If Carla and Katherine had been doing this a long time, it made sense. But the question made my chest tighten. I wasn't sure I wanted the answer.

She laughed so hard I thought she might pee herself. That was my answer. My mother had likely sensed something. That's why Ruth had told her they knew...and yet she'd never said a word to my father. He'd been so caught up in his grief after her car accident, he hadn't even questioned if there was anything weird about how or why she died.

I would have to think about this later. Right now, I had to get out of here—alive. Carla's plan was flawed. The grate at the other end of the tunnels opened out into freedom. "Make sure you close the door behind us," I said.

She snorted. "I know what you're thinking, but I planned for every contingency." The gun was snug against the small of my back. "That's why I went ahead and bought a new padlock, just for you."

It was now or never. I had to make a run for it. She was high and drunk and something had happened between her and Katherine. Her world was imploding. I didn't need to be around for the final, cataclysmic bang. I opened the door and in one motion threw myself down the iron-rung steps, hands slipping and sliding and barely keeping me on track, then I hit the ground running.

"Oh, Kelly," came from above. "Kell-eeeeeeeee."

I didn't stop, although I had no idea where to go in the dark.

The flash of light said she was using her phone to find her way, just as I had done the night before. "For God sakes Kelly, you're going to die in here anyway. There's no way out. Didn't you hear me? I've secured all exits. You're the rat and I'm the rat catcher. You're in my maze. And I'm going to end you this time."

Her analogies were past the point of annoying me. I found an old wood wheelbarrow and ducked behind it. I grabbed my phone out of my jacket, thankful I hadn't put it in my purse along with my gun too. *No bars*. The bricks and the building above blocked reception.

Carla's footsteps crunched in the dirt and rock. I tucked my phone back in my pocket. "There's no way out, Ms. Kelly. The tunnel ends in about twenty-five yards. Don't you think I know this place like the back of my hand?"

I ignored her, frantically looking around for a weapon in the dark. Using the touch method, I found a couple of bricks. I'd almost tripped on them going in and now I would use them to take her out. Throwing them at her wouldn't work to take her down though. I had to use the element of surprise. The tunnel was pitch black, but with her phone lighting the way, I could track her movements, while she couldn't see mine.

Hiding behind the wheelbarrow would be too obvious if she knew the tunnel as well as she said she did. I stood and flattened myself tight against the wall, holding my breath.

She was close, close enough that I could smell the alcohol on her breath. "For God's sake, come out here and die like your mother, will you?"

My brain snapped. I hadn't wanted to put the two pieces together, but I had known Carla was involved the moment I'd figured out my mother knew. Any hint of restraint, any lingering hint of friendship I'd once felt for Carla, exploded into rage.

I raised the brick above me and with every ounce of energy I had, slammed into her, crushing the rock right into her skull. The gun flew out of her hand ahead of her. I picked up the other brick and crashed it against her forehead for good measure. The level of fury that rippled through me scared me half to death.

Gritting my teeth, a violent tremor rattled me. I believed her when she said she'd killed my mother. She'd changed everything about my life. My breath stuck in my throat.

I backed off and stood over her body. I wrapped my arms around myself but couldn't get warm. She lay motionless. I hoped I hadn't killed her—I wanted her to face her accusers, stand trial, do time—but I couldn't bring myself to check her for a pulse to find out.

Turning on my cell flashlight, I found the gun and secured it in my waistband. Shaking, I moved back to the doorway where I dropped onto the stoop between the offices and the tunnels. My breathing ragged, my heart tight, my whole being split to the core. I managed to call the police and an ambulance. When I hung up, I cried at all that had been lost—and all that had been found.

I called Kyle. This time he answered.

* * *

The ambulance came. The police arrived. Detective Enloe didn't even give me the third degree. I was cleared of all charges in connection with LuAnn's death. Carla, it seemed, had been a busy girl.

Hannah-banana, I texted, *tell Robyn we've got them. All of them this time. Amber can come home, now.*

The dominoes would fall. Carla had been working with Katherine for decades. Bow-Tie Man would to be implicated—how could he not be—along with the senior nurses at Saving Grace. Whether Nettie and Gordon were pill pushers or not remained to be seen, but with the full force of the Portland PD, no one would go un-scrutinized.

My phone lit up. Robyn. *Shantytown. Meet us there.*

I grabbed Kyle's sleeve. "Do you need me to stay here?"

"I'm on duty, hon. And I plan to interrogate Carla as soon as I'm able."

I stood on my tippytoes and kissed him. "Love you, Hot Stuff, but I've got to run."

"Let them check you out first." He motioned towards the back of the ambulance. I knew what he wanted of me, but I didn't have time. Amber was coming out of hiding. I needed to be there.

"As soon as I get back." I hurried toward the door and looked back. "I promise. They can take me in and check my tonsils and whatever they want then, but I have to go. This is what it's all been about." I pushed open the door. "She's alive. She's safe. We're going to get her now."

* * *

I booked it all the way to Oregon City, singing at the top of my lungs. Terrible things had happened over the last few weeks: Maria had been killed to frighten Amber. Carla had tried to silence me when I was tracking LuAnn. LuAnn had died trying to protect the girls (sorry, Mitz, women). Amber had gone into hiding. Candy had died. Who knew what she'd stumbled into? Maybe we'd find out, maybe we wouldn't. Katherine would have powerful lawyers on her side and they'd throw Carla to the wolves the second proceedings got underway.

But Amber was alive. She'd been smart. She'd hidden herself away and her friends had covered for her and she'd managed, somehow, to stay invisible while I worked my way through the insanity that Carla and Katherine had wrought. An insanity that had included my mother. I would have to reconcile that…but later.

It was pitch dark by the time I reached the tent city. Hannah had accompanied Robyn and Trinity in Trinity's car. I was so relieved Arlene was not there. She was taking care of Mitz in her box fort. How lucky was I?

"You good?" Hannah slung her arm around me.

"I'm fantastic." I meant it. That one girl didn't have to live the rest of her life in the shadows was everything to me in that moment. I'd battled to find Amber. If it hadn't been for my sister, I might never have found her. I hugged Hannah. We were sisters in arms, at last. The tears made my nose fizz. My dad, no, OUR dad, might have been stunned at how it all transpired, but I also believed he would have treasured this moment.

"Stay here." Robyn issued an order rather than a request. She and Trinity wove through the darkened outdoor city, greeting toothless, grimy, bedraggled humans like long-lost friends. Towards the far edge of the camp, they ran into the Wall of Muscle who'd protected Robyn when I'd come looking for her. He scooped Robyn off her feet and twirled her around a few times then did the same with Trinity.

The flap to his tent opened and a young woman peered out. The way she squealed when she saw Robyn and did a running dive at her friend, catching her around the middle, left no doubt that she was Amber.

The three of them, girls on the brink of womanhood with everything to look forward to, linked arms and made their way towards me and Hannah.

I was so relieved and excited and overwhelmed and grateful that I could barely speak. "Bernie…" was all I managed before I broke down.

"Papa never gave up on me," said Amber. "He built a place where Grace could find refuge but when my life fell apart, it caught me."

Wow. She'd given that some thought. He'd be out-of-his-mind happy when he heard that. "Want to go see him?"

"Yeah," she nodded. "I do."

The girls piled into my Ford, while Hannah navigated Trinity's car behind me. The ride back to Bernie's place was full of chatter and stories and gasps and tears. Floyd got top billing, of course, but Hannah and Arlene had made a decent impression, too.

"They're not bad," said Trinity. "For civilians. Hannah, especially, gets it. She lived in a place like this up in Seattle."

I hadn't known that about my sister. In fact, I knew precious little about her life. I'd been so focused on my own hurt that I'd failed to consider hers. That would change.

"Mitz is super cool." Robyn was bubbly, enthusiastic. She'd lost that veneer of cool that she'd had since I first met her. "She wants to be a vet."

My lovely girl. My heart burst with pride. Of course she did. She'd always had a soft spot for animals and making things whole again, nursing them back to health, was the perfect way for her to express her sweet nature.

"She's going to open the first interpretive veterinary hospital for the deaf, but it won't only be for the hearing impaired. She's going to treat the throw away animals and raise consciousness around deafness, blindness, chronic conditions, and…"

I had to pull over I was sobbing so hard. Not because Mitz had shared this with them before she'd shared it with me, but because the best thing in my life was turning into the best thing in the world: Mitz forever, forever and ever and ever.

CHAPTER 29

We hung at Bernie's for at least an hour while Amber dished dirt on Carla and Katherine's empire. "It's not just a pill mill," she said. "That's peanuts compared to the real operation."

"Real operation?" Bernie hung on her every word.

"They were scamming Medicaid." Robyn waved her card in Bernie's general direction. How I hadn't managed to work that out was nuts. I'd seen the paperwork. Known they were registering patients. I was so focused on the street crime I'd been oblivious to the wholesale theft of benefits.

"They bring people from all over the city," Amber said. "Different people every day of the week. They bus them in, register them, then use their information to bill the State."

Bernie paced the room, angry and anxious and beating himself up, just like me. "Was Gordon in on it?"

Amber jiggled baby Thomas on her knee. "They were all in on it in some way, Papa. That's why I had to lie low. Once I told LuAnn what I knew, it wasn't safe for me."

Bernie groaned. "Why didn't you come home?"

Amber shrugged. I knew what she meant, but I prayed Bernie didn't. Candy had died in this very house. She hadn't been safe from Carla's reach.

"Red, white and blue," said Robyn, "let them do what they do."

I swung around to face her. "You knew and didn't tell me?"

"I told you as much as I knew. I mean, I didn't know every little thing," she barked. And despite that, she had helped me. She'd brought me her card, wrapped around her bottle of vitamins, and pushed it right in my face. She'd told me without telling me. I'd missed it. But perhaps my not knowing had kept Amber safe.

Eventually, Hannah and I left them to their chatter and made our way home.

Arlene and Mitz had taken their blankets and comforters down to the basement and made themselves a bedroom inside the fort. I ran my hand over Mitz's hair, careful not to wake her. "I love you, Ladybug. I'm so proud of who you are. I hope you know that. I just love you."

I slept in the chair where I could see her and dreamed of her bandaging up the lost and broken and setting them back on their paths.

* * *

Just as we had hoped, Katherine was charged, and Carla racked up multiple counts between her involvement, attempted murder for setting my house on fire, and the actual murders of LuAnn and Candy. Bow-Tie man and Nurse Ratchet were arrested. Nettie faced criminal prosecution, as did Gordon. Bernie was busy down at the shelter, interviewing new staff and trying to keep the place running. Someone from above was watching for him to even be alive. Carla had really come for him that night—but found Candy instead. Hoping it would take him away from investigating any further, she'd figured killing his wife would be the next best thing.

My friend Jessica had offered to help at the shelter while they found their feet and I've never seen a man so grateful to find a smart, hard-working, big-hearted woman to sort the wheat from the chaff and set up new processes and procedures to keep Loving Grace operating as a genuine haven for the people who'd fallen through the cracks.

But with the case in the hands of the police, I was at a loose end.

How do you start over, find a new way forward? My house was under repair. And thanks to Carla, my ability to trust women was hobbled, but not destroyed. I had too many good women in my life for that to occur. But the terrible truth of what had happened to my mother—murdered for doing exactly what Amber had done and what I had tried to do—had all those emotions I'd crammed down for years, bubbling like hot lava through the Earth's crust.

Kyle and I had gone for a cup of coffee and were just heading back home when he reached his hand over and squeezed my leg. "You going to be okay?"

I rested my hand over his. "Eventually." Carla's revelation about what she did to my mom had me out to sea. She hadn't had a car accident. Barbara Pruett, my mother, had been murdered. It was like losing her all over again.

Even worse, Crazy-Ruth had known something terrible was headed in their direction, which meant my mom had to be scared when she went out to that final meeting—whatever that was. We would never know. Not unless Carla traded long-lost secrets for time off her sentence. The hardest part was that my father, so engrossed in his detective work, had missed it. He'd failed to pay attention to the people who loved him and lived with him every day. While my mother clearly hadn't shared her suspicions either, the whole thing made me sad, and yet on some level proud that I'd found the truth—something my father hadn't done.

Whether I'd understand more of what happened again hinged on Carla's willingness to talk. A part of me wished she would. I longed to learn what my mother had been like during that time, what she'd been doing, whether she'd thought of me in her final minutes. I'd had her as a kind of "passive mom" figure all these years, but she was anything but. She was a firecracker who broke the case before anyone even knew there was a case to crack. The tears rolled down my face and dripped into my lap.

"You did a great thing." Kyle rested his hand on my leg. "You saved scores of lives, not just Amber's."

"I'm not sure about that." We both knew what was bugging me. I'd rumbled Carla, but hadn't uncovered the whole operation. Amber had been the one to fill us in on that. I'd been over it so many times in my mind since that night, but at the end of each cycle I came to the same conclusion: "I wasn't the hero of this piece, the girls were."

Kyle yanked the car to curb and idled. "Okay, enough of that." He reached for my face and searched it. "You stopped an entire machine that's been taking advantage of the homeless and the system for years. You stopped a supply of fentanyl patches from hitting the street. You brought Maria's killer to justice. And LuAnn's. You found Amber and gave her back to her family. Do you have any idea how many lives you saved?"

"If Carla survives to stand trial."

"She will. Her concussion was traumatic, not devastating."

I sighed and kissed him. "I thought I might have killed her when she told me to die like my mother."

"Well, you didn't and she's well enough that she's already trying to throw Katherine under the bus for the entire thing. She and Katherine had a falling out when Amber went underground. They'd been a team for two decades—scamming Saving Grace and splitting the proceeds, 70-30 in Katherine's favor—but the wicked witch drew the line at Carla wanting to kill her granddaughter."

"Katherine was definitely involved? We've proven that?"

He nodded, fast and emphatic. "Up to her eyeballs. Part of what Carla told you was true. Katherine was desperately jealous of Bernie's life—first of his career, and Grace, and then the divorce and Candy. I think she only got cold feet once the bodies started to hit the floor."

"There's so much to unpack. I'm having trouble wrapping my head around it."

"Yeah, it's complicated, but there's a paper trail." Kyle kissed my hand, then my cheek, then my lips. "Because of you."

I returned the kiss with enthusiasm. "I do love you."

"And I love you. Maybe soon we can make that more official."

I smiled. "Why Hot Stuff, is that a proposal?"

He smiled back. "Would the answer be yes?"

"It might be."

He laughed—only the second-best sound that had ever hit my ears next to Mitz's laughter. "Good to know," he said. "You ready to go home?"

"Actually," I said, "I need a detour. Would you drive me to Vancouver?"

* * *

I'd just watched an entire family collapse under the weight of their past. It was time to set mine right. No more misunderstandings or holding each other at arms-length. We might not be a family in the traditional sense, but we all loved Mitz. She loved her daddy the way I had loved mine: without reservation. She loved Mommy Linda and her new little brother, Seth. I wasn't so small-minded or petty that I didn't see that or would take that away from her.

But there had to be another way to heal this rift between us. Afterall, we shared a similar view of each other. Maybe we could find some common ground. And I knew Linda would be home.

Kyle waited in the car.

I rang the bell. Linda answered. She was by herself. There was no Jeff and no child on her hip. The baby was napping. "Can we talk?"

She wrapped her arms around herself and stepped out onto the porch. "Sure."

I'd rehearsed what to say. Now the words clutched in my throat. I swallowed. "You know, Linda, you have a lot going for you. You always have. You've always been pretty, and smart, and now you have this beautiful son and you and Jeff look like you're doing great together."

Linda looked away as I spoke.

"Truth is, I was always envious of you," I said.

Linda rolled her eyes.

"It's true. Things have always come easy for you."

She shook her head. "My God, why would you even say that? You've always been the cute and smart one. Way smarter than I could ever be."

"Right." I didn't believe her.

"You are. Look at you now. You're self-employed. You had a dad who loved you fiercely. You're independent."

"You had a lot of that too. And now you have a new family. Jeff is happy. Mitz adores you. So why this need to change everything about the house? Everything about Mitz's room?"

"Because I feel like I'm living in your shadow. Always being compared. Not being good enough."

That information slammed into my chest with so much force it nearly stepped me back. "My shadow?"

"Yes, your shadow. It's clear Arlene prefers you. Mitz talks about you all the time, which I get. You're her mother. But you are a Goddess to her. I will never be able to compete with that."

"Linda, I've been on that merry-go-round." I had. I'd been riding it for years with my father and only now felt like the spinning had stopped. "Don't do that to yourself. Or to me. You need to be you. Arlene is a big softy once you've spent time with her. And Mitz has a huge capacity for love. Don't compare us. We'll each have a place in Mitz's heart." The words pushed emotion into my throat, but I believed them to the core. "There's a place in there for all of us."

"How? You clearly hate me? I've felt it every time we've been around each other."

"Do you feel it now, Lin?"

She drew in a breath. "No."

"That's because I stopped hating you a long time ago."

Tears formed in her eyes.

My heart flooded. "Oh, Lin, we'll make it all work. Come here." I grabbed her into a hug, realizing how much I'd missed my friend and how very much alike we were in this moment. There had been so much pain between us. But we'd created a struggle that didn't need to be there. It was time to heal the wounds of the past and move on.

After a long moment, we stepped back from each other a weight that I'd held onto for the last couple of years lifting.

"I've got to go," I said. "And truly, I get it. It is time for you to make that home yours. But do it for the right reasons. Don't make it about me."

She nodded, a small smile crossing her face. "Maybe we could redo Mitz's room together?"

"I'd like that," was all I managed before I had to make a run for the car. I slid into the seat next to Kyle, and texted Jeff.

I have a proposition for you. If you can come for dinner tomorrow night at your mom's, I'd appreciate it. And bring the family.

A minute later. *Sure.*

* * *

The next night, I sat on Arlene's porch waiting for Jeff, Linda and Seth to arrive.

The whole gang was inside: Mitz, Kyle, Arlene, Hannah, Robyn, Trinity, Amber, Bernie and Detective Kuni jostled for room in the kitchen as dish upon dish was conjured out of nowhere.

Until the fire department released my house in a few more days, I would be staying in Arlene's downstairs bedroom. Mitz had one upstairs next to Grandma's room…which was perfect since Arlene liked to read to Mitz, like my dad used to read to her, and to me.

Bernie had insisted that Robyn and Trinity move in with them until they got back on their feet. Amber seemed pretty darned happy to have people her age in the house.

Things were working out all over the place. There was just one more wrinkle to smooth out and life would be pretty fine.

Jeff pulled up and he and his family got out. He escorted them up the stairs.

"Hey, Lin," I said as she passed by me with Seth on her hip.

"Hi, Kel," she said.

"Behind you in a minute," Jeff said and we watched as Linda and Seth disappeared inside.

We took a seat and I remembered how much I'd loved Jeff at one time. Perhaps if we'd been older when we married it would have all been different: if I hadn't had so much to prove, if I'd had a mother to guide me? I'd had all these thoughts swirling around my head since my talk with Linda. What would it have been like if I'd had that gentle, motherly presence in my life for a few more years?

I didn't want Jeff back. That marriage was over and done and Kyle and I were moving in the direction of forever. But I did want to mend any torn fences for Mitz's sake.

We sat in silence for a long minute.

"I spoke with Linda yesterday," I finally said.

"She told me. You really okay with her renovating the whole house?"

"It's not my house anymore. It's yours and Linda's, and Mitz and Seth's now. Your family. Your home."

He nodded.

"But I'm hoping you and I are good, too. You came at me hard about the homeless girls being here, and my previous cases."

"Didn't think it mattered what I thought."

"Of course it matters. And the thing is, it's not good for Mitz to feel the tension."

"Agree. I apologize," he said without hesitation.

My eyebrow arched.

"Really. I mean, I can't promise I won't have a reaction to these different situations that arise, but maybe if we talk about it more, communicate, we can be better."

"Apology accepted." I leaned back in the bench. "And I like that. Communication will be everything."

"Who would have thought we'd get to this place?"

"I hoped. I was never sure. But it's time to keep moving. As for my profession, well, that might be changing a bit. Bernie has offered me an in-house investigator position at his firm, and I'm going to take it."

"You're giving up your father's office?"

"I am. I've been thinking about it for a while. It's time I quit trying to be someone else." I had been living under my father's shadow for far too long. "I'm even thinking I'll hire Hannah to help me part-time when I need it."

Jeff laughed and bumped me with his shoulder. "You never do things by halves do you? You're all in, all the time."

He was right about that. But I had plans to do it differently this time. I wouldn't be "all in" like my dad. I would be "all in" like my mom *and* my dad. I was the daughter of Barbara and Roger Pruett, not just Daddy's little girl. As much as I loved my father, I did not want to do it the way he had.

"I think your dad would be really proud of you right now."

I smiled. "I think he would be too."

"So, what's this proposition you spoke of?" he said.

"I was thinking about your upcoming trip to Disneyland. Mitz is really excited to hang out with Mickey Mouse, and I wondered what you'd think about us all going…as a family."

"Like everyone?"

"Yes. Arlene and Kyle are already on board. I don't want to ever miss out on Mitz's first. Arlene feels the same way. It would be a great way for her to get to know Seth and Linda. And it would be good for Mitz to see us united." I was asking a lot. "I mean, talk to Linda, but if it's okay, I think it would be fun."

He reached out and squeezed my hand. "I already know her answer. It's a great idea."

I nodded, that damn frog hopping back into my throat. I might have to give him a room he'd shown up so often lately.

"You going to tell Mitz?" he asked. I looked at my ex-husband—someone I'd known since I was just a child, someone to whom I would be forever tied. Kyle might very well be my future, but Jeff would forever hold my past along with our shared love of our beautiful daughter. I smiled. There really was healing when it came to family. "Why don't we tell her together."

We stood to go in, but Kyle came out. Jeff nodded at him and went inside.

"We off to Disney?" he said.

"We are."

He brushed my hair away from my face and planted a kiss on my lips. "You're a good woman, Ms. Pruett," he said.

"I did okay, didn't I?"

"You did. You brought some peace into the family, and you brought home two girls and helped solve two murders. Enloe says you can't teach instinct. Maybe you should seriously think about joining the force."

I searched his face and then laughed. "Let's not go crazy."

"That's what I said." He kissed me again. "Ready? They're waiting for you."

We made our way into the kitchen where we were met with champagne and cheers.

Arlene, with Seth on her hip and Mitz at her side, handed me a jar of peanut butter and a spoon—not the healthy kind—the full-fat, full-salt, yummy kind I liked best. "To the greatest daughter-in-law anyone could ever wish for." She raised her glass.

The room exploded in cheers.

"To a great investigator," Kyle shouted.

"As good as her old man," said Bernie.

"To my friend," Linda said.

"And a great sister."

Oh my god, my face burned with embarrassment so much I thought I might die.

"You did good," said Jeff. "Look at her."

Mitz was reading lips but also getting simultaneous translations from Trinity.

Amber raised her glass. "Here's to never giving up on us. Even though so many others had."

"Here, here!" They crowed. "Here, here."

Mitz turned to me and signed, "To the best mommy in the world."

It was then that I knew everything would be alright.

EPILOGUE

"Ruth?" I'd been waiting outside the shelter since dawn. As soon as I saw her hunched shoulders and her stringy hair, I knew it was her.

"Barb!" she said, sprinting over the road with her skinny little chicken legs, hands grabbing for mine. "You're safe. You're safe. They told me your car went off the road, but you're safe." She hugged me tight.

"I have someone I want you to meet, Ruth." I waved at my car. A young man cautiously made his way down the sidewalk.

Ruth peered into his face and reached out a hand. "I know those eyes."

"That's right, Ruth." I wanted to take this slow. I had no clue about what she remembered or what she'd forced herself to forget.

"This is Anthony."

"I knew an Anthony." Her eyes were pools of pain and hope. "A long time ago."

"Hi, Grandma," he said. "We've been looking for you."

Ruth shook her head. "Me? No one looks for me."

"Daddy says you just up and disappeared one day."

Ruth nodded. "I had to disappear. He was going to kill us all."

Anthony turned to me. "The story goes she was married to a violent man. Adam Sims, my grandfather. Communicated with his fists. Landed her in hospital ten times or more. Broke her jaw. Knocked her about until her brain was barely a brain."

Ruth's hands clung to mine, but she was listening. Tracking. She knew this story. She'd lived it.

"One day it was just one session too many. She took her kids—all five of them—and left them with a cousin one state over."

215

Ruth nodded. "I had to leave my babies behind."

"He said he would kill them if she didn't come home." Anthony reached out and stroked her hair. "So, she went away."

Ruth was trembling and Anthony had waited a long time to find her. I didn't feel right being part of this huge moment but I couldn't leave Ruth with this bombshell landing on her.

"I ran and ran and ran," said Ruth. "No one knew where I was or who I was and soon that was true for me, too."

I'd seen her medical file. She'd numbed her pain every way she could, and why not? If I'd had to leave my Mitz, I'd be nothing.

"He died, Grandma. A long time ago."

"Adam? Adam's dead?" The dreamy far-away look fell away from her. It was like stripping rotten wallpaper off a wall and finding perfect plaster intact underneath.

"When Auntie Julie told us about you, we searched." He took her hand from mine and held it gently. "We've been looking for you all this time."

Ruth smiled. "Thank you, Barb."

I had nothing. All I could do was nod.

"I'm going home, now." She looped her arm through her grandson's.

Sometimes being a private investigator is the best job in the world.

After being a mom, of course.

THE END

ABOUT THE AUTHOR

MARY KELIIKOA is the author of the Lefty, Agatha, Anthony and Shamus award nominated PI Kelly Pruett mystery series and the upcoming Misty Pines mystery series featuring Portland homicide detective turned small town sheriff slated for release in September 2022. Her short stories have appeared in Woman's World and in the anthology Peace, Love and Crime: Crime Fiction Inspired by Music of the '60s. A Pacific NW native, she spent a part of her life working around lawyers. Combining her love of legal and books, she creates a twisting mystery where justice prevails.

When not in Washington, you can find Mary on the beach in Hawaii where she and her husband recharge. But even under the palm trees and blazing sun, she's plotting her next murder—novel that is.

For more information, please go to www.marykeliikoa.com.